Alfie's Diary

*Dog enough not to be human,
human enough to be a pet.*

Alfie Dog

&

Rosemary J. Kind

Printed in the United Kingdom

First Printing, 2015 Alfie Dog Limited

The author can be found at: authors@alfiedog.com

Cover image: Red Jester Photography

ISBN 978-1-909894-26-6

Published by
Alfie Dog Limited
Rose Bank, Norton Lindsey,
Warwickshire, CV35 8JQ
Tel: 07712 647754

DEDICATION

To

Anka vom Bogenthal and **Elio vom Schärlig**

without whom none of this would have been
possible
and of course to

Sonja van den Durpel

with thanks from your loving puppy

Alfie
(Einstein van de Tiendenschuur)

CONTENTS

ACKNOWLEDGEMENTS

Emma and Buddy – for giving me the kick I needed to turn this into a paperback.

INTRODUCTION

Alfie's Diary began in 2006 when Alfie left his
mother, Anka vom Bogenthal and moved to live
with me in his new home. He has been writing his
thoughts ever since and his exploits can be found on
a daily basis at www.alfiedog.me.uk.

This is his book, but I'm sure he won't mind me
thanking him for all the wonderful times we have
together and for being the inspiration for so much of
what I do.

For those of you who don't know the breed, he is an
Entlebucher Mountain Dog and a more loving and
loyal breed of dog you couldn't hope to find. He is
my sunshine on a rainy day and a reminder to live
life to the full.

In his own words, 'Live life as though every day is a
new field of rabbits just waiting to be chased.'

Rosemary J. Kind

1

A TEN-WEEK-OLD PUPPY ARRIVES

Monday 23rd January
Welcome to my diary. Quite what you're doing reading my private thoughts I have no idea, but seeing as you're here – Welcome. I'm ten weeks old and still struggling to get my paws round the keyboard.

I find it much easier to put my thoughts down on paper. Other dogs rarely stand still long enough to have a good deep conversation and as for humans, well the main problem is that they don't take a dog seriously when he starts talking.

I don't want to talk all the time. It's annoying when I want to play and The Boss wants to work, but I've found the perfect solution. The Boss has always been quite fond of Miffy. As a 'moving in' present, she bought me a 'Miffy' toy. If The Boss won't play with me, I get Miffy in my mouth and threaten to shake her unless I get some attention, something along the lines of blackmail. "Either you play ball, or Miffy gets it!" It's worked every time so far. How long do you think it'll take The Boss to realise how shallow I am?

Tuesday 24th January
There are some things humans just don't get. Only another dog would understand those times when you're in the middle of breakfast and you know you can't possibly go any further, until you've tried to chew the

corner off your cushion. And so it was this morning. I stopped dead in my tracks and then leapt from my breakfast to the cushion, in an attempt to introduce the element of surprise; that way the cushion isn't prepared for me. The Boss just looked at me as though I was crazy. Oh, the fun she misses.

I need to build up my energy for having my microchip fitted later. What is all that about? They've already given me a tattoo, so much for the European Union. Everyone recognises the tattoo system except the United Kingdom. I think there's someone deep in Whitehall with sadistic tendencies towards dogs. You can hear them now, "I don't think that young puppy has suffered enough having a tattoo in his ear. Let's make him have a microchip inserted too". When I rang the vet I didn't have the courage to ask where exactly he plans to insert the microchip. Do you think they test the process on humans first, to make sure it's safe? More importantly, will it enable me to automatically restock my bone store when it detects that I'm chewing the last one? Now that would make it worthwhile. If the chip could send a little signal to the butchers so they could send some bones round before I run out. Just think of the possibilities! My Master would be next in line, to get one that automatically restocked the Twiglet cabinet. Still he seems to have that one covered by having The Boss around.

Wednesday 25th January

It was less than minus eight centigrade last night. Did The Boss really think I was going to ask to be let out to go to the toilet when there is a perfectly good rug in front of the fire? I picked my moment carefully, for maximum annoyance. She'd just put tea out and was about to sit down to eat it. Too bad.

Regarding one of my comments yesterday, I take back what I said about the UK being mad on its requirements for me to travel. The vet (who I never want to see again) told me my tattoo would fade in two to three years. If I'd known that at the time, I would have chosen the dolphins or the heart with the arrow through it, rather than a random series of letters and numbers. I wonder if I borrowed a felt tip pen, whether I could join it up to make it into a picture.

I don't recommend having a microchip fitted, bone cupboard automatic restocking or not. Did you ever see such a big needle? There was no point in the vet telling me this wasn't going to hurt. It obviously was! And when the vet insisted on having a good feel to see if all my bits were in the right place I really didn't know what to do with myself. I heard The Boss making another appointment. I don't think so. I'm planning to be out that day.

I seem to have spent most of today in the car. First, The Boss was in the queue for the number plate office for an hour. It was the system where you take a number, then get depressed about how many people are in front of you. The best bit of the day was the 'thank you present' I got at the end for being so patient. Will she never learn? I am now the proud owner of a second Miffy toy, just as shakeable as the first one.

Thursday 26th January

Last night I was in trouble for dereliction of duty and today I'm flavour of the month. There is no consistency in the world. To be fair I was asleep and snoring heavily, when I was supposed to be map reading, but what does she expect? I guess when you're asking the question,

"How far along here before we have to turn off?" it's not that helpful to find your passenger not concentrating on the map. I told her she should get satellite navigation, but I don't think that really helped the situation.

The Boss gave me my first dog biscuit today. It was praise after a lovely walk in the snow. When I say praise, it was more of a guilt offering for the look I gave The Boss at the sight of her helping herself to a ginger biscuit when we got back and not offering me one. I took my prize to my favourite rug to eat. Not the same spot I peed on the other night you'll be pleased to know. Even I have standards.

Friday 27th January
It's taken me all week to get the hang of climbing onto the settee and today a new one arrived. It doesn't sag as much as the old one did, so I'll have to start practising all over again. On the positive side, it has got more bounce in it - a perfect doggy trampoline.

I must learn to disguise my true thoughts better. We went for a lovely walk earlier today, when suddenly, for no apparent reason, The Boss burst into what vaguely resembled a jog. I stopped in my tracks and just looked at her. It was when she said, "You're looking at me like I'm completely stupid," I realised I may be being a little transparent.

You wouldn't believe the lengths she's tried in order to fit the new number plates to the car. She found the holder she'd bought was too big for the car. Now the holder is the right size and she doesn't have enough screws. Still it was fun chasing the screw I found round the floor of the garage whilst she was doing it.

Saturday 28th January

When we got back from today's walk, The Boss gave me a dog biscuit. I immediately took it to my room and ate it over my bowl. What is she like? She started praising me for being a clean, tidy puppy...duh! Has she got no sense? I wanted to make sure I got it all. I've lost some crumbs from the last one in the tufts of the rug and much as I scratch at it, I just can't seem to get them out.

I suffered the trauma of being force fed a worming tablet today. If it's anything like the last time, I shall get my own back pretty quickly. I had an upset stomach for a couple of days after that one.

There I was sitting outside the changing room in a men's clothes shop and the sights you see. First, there was the bloke with a paunch trying on jeans. He came out to admire himself in the mirror. I just wanted to say to him, "The jeans are great, but will you not just try and lose the stomach?" Then there was the lad in his early 20's with a woman probably in her 50's. I wanted to call out to him "Don't you think you're too old to be shopping with your mother. Please tell me that's your mother? Otherwise, whatever are you thinking of?" But hey, who wants to listen to a dog?

Sunday 29th January

The question came up yesterday, 'what am I going to do when I grow up?' I was a bit nonplussed by this. When you say 'do', what exactly did you have in mind? I thought maybe sleep on the couch, chase a few cats, bark at the postman. You know, generally the sort of thing that every puppy aspires to when he becomes an adult. No, it seems The Boss has in mind that I should earn my keep. This is going to take a bit of thought. If I really have to work for a living I guess 'stud dog' sounds the most fun or how about film star, like Lassie? For either of those, I would have to pass lots of tests, so I've gone back to the drawing board.

I've learnt to climb up the first 5 steps of the staircase and what's more I can get back down. The Boss seems a bit concerned as there are no backs to the stairs and I keep poking my head through to have a look. I tell her it's not the looking, that causes the injuries, as much as the falling.

On reflection, perhaps The Boss did do something nice for my eleven week birthday. I had 'accidentally' torn half of Miffy's ear off, and she kindly sewed it back together, so that I can chew it off all over again.

Monday 30th January

Why don't humans eat acorns? Just one of the thoughts I pondered on my walk earlier. There I was happily tucking into my first acorn of the day, when The Boss made me spit it out. What is all that about? Do I make her spit her breakfast out, or question the things she eats? No. Live and let live, that's my motto. After the indignation about the intrusion into my happy munching, I started wondering why don't humans eat acorns too? They eat lots of other seeds and nuts, so why not acorns? Anyway, for those who are considering it, I would just like to say that they come with my wholehearted recommendation.

When we went for a walk through the woods yesterday, I couldn't help noticing, (mainly because they kept tripping over me), there were large numbers of humans going in the opposite direction. I know there's nothing odd about that in itself; humans are of course perfectly entitled to go for a nice Sunday afternoon walk, but a disproportionate number of them were wearing woolly hats with pom-poms on. Have they no shame? I've thought of Belgium as a chic, trendy sort of place, until now. But bobble hats! It has made me go back to thinking about my career options. How about 'Alfie Dog - fashion consultant to the stars'? Admittedly, as yet I don't know any stars but there's plenty of time. I can hear you, "Who's going to take a dog seriously as a fashion consultant?' Think about it, what do most men know about women's fashion? Zip, zilch, absolutely nothing and yet some of them have even gone as far as being successful designing women's clothes. So if they can do it why can't I?

Tuesday 31st January
It's been an odd day really. First, I see a man with a gun walking past the gate at the end of my garden, then when he's gone, out come two pheasants that were hiding behind our hedge. Now I don't know whether the bloke meant them any harm, but it was funny how they hid until he'd gone.

When we went out, I tried to see if I can bark and growl properly yet. I tried to bark in greeting to a 'Westie' who came to see me at his gate. I don't think he even heard me; my bark was so quiet. Then we came to a field of horses and I thought I'd make clear who was boss, so I tried to growl. Well, it's safe to say they certainly won't have gone away scared by me.

I've been rethinking my career options. I may have been a little hasty with the idea of fashion consultant. Who is going to take seriously someone who turns up in the same clothes every day? I've been thinking more of advertising and working on one or two slogans while I was walking. How about, 'Acorns, one bite and your hoaked'. Or 'Mud - every puppy's dream. You can roll in it, squelch it through your toes, eat it and it comes with the added attraction of being useful to repulse your owner.' Not as catchy as the acorn one, but it has appeal to the buying dog. Alternatively I could launch a doggy safety campaign, 'Bones - you can chew them, gnaw them, bury them but best not to break them.' No maybe I'm not cut out for advertising either.

Looking through the paper last night, just before I peed on it, I have to say there really weren't many companies advertising for dogs. Perhaps it's time to start a campaign to extend the discrimination legislation a little further. Not only should it not be all right to say you want a man or a woman for a particular job, why can't it be illegal to specify they have to be human. There are so many jobs a dog can do and for that matter perhaps the current jobs that are exclusive to dogs, should be opened up to other species including humans. You could have a 'guide cat for the blind' and maybe a hamster might want to carry a barrel in a rescue operation instead of a St Bernard and thinking of it from the perspective of other species, why should dogs have all the fun sniffing out drugs?

Wednesday 1st February
Well I've been practising being a 'sniffer' dog. I reckon I can now sniff an acorn out from 50 metres. I haven't tried with drugs yet. I would probably need to slip over the border into the Netherlands to give that a go. In the meantime, I can lead the way to any acorns stashed away by rogue squirrels.

I love some words in Dutch. The word for squirrel is 'eekhorn'. Do you think the word for acorn is 'squirrel'?

The Boss may be taking feeding the birds a bit too far, the pheasant is back and is sitting outside the front door. It looks nice and plump and would be easy pickings for tea; perhaps we could roast it over the log fire. Does it count as poaching if the bird comes to you?

We met another lady walking a dog today. It's very exciting when you're 11 weeks old to meet another dog, so I duly rolled in the dirt to show my appreciation. Then the indignity of it, while The Boss was busy talking to the other lady, her dog climbed on my back and I wasn't sure whether I should be shouting, "I'm only 11 weeks old" or "In case it's escaped your notice, I'm a boy too." Fortunately, the other lady pulled him off. I hope that isn't what happens every time I meet a new dog. He then showed off by cocking his leg against a tree. I'll show him I thought, so I tried cocking mine against a twig and fell over. I really must master this balance and co-ordination thing.

Thursday 2nd February
How is it that I get the same dog food every day and they get to eat steak? The Frosties and the crisps sometimes fall off the plate onto the floor and I get a little bit, but the best thing I got last night was apple peeling. I'm starting to understand how things work around here and I'm not sure I like it. Still all that will change when I have my own income. You wait and see. There they'll be, sitting down to the meal they have had to cook themselves, when the doorbell will ring and it will be the pizza delivery I've ordered. You wait 'til they try asking for some of my pizza. I'm not sure if I shall simply say "No", or drop a few crumbs on the floor, for them to lick up.

I really need to move this 'getting a job' thing forward.

Given that I'm a cart dog, I was wondering about working for Santa. I went to see the deer that live in our wood, but it didn't go well. I got off to a bad start when I got a bout of hiccoughs as I introduced myself. Now being 11 weeks old, and a dog, it was going to be difficult to get them to take me seriously at the best of times. But I guess even I can see that faced with a puppy with hiccoughs, saying he wants to learn to pull Santa's sledge, it's not altogether surprising that the whole group of them fell about laughing. The stag in charge said it was the best joke he'd heard all winter.

One of the younger ones was a bit kinder and sat down and talked to me for a while. Apparently, there are so many deer wanting to do it as their 'calling' that they're willing to do it for nothing. On top of the need to be very fit, be prepared to spend six months of the year training at the North Pole, and being a 'deer', you really need to have money of your own, or be able to get sponsorship. Having already established I'm not cut out for a career in advertising, I can't see sponsorship being very likely and I still need to get round the lack of discrimination legislation, meaning they can still advertise the post as being for a 'deer'. All in all, the fact that I don't fancy the temperature at the North Pole, assuming global warming doesn't get a hold, is immaterial.

Friday 3rd February
How would she like it if I said to her 'You smell and you need a bath'? Yet that is exactly what The Boss said to me today. It's not being told I smell that I object to, as a dog I take that as a compliment. It's her telling me that I have to have a bath. Is there no respect for the fact that it's taken me two weeks of rolling in everything I can find, to

perfect this 'classic' odour. I've been seriously thinking about developing it as an 'off the shelf' cologne, to save the hard work involved in endlessly rubbing myself in dirt, puddles, bushes and acorns. Sadly, the Boss has gone to the lengths of washing cushion covers and my bedding to destroy the formula.

Following my return of the worming tablet I was given last week, The Boss got me some new stuff from the vet. This time The Boss got a syringe of paste that she squirted onto the back of my tongue. Being a typical dog I'll try eating anything and I'd swallowed before I'd really thought about the fact I was supposed to be objecting on principle.

My Master wants to know why, when he tells me to do something, I answer back? We got into an almighty row both last night and this morning. He says he wasn't shouting he just has a loud voice. When he told me to get down, I just barked like mad at him. I think it's because he's so easy to wind up, that it makes it fun.

I was thinking about not being able to apply for the position of pulling Santa's sledge. There might be legislation I could try suing Santa under. There has to be something that covers the rights of dogs to be considered for all types of work; there's European legislation for almost everything else.

Saturday 4th February

Misskin the cat thinks I have an easy life. The cheek of it. She didn't have to sit patiently for half an hour in the car with the car alarm going off the whole time, because my Master hasn't figured out which switch stops me activating the sensor. Easy life indeed.

I've spent much of the day trying to find things to roll

in to get my smell back. It's been fairly successful but I have a way to go yet.

I'm still thinking about suing Santa. I did a bit of research on the internet earlier and although not relevant to my case, I found some very detailed regulations on what counts as a pair of pyjamas. It goes to prove that there really is legislation that covers just about everything. The boss was a little taken aback when I told her that I was unsure whether her Miffy pyjamas would count as 'constituent fabric' and may in fact not have been a pair of pyjamas at all. The regulations actually say they should be 'designed to be worn together by one person'. As opposed to being worn together by 'two people' I presume.

I thought about the poor person spending his working life, sitting in some windowless office, dreaming up bizarre wording for VAT regulations. I guess you have to end up using terms like 'constituent fabric', to feel there is any value to what you've written. A document that said, 'A pair of pyjamas shall be deemed to be that garment that normal people would wear in bed' doesn't really justify the salary.

On a more mundane note, yesterday I polished off (if you'll pardon the pun) half a cleaning cloth. Being a cleaning cloth, do you think it was any nicer for my Master to clean up when it had worked its way through me and came out the other end to be deposited in a neat pile just inside the front door? He had only taken his eyes off me for five minutes, but I took my opportunity.

Sunday 5th February
I'm twelve weeks old today and yet again no party. I had a celebratory acorn when I went out first thing this morning.

I spent last night and this morning moving two tonnes of wood. When I say 'moving' that might give the wrong impression. I was more worrying it, while my owners did the moving. I sort of barked at it occasionally and got under their feet.

After staying up late last night with my Master, I now understand a bit more about what The Boss is doing when she kicks a ball round the garden. She's clearly expecting me to join in. What is all that about? What is the point of chasing a little ball all around some grass, let alone watching 22 men doing it? I still think it's more fun to bite her shoes when she goes to kick the ball. At least she hasn't tried to introduce the offside rule to playing in the garden.....yet! Just in case, perhaps I need to pay a bit more attention. Did it mean I can't go the other side of her when the ball is near the house or near the footpath?

I've been thinking about how I'm going to get one of those pheasants for tea. They're clearly not going to issue a shotgun to a puppy. Even I recognise that twelve weeks old may be a little young. When we were out for our walk yesterday, we saw a very big bird of prey. My owners said it was a Buzzard. I was wondering if I could do a deal with him, where we might go 50:50 on a pheasant, perhaps he'd catch it if I offered to do the cooking?

What a walk I had today. It's raining and the temperature is above freezing. Some off-road bikes went up the track earlier and left such glorious mud to roll in, thick, black, squelchy mud. I'm covered from head to toe and I'm sooo happy. I'm just off to lie in front of the fire whilst my Master watches a game where a load of men run round picking up a ball and throwing it to each other between kicks. Why don't just get it in their mouths and shake it, that's the obvious thing to do with a ball.

2
NOW I'M TWELVE WEEKS OLD

Monday 6th February

In respect of my discrimination case against Santa, I'm struggling to find legislation that covers it directly. I can't claim sex discrimination as the fact that I'm male has no bearing and no one seems to think that being a dog qualifies under any sort or racial or cultural grouping. All the discrimination legislation seems to start from the assumption that you're human. This is also the case with the 'Human Rights Act'. What about the rights of puppies? Surely I must have some rights? Neither does there seem to be any legislation protecting the rights of deer, so maybe we're on a level playing field. Do you think there is anything to prevent me claiming to be a deer, rather than a dog?

I only appear to be covered by legislation to make sure no one is cruel to me. Do you think I can claim Santa is being cruel not letting me pull his sledge? I don't suppose I would get much sympathy trying to accuse Santa of cruelty when he gives everyone so many lovely presents. It's my plaintive looks and big brown eyes, versus Santa's presents, – which one do you go for children? I'm cute, really I am.

I guess I'll just have to give up on the idea of pulling Santa's sledge and think about my other career options. I was wondering whether I could bring action against the European Parliament on the grounds that the 'Human Rights Act' discriminates against me as a dog. Perhaps I should start lobbying for a change in legislation. After all, if so much time can be spent protecting the rights of foxes, I would have thought there must be a bit of time free to consider the interests of man's best friend.

Tuesday 7th February
Now the ground has thawed out a bit, I think I stand a real chance of being a successful sniffer dog. There are so many new smells to sniff and wallow in. I can now sniff out astilbe, as well as acorns. Admittedly the astilbe is not that difficult, as it's right outside the back door, or rather 'was' right outside the back door. It's sort of inside the back door now.

Unfortunately, I think to be a proper sniffer dog I need to deal with either drugs or explosives. The only drugs I've found to practice on are coffee, which seems to be available in plentiful amounts and alcohol, which thinking about it, also seems to be available in plentiful amounts. I'm struggling when you come to the explosives category. It isn't the sort of thing that people leave lying around, thankfully. If I'm going to get some practice in, do you think curry powder would be a good substitute?

When my owners moved in to this house, there were moles living in the garden. As part of the move, the moles were asked to leave, but only went after leaving seventeen molehills in protest. Now I'm not sure if I should say something, but I think we're heading for trouble. As I went out of the back gate earlier, I noticed some freshly dug molehills just over the other side of the fence. I kept my ear to the ground. It was a bit difficult walking alternating between trying to be a sniffer dog and having my ear to the ground. The word on the street, or forest depending on how you look at it, is that the new holes have been dug by the 'moles' army advance party' coming to check things out. Rumour has it, that the massed ranks of moles are due to be gathering in a bid to regain their territory. I'm not sure whether to tell my owners or just sit back and enjoy watching the frustration as the molehills start to mount up.

Wednesday 8th February

I've been noticing something very strange happening recently. The car seat is getting smaller. Every time I get in, there seem to be more bits of me hanging over the edges of the seat than there were the last time. I've also noticed that every couple of days I seem to be a bit plump around the tummy and then overnight it's as though someone comes along with a rolling pin and rolls me out. The next day I seem to be back to normal round the middle but a bit longer.

The Boss is a bit on the clumsy side. On a bad day it means she stands on my paw and I yelp and hold up my paw for a bit of sympathy, but overall it rather works to my advantage. I've learnt that, when she's cooking, the best place to sit is on her feet, she finds it a bit difficult to move and has told me that this may be directly leading to her standing on my paws, but it's worth it. I'm there, ready and waiting for all the bits of food that she drops on the floor. I'm becoming particularly partial to a bit of apple crumble, and last night she managed to spill chicken stew all down the front of the work surface. I was there ready, with my tongue against the cupboard to catch it. If she would share it with me in the first place, instead of giving me dry dog food, I wouldn't have to resort to such lengths.

I was watching a DVD about Formula 1 motor racing

last night. Do you think I could be a racing driver? Do you think the FIA have any regulations that prevent the car being modified so that I can reach the pedals? I can see it now, on the podium in Monaco. The worlds newspapers with the headlines 'Alfie the first dog to win a Grand Prix', 'Alfie the Greatest Racing Dog Ever'. I can see the crowds, the applause, the fans. Oh what a life.

Thursday 9th February
Today The Boss received a parcel in the post. It had been squeezed through the letterbox and was a bit out of shape. I was appalled to discover that this is considered an acceptable method of transport for a teddy bear. I hadn't got over this concern when I was horrified to find The Boss putting the bear in the microwave oven and turning it on. What had the poor bear done to deserve that? No sooner was I starting to relax thinking that the poor little bear had survived his ordeal, than she said he was cold and put him back in the microwave again. I am beside myself with concern; this is really no way to treat a teddy bear.

I've hidden Miffy as there's no way she's going in the microwave. It was bad enough when The Boss put her in the washing machine and all I could do was sit and watch her helplessly going round and round.

I went up to the bear. It was a bit difficult, he's filled with some funny smelling stuff called lavender that made me sneeze. He didn't seem awfully pleased to meet me, but then I had just sneezed all over him. I gave his ear a sharp nip, to bring him to his senses. I explained it was for his own good, but I can only conclude that as bears go he isn't very bright. He said that as far as he's concerned, being put in a microwave is fine. He was told that's what he's made for. I think the microwaves have damaged his brain. He did say the microwave gives him a nice warm glow, however, he does find that his bottom gets a bit hot. It's like when I don't realise the car seat heating is on and my bottom starts getting really warm and I'm not quite sure if it's just me or if there might be something wrong.

Friday 10th February

I'm not prone to jealousy but I'm starting to lose sympathy with the bear. Firstly, he gets to sit on The Boss's knee while she's working and I don't. She said it's because I don't fit on her knee quite so easily now. That may be true, but I'm not happy about the principle of it. I demand an equal right to sit on her knee. The Master laughed when he heard me say that. He thinks I've been spending too much time with The Boss and am starting to sound like her. What really upset me is that when I moved in, we had a long discussion about the fact that I wasn't going to sleep in their bedroom. We also had a long discussion about the fact that I was not sitting on the settee, but I won that one. Fair enough, I don't mind too much, I have my own room and I can leave it as messy as I like, which is more than can be said for my Master. However, what I'm not happy about is that the bear told me that he does get to sleep in their bedroom. I'm not happy. As far as I'm concerned, microwave or no microwave, the bear is on his own.

I've worked out the nationality of the birds in our garden. There are many different varieties, but I think they all come from the same place. You might wonder how I've arrived at my conclusion. Have I for example been reading up on the migratory habits of the robin? Have I studied the direction of the flight path of the nuthatch? No, it has been much less scientific than that. It has all been a simple matter of observation and deduction. I've been watching from my vantage point in the office and notice that they all form an orderly queue along the hedge, waiting for their turn on the bird table. They queue up even when there isn't anything on the bird table. Well it's obvious isn't it, behaviour like that, they must be British.

My deductions regarding the birds have made me start wondering whether I should consider a career as a detective. If I could use my inspired thinking, together with my ability to track a scent, there would be no stopping me. 'Alfie Dog from the CID' sounds quite good, and I'm sure it would impress all the girl puppies.

Sunday 12th February

I'm not sure I understand this whole Valentine's Day thing. The Boss has spent absolutely hours doing something as a surprise for my Master. I keep asking what it is, but she won't tell me because she thinks I might blab. I ask you, me blab? I'm discretion itself. And she needn't think I'm going to let my Master anywhere near reading my diary. Not after some of the things I've written about him.

I've been having a close look at the plants in the intensive care unit. That's what The Boss calls the ones on the kitchen window ledge. When I say look, I may actually mean nibble. Surprisingly, this seems to be an area where humans and dogs have different expectations. You can't tell if a plant is getting better just by looking at it. You need to know if it has the right taste. I can report the branch that accidentally came off in my paws, tasted just fine. I tried telling The Boss, the rest of the plant may look a little lop-sided, but I hear that's the latest fashion in house plants, at least in this house.

Monday 13th February
32! "32 what?" you might ask. Go on then ask. Well the answer would be molehills. 32 molehills, one of which is now 2 feet from the back garden gate. I don't mean to sound alarmist, but I really don't think it's going to be long before they start their attack.

I haven't been feeling at all well today. I think it may be from eating a large number of acorns yesterday. Right now I'm at that 'I'm never going to have another acorn again in my life, until the next time,' sort of phase. The thought of food makes me feel quite queasy.

I'm now three months old and The Boss says this birthday is a special occasion. It still seems however that cake is not on the menu, which given how I'm feeling is probably a good job. As a special 'treat' I get to visit the Vet tonight to get my rabies jab. Am I missing something here? I thought you got nice things on birthdays. Apparently, it also means I'm old enough to start 'puppy training classes', I'm not sure if that's good or bad. On the upside, I get to meet lots more 'kids' my own age, on the downside, I have to learn to do as I'm told. Yeah right! I'm told it's all part of growing up, but from what I can see growing up is a bit on the boring side. I met a lovely dog called Mackensey. When I say dog, I really mean bitch. When I met her, I asked her very nicely to play, but she's six years old and didn't seem to notice me. I barked at her and she still took no notice, so I barked some more and she still didn't show she wanted to play with me. What does a puppy do in circumstances like that? I barked and barked and barked, and then I barked some more, and some more. Even then, she ignored me. Why don't adults play?

Tuesday 14th February
So much for Valentine's Day, no card, no flowers, no chocolates. Admittedly, I haven't sent any. I wanted to, but I didn't have enough left from my pocket money to buy anything. (Is it still pocket money if you haven't got any pockets?) I did try stealing some paper to make a card but The Boss thought I was being naughty and told me off. How was I supposed to know that that particular piece of paper was important and didn't want to be chewed? How is it that The Boss sent a card to my Master and he sent one to her, but neither of them thought to send one to me? I'm just the dog.

Last night's visit to the vet involved rather more prodding of 'my bits' than I'm happy about and on top of that he made me get on the scales. One thing the vet did say, was that in the next week I'm going to start losing my baby teeth and getting my adult ones. I asked The Boss where I should leave them for the tooth fairy and whether she knows what the going rate is. She says I'll have to wait and see.

I had a strange thought when we were out walking the other day. Why are the places that are called things like 'Hope Street' always so run down and dismal? Do you think they were like that before being given the name and it was a vain prayer for improvement, or do you think being given that name has been their undoing? Perhaps they were really grand roads until someone cursed them by calling them Hope Street and since that day everything has gone wrong.

Wednesday 15th February

I saw a plane going overhead and started wondering where it was going. I've been wondering where I might like to go for my summer holidays. The world is an awfully big place for a little dog and there are so many places I would like to see. I think the Isle of Dogs and Hound Tor sound quite exciting to begin with. I came back and sat by the fire dreaming of being on a plane and being able to press the call button whenever I wanted, to ask the stewardess to bring me another dog biscuit. Just another seven months until I get my passport finalised.

Thursday 16th February

She has got to be joking! When she told me we were going out in the car last night I thought 'Oh no, we must be going to the vet.' I ran into the other room and refused to come and have my collar put on. I can honestly say that after the way the evening turned out, I wish we had been going to the vet. When The Boss coaxes you to the car telling you that it's going to be 'fun' and you're going to get to play with lots of other dogs, it builds a little puppy's hopes up. I went along with the plan.

The 'puppy class' was held in the middle of a field. So what? Well it rained yesterday. Not the little bit of drizzly rain that makes no difference, no, the full-blown soaked to the skin and little brook is now a raging torrent, sort of rain. I think you may be starting to get the picture. There I am in a field, on a February evening, with floodlights in the distant corner, leaving the 'puppy ring' very dark, standing in three centimetres of muddy water. I don't just mean it was damp, I mean I was up to my ankles in water. And there's The Boss in white training shoes. I really don't think she'd thought it through very well. What was I expected to do? It was bad enough that the bloke spoke in Flemish and neither The Boss nor I had much idea what was going on. I think she understood about one word in ten and for reasons that will become apparent, the ones I did understand I thought it best to ignore. The Boss has taught me to sit, stay, fetch and I will roll over for just about anyone, but when you're asked to sit, lie down and roll over in three centimetres of muddy water would you cooperate? I just looked up at her and in fairness she couldn't bring herself to make me do those things either. I enjoyed meeting the other puppies and I had a lovely run round. I was happy to come when called, but whatever they said, there was no way I was going to put my delicate little bottom down in that amount of muddy water. Overall The Boss had a really bad evening too. She hates going into situations where she doesn't know anyone and when she gets there to find there is very little English spoken. Then she had to spend an evening in a muddy field feeling completely and utterly lost, well you have to feel a little bit sorry for her, and I don't think her training shoes will ever be the same again.

Friday 17th February
In my desperation to eat acorns, I've searched the Internet to find where I can buy them. I can find music about acorns, paintings of acorns, books about acorns and rugs with acorns on. I can find postings by people wanting to buy acorns to supplement the diets of their local squirrels, but I cannot find anyone selling acorns. I even found a property rental company that goes by the name of 'Acorns', but unless I want to move home that won't help either. If I can't get acorns, apparently, 'filbert nuts' are better for squirrels than peanuts, but is this also true for

dogs? I do find this a little confusing. Filbert is the name of the fox that's the mascot of Leicester City Football Club and I'm sure that a fox isn't better for squirrels.

I'm also disappointed to report that 'rubber chicken' (he replaced Miffy as my favourite toy after The Boss insisted on putting Miffy through the wash,) has lost his squeak. That is to say, due to the hole that has mysteriously appeared in his foot, he no longer makes a noise when I bite him. He's still good for shaking and racing round the lounge with, but it's so much harder to wind people up if your toys lose their squeak. It's not all bad, Miffy never did squeak so I don't really mind, and he can't go in the washing machine. I'm working on the basis that if I pick him up by his ear and forlornly dangle him in front of The Boss, she may take pity on me and buy me a new one, or maybe if she can sew Miffy's ear back she could stick rubber chicken back together too.

I really need to get back to thinking about my career options. Even if I had found acorns to buy, or filbert nuts for that matter, I don't think I have enough pocket money left. I know I don't want a job that involves spending too long in a muddy field. I may be a Swiss Mountain Dog but either they don't get that much rain in the Swiss mountains, or I'm a fair weather Mountain Dog. I'm going to skip the usual roles of cattle herding and look for something more desk or fireside based.

Saturday 18th February
It's a funny thing growing older. It seems to be mainly about hair. Hair grows where it didn't used to grow, usually in places you don't want it. Hair stops growing in places where you did want it, and in my case the lovely soft puppy hair starts to go coarse. I've noticed that, with

the black bits down the middle of my back, one minute it's all soft and fluffy the next it's all coarse and shiny, strange process when you think about it. No sign of the tooth fairy yet though, I'm really hoping that I might get enough money to buy some nuts.

On one expedition today, the computer actually hit me. Up until now, I've seen it as a friend, without whom I would have difficulty writing my diary; whoever heard of a dog being able to hold a pen and write? Today, however, all that has changed (not the bit with the pen – I really can't get the hang of that, I can't even work out if I am right or left pawed). I simply sniffed it. When you're a dog you do that to your friends, have a good sniff to say hello. When I sniffed the computer today, a little draw came out and hit me. Perhaps it doesn't like that particular button being sniffed.

Most of today has gone into thinking, reading and sleeping, but maybe not in that order. I was reading about some giant rabbits that grow over three feet long, in an old copy of a newspaper that The Boss left lying around. (Having reread that sentence it dawns on me that language is a brilliant thing and grammar was probably invented for a purpose. I didn't mean to say that they 'grow in a newspaper' I really meant 'I was reading in a newspaper' a subtle difference that even I can appreciate.) I find it hard to imagine a rabbit that's bigger than me. I asked The Boss if I could have one as a pet, but she said I would have difficulty looking after it. Imagine being bounced on by a three foot tall rabbit, mind you The Boss pointed out that she has to cope with being bounced on by me. Where do you get a hutch for a rabbit that size?

Sunday 19th February

I was wondering if boredom is a bad thing, or whether it's just nature's mechanism to stop you wasting time. I then spent an hour gazing out of the window at nothing in particular and wondered what it would be like to get bored.

I still need a good idea for a career. I did wonder if I could be an actor, like Lassie or Benji, although that involves a bit more moving about than I feel like today. I need more of a Bagpuss type role, although in my more energetic moments I'm more like the mice on the mouse organ. It would be no good playing a 'bit part', I want to be the hero of the movie, suave, sophisticated, brave and lavished with praise and dog biscuits. I see myself as a dashing and brave knight, coming to the rescue of a poor maiden, who would throw herself into my paws and declare her undying love. You can see the name of the film up in lights, 'Alfie the Wonder Dog'. Oh the applause, the accolades, Best Film, Best Leading Actor and me at the Awards nights, walking up the red carpet and cocking my leg nonchalantly against the large pot plant in the hotel foyer (and hopefully by then not unbalancing myself and falling over in the process). Every dog must have his dreams.

3
14 WEEKS AND GROWING

Monday 20th February

Yesterday we went to see my Mum and Sister. I haven't seen them for four weeks. I spent some time with my Mum where she briefly checked I was ok. We had all the usual "Haven't you grown!" and "Are they looking after you properly? Are you eating enough? Are you behaving as I taught you?" Then she proved she could still outrun me by chasing round the garden. I got quite dizzy at one point. I really need to practise cornering; every so often I'm going so fast in a straight line that when I start to turn, my head goes round the corner but the rest of my body carries on in a full skid. On the plus side it is quite fun. Then my sister Esther came out. Wow, is she scary? She wanted to be quite clear that she was top dog and that I should know my place. I'm happy to roll over for anyone; I don't need to be in charge, I seem to get much more fuss by pretending to be all soft and cuddly. Esther jumped on me, growled at me and held her tail in the air. The Boss said that brothers and sisters are often like that. I only went in the pond once.

Apparently, I'm not supposed to drink from the pond. Nobody explained why; it's all just water to me. Now that I walk off the lead I'm finding puddles taste quite nice too.

Apart from seeing my family, I don't think The Boss was very impressed with both my Master and me; we spent most of the weekend asleep in front of the fire. 'Why go out when I've got a house that needs to be lived in and a television that needs to be watched?' They were actually my Master's words rather than mine, but I thought they summed it up quite well. We did go for a lovely long walk and I was allowed off my lead for the first time. The Boss was quite nervous about it but where exactly does she think I'm going? I know which side my bread's buttered. It's the same with my Master really, if he went off very far he'd come back when he got hungry. Sometimes I really don't think women understand men at all.

Tuesday 21st February
I've been thinking about the trip to see my Mum and I really wish I could see my Dad too, but he lives a very long way away. I've been looking at what I'd have to do to catch the train and it seems I can travel on a child's ticket, which you would expect as I am only fourteen weeks old, but the problem is, I seem to need an accompanying adult.

It's only now I'm a bit more familiar with the world that I've realised that 'rubber chicken' is in fact a rabbit. Not one of the giant rabbits, in fact not much like a rabbit at all when you think about it, but he is none the less a one legged rabbit. The Boss couldn't fix him and now I've chewed his leg off completely. Well more half his body and his leg if I'm being honest, so I can understand why she may be refusing to put him together again. I had almost managed to get the corner off the cushion to get the filling out, but The Boss has sewn that up again. Just to reassure you, it is my cushion I'm talking about; I haven't started on the house cushions, yet. I have sort of nibbled a piece of The Boss's jigsaw though. She may not have realised, but when there is a bit of the picture missing at the end I'm sure she's going to guess it was me.

My sister was telling me about her training, she said she wouldn't do as she was told simply because she wasn't having a human lay down the law to her. If she wants to sit she'll sit, but why do it because someone else wants you to do it? I do admire her free spirit, but I like all the fuss I get when I do what I'm asked. I'm quite a simple soul at heart and when I'm bribed with ginger biscuits who can blame me?

Wednesday 22nd February
The Boss must think I'm stupid. There she was putting the cardboard out to be collected for recycling and there were about five or six lots to carry down the drive. Did she really think I was going to walk up and down the drive that many times for absolutely no reason? Let's face it, I can't help carry the cardboard, so it was all a bit of a pointless exercise as far as I'm concerned. I walked down the drive with her the first couple of times, just to make sure she was going to be ok and then I watched from the warmth of the garage, as she wandered off into the rain on her own for the other trips.

In my experience cardboard has only three uses. It can be chewed, peed on or used to light a fire. At least two of those leave it in no fit state for recycling and the third is questionable!

I've started to make a thorough investigation of the bases of all the trees, by sniffing them in turn. It may take me some time to cover them all, as The Boss seems to object to me stopping at every single tree and I've had to restrict it to about one in six. I hope she isn't like this when we walk anywhere with lampposts. It's essential as a dog to be able to sniff every lamppost in case anyone has left you a message, it's like the doggy equivalent of email!

Thursday 23rd February

Good news, The Boss concluded we wouldn't go to dog training this week. I know I should be excited about seeing all the other dogs, but it's winter and I've got a fire to sit by and if I'm being honest, two of the dogs were Jack Russells, who shouldn't be included as dogs; their yapping and irritating ways give us dogs a bad name.

I don't like to publicise this, in case it becomes more widespread, but I think our bird table is being used as a sort of 'singles bar'. Now I could just be imaging this, but from my pretty good vantage point, where I can lie quite comfortably with my head on my paw and see the bird table, it would seem that a lot of birds turn up on their own, but then fly away a little while later in pairs. At this rate, there could soon be a serious amount of nest building going on. Do you think I could supplement my pocket money by helping them a bit? If I took down a few details of the sort of characteristics they're looking for, you know the sort of thing; species, age range, temperament, I could then start helping with the introductions to other suitable birds. Robin has certainly been looking a bit lonely; maybe I could find him a partner? Alternatively, I could set up a sort of 'speed dating' for birds. If I could find twenty males and twenty females, they could all rotate round the table and see if they wanted to see any of the others again. I might have to ask the buzzard and the carrion crows if they would mind NOT taking part.

Friday 24th February

I've been watching the winter Olympics on television and would like to try my paw at one or two of the sports. What is curling all about? Where is the excitement, the speed, the 'sitting on the edge of your seat' feeling? No, I think for me I need something with a bit more of a kick to it (though I have long since concluded that football seems a bit of an odd thing to call sport! The bobsled looks fun, as does speed skating; all I need now is a bit of ice to practise on. I don't think I've quite got the coordination or poise for figure skating. I wondered whether in the absence of ice, I could possibly get some roller blades as a starting point. The Boss tried roller blading once, but it ended with a hospital visit. At least the vet is only just round the corner if I need him.

With not having gone to my puppy training class this week, The Boss has been making me practise at home. 'Sit' and 'stay' aren't too bad, but she's been making me practice 'leave'. When we did it in training, she tried it with a dog biscuit. Well what do you expect? I'm given a biscuit one minute for being good and the next minute I'm supposed to understand that the one being offered to me is not for eating. At home, she's trying with something other than dog biscuits, however using my Master's sandwiches in this way really is asking for trouble at some point.

Saturday 25th February
I'm having difficulty getting hold of four 'paw sized' roller blades. It doesn't seem that dogs are very well catered for with sports equipment, at least not for this type of sport anyway. In fairness, there's a lot more for dogs than for rabbits. They said I can try agility or flyball, but I have to be older before they'll let me do those. I really do need to get the hang of cornering before I try agility; I suppose the same would be true for the roller blading.

Before I start my roller blading, I'm going to practise

both cornering and stopping. I'm also going to see if The Boss's knee pads and wrist pads will fit me; I fear they may be a little on the large side.

I heard somewhere that aloe vera is good for you and that you rub the juice from the leaves into your skin to soothe it. I've been working on the assumption that it must also be good to eat. The Boss has an aloe vera plant that sits on the window ledge in the kitchen, just along from the plant 'intensive care unit'. I should perhaps say 'sat'. I'd been chewing the leaves as I would on any normal day, when the plant pot decided to extract revenge and jumped off the window sill, causing the aloe vera plant to hit me, before landing inelegantly on the floor surrounded by its soil. There was a classic moment when The Boss came in. The plant and I, in unison, pointed to each other and said, "It wasn't me it was him." Well I'm sure The Boss must have believed me over the dumb plant, although the plant certainly seemed to get more attention for his injuries than I did.

Sunday 26th February

Only a few weeks ago I'd never come across an acorn and now I'm addicted to them. I feel guilty every time I eat one, but I just can't stop myself. The rate I'm going I shall have to ask The Boss to take me to Acorns Anonymous.

We're reaching crunch point on the jigsaw. In one respect I'm looking forward to finding out precisely which piece I ate last week, but in another I know there's going to be trouble. I wonder if The Boss would be happier if it was just a nondescript piece rather than a piece of Santa and his reindeer? Unfortunately, until she finishes, I shan't actually know which it is. If I could have worked out where it went at the time, I'd have fitted it, rather than eaten it in frustration.

There are odd times that I think The Boss can be very unreasonable, a point on which I regularly find my Master agrees. There I was, under the table, minding my own business. Incidentally this is not usually the location you can find my Master when he thinks The Boss is being unreasonable, in fact I don't think I've found him under the table very often, if at all. Anyway, there I was, minding my own business, when I was told off for chewing. "Oi" she said, (not the politest of introductions,) "Give me that". I politely refused. "No, it's my twig. I brought it in from the garden. If you want one then please be kind enough to go and get your own." What is the world coming to when a dog can't chew his own twig in peace and quiet?

Monday 27th February

What an exciting discovery! I've found out that if I angle it just right I can chase my tail. I can't quite catch it, as it goes at almost exactly the same speed that I go, but if I do it for long enough I'm bound to get there in the end.

It's very strange living in a country that speaks two languages. One of the biggest problems is finding places. Maps are difficult enough for dogs to read at the best of times, but when you're looking for a place name like Antwerp and find that it's called Antwerpen, unless you're in the French speaking part in which case it is Anvers. Surely one place can't have three different names? I'm still trying to work out where Luik is. I'm told it's Liege but that seems ridiculous; they're nothing like each other. In Great Britain, although you may wonder about the dialects and have serious difficulty understanding what people from, for example, Glasgow, are saying, at least when it comes to spelling place names there's no change. Me and The Boss are still struggling to speak and understand Dutch, or rather Flemish. It's a little more simple for me, I just have to remember 'blijf' means 'stay' and 'zit' is 'sit'. I'm hoping when I get a little more confident to try learning the French commands as well and be a tri-lingual dog.

Tuesday 28th February

What is it with The Boss? Hasn't she got enough toys of her own? Granny has bought me a Miffy colouring book. It's brilliant. It has lots of different pictures of Miffy that I can chew. I would colour them in, but the book didn't come with any crayons. I pulled a few things off The Boss's desk to get the ones I could see on top of a big pile, but I'm having some difficulty getting my paws round them. Short of actually taping the crayon to my paw I'm not sure what to do. I did briefly try with my mouth, but at this point, I had to conclude that crayons don't taste awfully nice. Anyway, rather than being in trouble for pulling the crayons off the desk, I found The Boss happily sitting down using them to colour in my book. How is a puppy expected to enjoy chewing a picture of Miffy when it tastes of crayon?

I've noticed something very strange with humans. The minute one of them suggests they have an item that is broken and won't work, there is always another one eager to take it apart and see if they can fix it. It doesn't matter how little they know about the item in question, or how unqualified they are to deal with the situation, they're always convinced they can do it. To be fair to The Boss's sister, it did turn out to be the case and she did have a thoroughly enjoyable time taking the entire vacuum cleaner apart, and I really do mean the 'entire' cleaner. There she was painstakingly dismantling it piece by piece. Just enough force to separate the parts and not break them, totally ignoring the advice from every other adult, all of whom thought they knew what to do and all wanted to take over if she failed. Well I was convinced that she wouldn't be able to work out where all the parts went, or how they fitted back together, but to my and everyone else's amazement not only did she rebuild it, but it worked. She had no idea why it worked, but in her moment of glory that was irrelevant, by this time all the other broken gadgets were being lined up ready for her attention.

We all suspected that the long piece of coiled metal she removed at the start of the process may have been the culprit, but she took the rest of the cleaner apart before testing it, just for good measure. I use the same philosophy in chewing everything, but in my case, they never seem to go back together.

Wednesday 1st March

Well what a day. There I was going out to do my business as usual and the garden had disappeared under a blanket of white. I thought about not going out at all, but The Boss said that wasn't an option and she'd stay there as long as it took for me to come to my senses. She had a point and it didn't take long. It was fun to play in once I'd got used to it. The Boss showed me how to roll a snowball and then threw it for me to chase. I went hurtling across the garden, but there was nothing there. Then she tried to show me how to make a snowman, but it turned out that the snow was too dry. It was either that or the fact that I kept running over the bit she was working on.

The other exciting thing that happened today was that she finished the jigsaw and I'm delighted to tell you that what I ate last week was not the missing piece of the reindeer. As it turns out, it was not a piece of that jigsaw at all so it's no wonder I couldn't work out where to fit it. I think a 1000 piece one is too hard for me and I need to start with something a little less complicated. Do they make one piece jigsaws for beginners?

My Master was left alone for 24 hours, which proved long enough for him to serve up burnt fish fingers and set fire to the oven gloves, in two completely separate episodes. It all just goes to make him all the more lovable to me, but then I did have a bit of an issue with an apple crumble, so I really think it's only fair that we blokes stick together.

Thursday 2nd March

Despite a long walk in the woods and madly running round the house, The Boss still made me go to puppy training. My Master came too. I'm not sure if The Boss was hoping they would train him as well. It was a little more successful than last time, but the field still resembled a floodlit bog. At least they had the sense not to try to make me roll over in it this week, but I did point blank refuse to lie down. This time The Boss tried teaching me 'leave' using a ginger biscuit. These had been my favourites, but now I really don't know if I can have them or not, so have started to refuse them altogether. There was one funny bit where to get us used to lots of odd things, The Boss was told to behave like an aeroplane and fly at me. Now if you know The Boss, you will be aware that there are times when she's a sandwich short of a picnic. I could have assured the trainer there was absolutely nothing he could get her to do that would have even slightly phased me. I just stood and looked at her as much as to say 'So what is it this time?' and then got back to chewing the tissue I'd pinched out of her pocket when she wasn't looking.

Friday 3rd March

It's only the third day of the month and I've already run out of pocket money. It's so exciting suddenly having some money that I feel I have to rush out and spend it all at once, even if I don't really need what I spend it on. Then I get to the next day, I see something I really want and there it is, gone. I do need to give more thought to how I can earn some extra money. The only job I've come across recently that I think I would rather enjoy is secret agent. I could go out in disguise and follow people, develop secret codes and foil plots. I did wonder about practising writing secret code to stop The Boss or my Master from reading my diary, but I haven't yet come up with one that works so that it is both secret and I can still remember what it means.

I like the idea of secret agent, the whole lifestyle sounds so glamorous. "The name's Dog, Alfie Dog. I have a licence to kill." Of course, if you saw rubber rabbit you might think I'd already killed, but really I haven't.

Saturday 4th March

It's time to confess. The apple crumble incident, as it will henceforth be known, was just a simple misunderstanding that any puppy could make. It was me against the kitchen scales and this time out, they won. If my owners will have silly old fashioned scales that use brass weights on a cast iron stand what can they expect? The weights are not even metric. I'm just a simple Belgian dog, how can I be expected to understand imperial measurements? "Weigh six ounces", The Boss said, after we had got through the whole 'what's an ounce?' thing and she explained that was how they used to measure things in England. For the sake of ease of understanding (clearly in contrast with the difficult metric system), there were sixteen ounces in a pound and fourteen pounds in a stone and these were not the same pounds as you spend in shops. Just to make it easier ounces is abbreviated 'oz' when there isn't even a 'z' in the word and 'pound' is abbreviated 'lb' when there isn't an 'l' or a 'b' in the word, unless it is the type you spend in shops in which case it is '£' and I have no idea why that is.

Anyway, on one side of the scales I put the four ounce weight and the two ounce weight on their little stand. On the other side, in the pan, I started to pile a very large quantity of margarine. The tub ran out, so I got another one out of the fridge, or at least tried to. I find that even standing on my back legs I can't quite reach the very top of the fridge, so I had to ask The Boss to come and help. It was just then it all came to light. She said there was much more than that in the tub she'd already given me and I couldn't possibly need any more. I said I definitely did; it was nowhere near balanced yet. She came over to have a look.

Well diary, if you've been paying attention, you will already know what was wrong. I had included the weights 'on their little stand'. That would be the stand that is made out of cast iron and on its own probably weighs about a kilogram, (2 1/4lbs apparently.). Rather than trying to weigh out six ounces, it meant I was trying to weigh about one kilogramme and six ounces and even I know that that would have been an awfully big crumble. I'm sure I could have eaten it.

Sunday 5th March

My excitement knows no bounds. We went for the most amazing walk in a big park. I saw children riding bicycles with little wheels on the back to stop them falling over. I really want one. I started asking The Boss if I could have one for my birthday, but she said that was a very long time away and I might have changed my mind by then. Then we saw a child on a push-along scooter and when I said I wanted one of those The Boss said she already has one and I can try it some time at home. There were some deer but that wasn't exciting as I talk to them quite often in the woods. It was a bit sad, as they seemed to be in a cage whereas the ones I usually meet roam in the forest and go where they like.

The Boss has been telling me that I'll have my own email address soon so that I can send emails to my friends. It won't be quite as good as the excitement of going to the post box and finding one of the letters I bring in is for me, but so far that's only a dream. The only things that have arrived that should really have been addressed to me, have been my passport and a form from the council doing a census on all animals in case of bird flu and both of those were addressed to my owners. It really is hard being an educated dog and not being appreciated as such.

4

AT SIXTEEN WEEKS OLD

Monday 6th March

I've been wondering why humans eat so many different types of food. It's quite simple for me. I have dried dog food for breakfast, dried dog food for lunch and dried dog food for tea. I'm always excited to see it and within seconds it's gone. What's more, I get all the right vitamins and nutrients without having to think about how many portions of fruit and vegetables I've eaten. One shopping trip for one bag of food, every few weeks, no wasted food, no wasted time cooking, no wasted time doing lots of shopping, no money wasted on a cooker and a microwave, a food blender, knives and forks, saucepans and so the list goes on. Why are humans so stupid? Why do they make it so difficult for themselves? I hear The Boss ask my Master what he wants for tea and then he suggests something they haven't got. What is the point? I'm sure he could still have his beer with a bowl of 'human food' a dry food with all the right nutrients for humans. It could be just like my dog food, they could have different ones for all the different stages of development, with a little chart on the back saying how much you should feed for each age and size of human. OK so I'm occasionally found begging for odd morsels of their wonderful smelling human food and I am partial to the odd dog biscuit, but basically I think the point is valid. Humans waste an awful lot of time, money and energy on things they could do so much more simply.

Tuesday 7th March

I went round to make sure that Matilda the cat knew about the 'bird flu' census and in the process scared a pheasant out of the front garden. It seems a bit odd to do a return on all the domestic animals, when we are completely surrounded by wild ones that don't live at any one address.

This whole Dutch language thing just seems to get more confusing. Take the word 'roos' for example, it looks innocent enough and yet it has three very different meanings and they aren't ones you would want to get confused. It can mean rose, or bulls eye, or ...wait for it... dandruff! Now just think of the confusions that could occur in translation. Shakespeare could have written 'Dandruff by any other name would smell as sweet', whereas 'Head and Shoulders' may actually be a treatment for the roses in the garden. Playing darts could become interesting; you might score fifty for hitting your opponent's dandruff or the flowers on the table. Then again, if you were ordering a present to send to your loved one and doing it by phone, rather than in person, it would be an awful shame to find you had sent a dozen red bulls eyes; it could be the end of a beautiful friendship.

Wednesday 8th March

Being a secret agent is fun, particularly when no one knows that's what you are. You can be having a dreadful day, doing lots of things that could be regarded as mundane, but all the time you know you are part of something much bigger. Only you know that you're waiting for communications of secret meetings, or following people, searching for valuable information.

Admittedly it was much easier to work out where footprints went when there was some snow, but it was also much easier for my suspects to realise I was following them. There we were walking along, The Boss out in front; every so often turning round leaving me to have to hide behind a tree to make sure she didn't know I was there. Then last Thursday she got lost and ended up walking a very long way and I really wanted to go up and ask if she'd mind carrying me, but, as a secret agent, it really wouldn't be good to blow my cover. The worst bit is when I get the scent of something else I want to track, but know if I let her out my sight, I'll never know which way she went. I've managed to get a good copy of a set of my Master's fingerprints, from a beer glass, just in case I need them and earlier I found if I hid behind the curtains I could listen in without them knowing I was there. I actually caught them plotting to go out without me, now I just need to work out how to prevent that happening. Do I go for the cute cuddly approach, feign illness, or try the devious 'pinch the car keys' method?

On the downside, it has rained solidly for most of the last 24 hours and on the upside it means I get a reprieve from puppy training tonight. When we went for our walk earlier, The Boss tried out some bits of training with me and I did my best in the hope she'd decide it wouldn't matter if I missed this week. I still won't sit or lie down when it's wet, but I've tried it out on her and she won't either. I knew that the battle had been won, when the rain got even heavier and she asked if I'd like to spend the afternoon building an ark.

Thursday 9th March
After much hard work, I've finally managed to separate

Miffy from the teething ring she was attached to and what a relief that is. It's so much more satisfying to chew Miffy, than to find your teeth around a piece of hard white plastic, apart from which I cannot believe for one moment that it was very comfortable for her to be strung up by her arms and legs like that.

Friday 10th March
Funny thing watching Star Wars, now it may just be me but have you noticed that if you see the start of a fight scene, you can then go and do something else for fifteen minutes and get back in time to find who won and feel as though you've missed absolutely nothing? I said that to my Master, but he seemed to think I was missing the point.

There's nothing like an evening sat by the fireside, all doing a 'Murder Mystery Jigsaw' together. The Boss and my Master worked on a 999 piece jigsaw, whilst I created my own 2 piece one out of the remaining piece. It wasn't meant to happen that way, but they kept ignoring all my suggestions of where to put the pieces and it all got very frustrating. I took a piece and held it hostage. Then I sent them a little ransom note saying if they didn't take some notice of me, then I was going to cut off the corner of the piece I'd taken. They didn't believe me, which meant even though I didn't really want to, I had to carry out my threat, so I chewed the corner off. I felt guilty straight away, so I carefully nudged the two ends together in the hope they would think I was trying to help rather than spoil their fun. I'm not sure whether it was a vital clue that I decided to work on, as they haven't finished the rest of the jigsaw yet, but despite my attempt to help they really didn't seem awfully pleased. I was also somewhat disappointed to find that my Master totally refused to share his Jaffa Cakes, which in fairness was what led me to steal the piece of jigsaw in the first place. Share and share alike, they are always welcome to play with my toys and could join in eating my food if they were ever quick enough.

Sunday 12th March

We play a great game. The Boss, mistakenly, thinks she's in charge. She calls it 'Dog on a stick', but I prefer to call it 'Keeping The Boss at arm's length'. Basically, I get her to find me a nice big stick and then I let her hold one end of it, while I alternate between chewing it and hanging from it. At any point, I know I have her at precisely one stick distance away, which is a nice and safe place for me to keep an eye on her. It seems to keep her amused for a long time. If the stick breaks, I get her to find me another and so the game goes on.

Monday 13th March

I'm now a little confused. My owners completed the murder mystery jigsaw, but had no more idea what the solution was when they could see the picture than they had at the start. Fortunately, the bit I had 'rearranged' did not make any difference to what detail you could see, at least not as far as I could tell. Quite apart from how they were supposed to get the solution from the picture, what confused me was, why would you carefully put a thousand little pieces together to make a picture and then as soon as you've finished, break it all up again and put it back in the box? Humans do some funny things.

I'm four months old and it seems that I now look more like a dog than a puppy. Fewer people stop and say 'Isn't he lovely?' when we're out walking, though of course I am. I've even noticed that I look a bit different now too. The fact that I can notice is a bit of a giveaway, as it means I'm now tall enough to see myself in the hall mirror. It was a shock at first, but now I've got used to it, I stop and admire myself each time I go by, just checking that I look my best, in case anyone should call round unannounced and because The Boss rarely gives me much advance notice when we're going out. I barely get time to get my collar before I'm whisked out of the door. On the plus side, she rarely keeps me waiting on the odd occasions that I'm ready first.

Wednesday 15th March

I saw another of those strange road names, 'Badger Wood Glade'. I got all excited given how fond I am of the woodland animals and the forest near here. There I was wagging my tail and running round in excitement, but it was nothing short of fraud, no badgers, no wood, no glade, in fact not so much as a tree in sight. I think on that basis I should rename where I live 'Concrete Jungle Freeway', so that it's just as far from the truth as all the other road names I see.

I was taken to the vet again yesterday. The Boss said I didn't need to worry because it was only for a blood test. What she didn't tell me was that a blood test also involves having a needle stuck in me. Why didn't I need to worry? How does that differ from an injection exactly? The good news seems to be, that as long as the result is ok I can travel to England in six months' time. I'm not sure why that might be good news. Are English lampposts better than the ones in Belgium? Is there an endless supply of acorns? Do English dogs smell different? I wonder if there is a travel guide to England, written from a dog's perspective?

I was talking to The Boss yesterday and I can't believe how odd humans are. She was telling me that when she was little, they didn't have home computers. Can you believe that? No internet! She used to type on a thing called a typewriter that didn't save any of her work. If she made a mistake, she had to either cross it out, or start again and there was no built in spell checker, she had to use a real paper dictionary. She was trying to explain to me how every so often she had to change the ribbon on the typewriter and how it was a bit like the printer cartridge except you used to end up with ink all over your paws. I said I still do that with a print cartridge, but she said I would have been even worse with a ribbon.

Thursday 16th March

I've been looking at my family tree. It all gets quite confusing. To begin with, it seems I'm not called Alfie at all. My real name is Einstein; it's a shame I'm not as clever as the real Einstein. My last name isn't really Dog either, it's something quite long and difficult for me to pronounce correctly. Mind you, if I think that one is difficult to say, it's nothing compared with some of my ancestors. All that is not as bad, as finding out that the same 22 dogs appear to be 64 of my ancestors in the last six generations. One dog seems to be my great great great grandfather three times and my great great great great great grandfather three times. I'm quite shocked. I was wondering if any of them were famous and how many of them are still alive.

It was puppy training last night. I like to think that I'm not a badly behaved dog, but then I like to think that I'm handsome, sophisticated and intelligent as well. I just didn't want to do any of it last night. It isn't that I can't, I'll sit and come when called at home and you know how much I love playing fetch, but last night I just didn't want to. I was probably showing off a bit, because I had an audience and I was testing out some of my new-found strength. I felt a bit mean by the end of the night, as the poor Boss was really quite upset about it; she does try very hard. I suppose looking after me is quite hard work, perhaps I should have put in a little more effort. One good thing that came out of it was that she's given up on the idea of training me using affection and praise. She's finally realised that bribery is much more effective, yet again – the dog wins! I suppose on the downside I'm now threatened with spending more of the rest of my week doing training so that I can advance past the starter class, but at least it'll mean lots of treats along the way, so it can't be all bad.

Friday 17th March
One very exciting thing that has happened this week is that The Boss has sorted out my email account. I can now be emailed at alfie@alfiedog.me.uk I just hope that someone writes to me, as it'll be very sad to have an email account to check every day and find there's nothing in it. I wonder if there's much spam directed at dogs. I know you get all sorts of spam that I may not understand and I'm sure I've had enough prodding from the vet, not to want to try any unnecessary surgery.

Saturday 18th March
It was really cold at the park yesterday. Despite my barking at the goats to keep warm and then shouting a

few greetings to the deer, The Boss thought it would be a good idea to go into the restaurant to have coffee. I thought it would be boring, but its amazing how much fun small boys and puppies can have in all situations. Besides which, me going into a restaurant, I've never done that before, I didn't know what I was supposed to do. It was hard to know which order I was supposed to lick the cutlery. Do you start with the ones that are easiest to get to, or should you lick the ones on the neighbouring table first? Is it good practice when you're lying on the floor, to nip the ankles of passing customers, or should you only bite the waiter? I was struggling with all these thoughts when the waiter brought me my very own biscuit to keep me quiet, but it was much more fun to try to pinch the ones that were for the rest of the group. One of them got chocolate all round his mouth and The Boss didn't seem very pleased when I offered to lick it off. I had mud on my nose, so James was laughing at me too. He did refuse to lick that off for me so I had to do it myself. It was brilliant fun, but I could see The Boss looked a little strained by our antics.

Sunday 19th March

I've been listening to The Boss talking about money laundering. Not actually about doing it herself, but about other people doing it. Try as I might I just couldn't understand what was wrong with washing some money. She laughed at me and said "Oh Alfie, money laundering isn't about literally washing money." Well how was I supposed to know? It turns out that it's all about taking money from crimes, like selling drugs or stealing and then making it impossible to work out what the original source of the money was, so that the criminal can spend it safely.

It isn't about the times you leave your notes in the pocket or your trousers when they go in the washing machine, after all. I do wish sometimes that people would tell me what they mean rather than letting me misunderstand, leaving me to look stupid.

Monday 20th March

Would you believe, yesterday The Boss actually expected me to go for a walk before 9 'o clock in the morning? We got half way along the bridleway, it was cold and misty and I just thought 'blow it' so I stopped. The Boss carried on walking for a bit before she realised I wasn't with her. Then she turned round and called me to join her and I just said 'Look, it's Sunday morning, I wanted a lie in.' Fortunately, she said she hadn't been too fussed about getting up either, so we turned round and went home, another minor victory to the dog.

Following on from the walk, it turned out to be quite a day. James was flying back to England. The exciting bit, for me, was that The Boss said, as I had been so good in the restaurant, I could go and wave him off. I'm now proud to say that I've been to Schiphol airport, near Amsterdam. I can't actually pronounce it properly but I have at least been there.

We stopped at a service station for lunch on the way. I wanted to go to 'KFC', but James said he wanted to go to Burger King and The Boss said she'd brought dog food for me anyway. She really is a killjoy at times. The first piece of excitement was getting inside and encountering stairs. Now, I've already told you that I'm only just learning how to do stairs and am struggling to master the ones at home as they are slippery and fairly narrow, but here I was in the service station with several flights of stairs separating me from begging for a bit of burger. I took a deep breath and carefully followed The Boss. As it turned out these were not slippery and were quite wide, so I found I could do them just fine. Then there was another flight that were narrower, but I found if I criss-crossed right to left and back again, I could do these too. We had to go over a bridge with lots of restaurant bits and loads of people. Despite my best endeavours to nip the ankle of a bloke in the queue at the checkout, The Boss managed to pull me back just in time and we got to the other side without incident.

This is where I discovered the truth of the old adage 'what goes up must come down' and in this case, it was me. Suddenly I found myself faced with several flights of stairs that went in the opposite direction to the ones I had just climbed. I followed gingerly behind The Boss and caught my breath when we got to a little landing, then did the next bit and eventually got to the bottom. After all that, what do you think my reward was when we got to Burger King? Do you think I got the bacon double cheeseburger and large fries I asked for? Do you think they even brought me back a Coke to drink? No. The Boss gave me a dog biscuit and a pat on the head and one of the waitresses offered me a bowl of water. To say I was disappointed would be a massive understatement.

What I hadn't bargained for, was that having walked up and down all those stairs to get to Burger King, only to have to sit and watch, I then had to walk all the way back to the car. This time my Master suggested I try the escalator. What kind of nutcase steps onto something that is constantly trying to move away from them? Not this one that's for sure. The Boss took me back over all the stairs and I started to find I was getting the hang of it.

When I found I really was being taken straight back to the car and they weren't going to buy me so much as a bar of chocolate. Well that was it! I got my own back by leaving a large pile on the service station floor. The Boss was mortified. My Master was oblivious, until of course she called him back to take me out so that she could clear up. I felt pretty bad about it, given how upset she was, but she really does need to learn that I like burgers too.

Back at the car, outside the service station, I was given a lunch of dog food and water which soon stopped me feeling bad about the pile I'd left in protest inside.

At the airport, the first thing I noticed, was the decided absence of green. There appeared to be absolutely no grass, except on the roof of one building - very strange. It was just concrete everywhere. It didn't seem very well designed from a dog's perspective.

There were trolleys to watch out for and people who didn't look at my level to see if they were running into anyone. Worst of all, every time I lay down it was hard finding a spot where my nose, paws and tail weren't exposed to passing feet and trolley wheels. I was watching everything as carefully as possible so that I'll know what to do when they let me travel on my own. There are special check-in machines that you insert your passport into, to get your booking to come up, but I'm going to have difficulty reaching to follow the instructions on the screen.

I even made one or two new friends, including a lovely man who said he wasn't allowed a dog where he lived and made a real fuss of me. I wondered if I went home with him whether he'd give me a bacon double cheeseburger.

I think the best bit was sitting watching the people go

by. It did make me go back to my earlier idea of being a fashion consultant. Now to be fair, if I started on The Boss I'd have my work cut out, but at least she doesn't go out in public wearing something that looks more like pyjamas, or in clothes that clearly don't fit her. She has no fashion sense, but she's generally not embarrassing, scruffy yes, but not downright embarrassing.

When we got home, The Boss went upstairs and as always left me downstairs to play for a few minutes. Well I wasn't having any of it. Not now I've learnt to climb stairs. I followed her up and made her jump by tapping her on the leg when she wasn't expecting it. One minor problem is that I can't walk down the stairs at home yet, so if I try that one at the wrong time I'm going to be stuck, until someone comes to find me. I'd better make sure it doesn't happen at meal times.

5
EIGHTEEN WEEKS AND GROWING

Wednesday 22nd March

Now here's a strange thing. Can you believe that mobile phones were once the size of bricks? What would be the point in trying to call that 'mobile'? You would need awfully big pockets to fit that in. Apparently, only 20 years ago it was like that and the batteries only stayed charged for about 2 hours. What kind of world was that? I just can't imagine what it must have been like. The Boss was telling me that portable computers were the size of the one I have for my desk. How on earth are you expected to carry that round with you? Were people bigger then, so that things were more in proportion? Have humans evolved into a small size now, as they don't have to carry big mobile phones and computers?

Another thing I've been wondering, is life real or is it just a film? Are all the people and creatures around me just playing 'bit parts' in a film about my life, or am I just an extra in a film about one of their lives? If this is a film about someone else, do I know the real person or are they just being played by an actor? Maybe my Master isn't who I think he is, maybe he is just an actor pretending to be my Master and I'm playing the part of my Master's dog, whilst obviously not being the real dog at all. Sometimes my trains of thought just get too complicated for even me to deal with.

Much as I have been doing little dances round the garden, I have failed to summon up the rain clouds. This means that short of my having a really imaginative idea within the next few hours, I will have to face the fact that The Boss is going to take me to puppy training again. I've contemplated feigning illness or pretending to limp, but she isn't soft enough to simply say it's ok to stay at home. She is most likely to say something like if I'm not well, then I will just have to go to bed early and clearly won't be able to go out and play tomorrow. I did try hiding and not coming out, but she threw a toy and shouted fetch and before I knew what I was doing, I chased it and then pulled up sharp when I realised I was supposed to be in hiding.

Thursday 23rd March
Last week we played 'hide and seek', The Boss counted whilst I stayed with her and James went to hide behind one of the trees. Well in fairness, it wasn't that hard as I'd only pretended to close my eyes, but I would run and just stand there for a while, pretending I didn't know where he was. Then he'd move or call 'Alfie' and I'd go bounding up to him. I did try doing it by smell, but unfortunately, The Boss in her lack of understanding of boys, had made James wash, so he wasn't so easy to find, until I remembered to follow the smell of soap.

After all my concern about puppy training, I didn't go last night. I was almost sorry. It is one of those things that you pretend you don't want to do, because it doesn't seem cool to want to go to 'obedience training', but privately you think it's really fun to see all the other dogs and bounce on them, in a way you can only get away with while you're a puppy. The problem with pretending you didn't want to do something, is that you can't then mope about with disappointment when you don't get to do it. I spent all evening having to pretend I was happy.

Friday 24th March
The Boss went to the vet without me yesterday. On the one paw, I'm very happy that she didn't take me and on the other paw, in my role as a secret agent, I'm concerned that there is a conspiracy going on. She claims that to cheer me up, because I can't go to see my Mum and Sister, she's taking me to see the place in Switzerland where my ancestors came from, the village of Entlebuch. I will believe it when I see it; I think she was just plotting against me with the vet. Do you think this is how paranoia starts? I might try to look in her diary later to see if she has written an appointment down. She did show me the special stamp that the vet has put in my passport and told me that's what I need to get into Switzerland, but as I managed to go to the Netherlands last week without one, I'm a little dubious as to what the difference is for Switzerland.

Saturday 25th March
I'm so excited. Now I know this may seem strange, but if it was your first time going into a supermarket, you might think it exciting too. The Boss is going to the do-it-yourself store later to buy me some more dog food and I can go too. When she was in there the other day, there was a person in front of her with a particularly ugly dog, the sort that only an owner could love, so she came home and said if that person could take his dog, then the next time she went I could go. This means I'm going to get to do that old tugging at the coat thing, 'can you buy me this?' 'can I have one of those?' 'this toy looks great. If you don't buy me one I'm going to cry and make a scene.' I can be

just like all the other children. Oh the joy of the things you can get away with when you're only nineteen weeks old. I'm going to sniff all the other foods to see if there's one I prefer and be all cute and beg for dog biscuits. I'm not sure how I'm going to contain my excitement until this afternoon.

For the trip to Switzerland, I plan to watch a dvd. I'm trying to decide which films I want to watch. I wanted to take 'Wallace and Gromit and the Curse of the Were Rabbit', but The Boss says it's a nightmare trying to drive with me chasing rabbits behind her. I have to make sure I put my ears up before putting on the headphones, otherwise I can't hear very well and The Boss gets annoyed if I keep asking to stop to get her to sort it out. I can use the journey as an excuse to ask for some sweets when we go shopping this afternoon. I'll probably have eaten them before Monday but that's not the point.

Monday 27th March

I asked if I could have some extra spending money if I was going on holiday, as all my pocket money went ages ago and The Boss said she would see. She did confuse me by telling me it would have to be in something called Swiss Francs, instead of Euros, as they use different money there. Why?

The bad news was that I did have to go for an early walk. I grumbled all the way, but it wasn't too bad as we met a few other dogs on route. They were all grumbling that their owners took them out early and seemed quite jealous when I said that we usually preferred to go out just after lunch. Most owners just have no idea what a dog wants. There are times that we're about as keen on exercise as they are, but does that stop them? No, it does not. They march us off because it's 'good for us'. Pah, a nice warm fireside and something to chew, that's what we really want.

I did manage to get The Boss to buy some sweets for the journey, but she wouldn't let me have them early. I tried to get her to give them to me before we got in the car, by arguing that I would get sticky paws on the car if I ate them as we went along. She was one step ahead of me and said I shouldn't have used the excuse they were for the journey, if that wasn't what I meant.

Anyway, Switzerland here I come. Do you think I need my bucket and spade?

Tuesday 28th March

Well I packed my bucket and spade, but The Boss took it out again before we set off yesterday. Then she showed me the map and it turns out that Switzerland doesn't have any sea round it.

What she hadn't told me was that I get to stay in a hotel. I'm not sure where I thought I might be staying, but having never done this sort of thing before, I hadn't really thought about it. Annoyingly, they have not booked me my own room and The Boss has brought my bed from home, so I don't even get to snuggle up under the duvet. Apparently, because I was so good in the restaurant the other day, The Boss decided I was ready to stay in a hotel. It just goes to show you, behaving properly might be boring but it sometimes pays off.

I don't know what The Boss is planning to do today, but I just hope it doesn't involve climbing up any of those mountains. I know I'm a Swiss Mountain Dog, but you can take going back to your roots a little too far.

Wednesday 29th March

What an odd day it was yesterday. Not only did it rain all day, but I had to eat my meals at the back of the car in the Hotel garage. Now I'm not what you might call fussy about where I eat, but when you have to pick up the bits you've dropped off a concrete floor, it tastes a bit dusty. It seems somewhat unfair when my owners get to eat in a restaurant, with me sitting drooling at their feet. We went for a drive around some fairly 'hairy' roads, where The Boss made an amazing discovery. If you drive round a mountain clockwise you stay close to the mountain and avoid the edge. Of course, this only works if you drive on the right hand side of the road. For those who still drive on the left, the principle needs to be reversed. There's still snow on the hillside. How does that work? The temperature is much warmer than freezing, so why hasn't it melted? I tried asking The Boss whether water freezes at a different temperature here, but she said that wasn't the answer.

I've really enjoyed meeting lots of new people. I always like it when people say, 'Oh isn't he lovely?' At least I'm interpreting that as being the translation, as there seems to be a small language hurdle that we're failing to overcome. At least in Belgium a lot of people speak English, which for the most part gives The Boss a fighting chance of understanding them, on her good days anyway. Bless her, at one service station, she got so confused as to what language to speak in which country, that I don't think she made a lot of sense to anyone anywhere. She even had difficulty being understood when she only wanted to order some fries and coffee and I thought the words for those were universal.

Thursday 30th March

I now understand why I'm a Swiss 'mountain' dog, a term that doesn't make a lot of sense when you're born and bred in a flat country like Belgium. I think I may be a bit on the soft side to identify completely with my roots and although I still want to find a career that means I have a little more money than I have at present, I can't see myself either herding animals or pulling a cart. I think I'd like to do something a little less manual and a little more indoors.

Friday 31st March

Yesterday we saw another Entlebucher. He was the other side of the park and I waved madly but he didn't come over. I wonder if he was a relative? For all I know he could have been my dad or my granddad or three of my great granddads.

Now you can call me naive if you want to, but somehow it hadn't dawned on me that my excitement at the prospect of going home, was going to be completely spoilt by the thought of a large number of hours in the car. In fairness, I don't think The Boss is all that keen either, but short of abandoning the car here, she doesn't seem to have a lot of choice. Maybe it won't be quite so bad. I have asked if we can stop at places other than motorway services, as I didn't really like them very much. Let's just see if she's been listening to me.

Saturday 1st April

Well it's good to be home. It's probably fair to say that no dog or human was ever so happy to be home. I ran around like crazy, just checking everything was still there and of course it was, but you can never be too careful.

Then I went for a skid on every rug in the house, just to make sure I still could and nibbled all the houseplants. Then most importantly, I peed in my favourite spot. My owners were very pleased to be back. But did I see them undertake any of these important rituals? No. In fairness, they may have peed in their favourite places, but I just wasn't there to witness it. Home isn't just the place you put your bed. Home is the place where you know where the dog biscuits are kept and you know which door to sit by when you want to go out. It's the place where the smells are familiar and the plants have nibbled edges. I can only conclude and with much enthusiasm, I love my home.

Sunday 2nd April

Fortunately, my Master managed to restart the central heating yesterday. For some reason it had gone off while we were away, which left me no choice but to sit in front of the fire when I wasn't running round. Then I had the problem of having to keep finding my Master, to make him put another log on the fire. I would do it myself, but I would so hate to burn my paws and I find the tongs quite difficult to grasp. Generally, I pick logs up in my mouth, but I'm certainly not planning to stick my head in the fire. Other than that, it's been a bit quiet since we got back The Boss is poorly. I did try taking her breakfast in bed. I got as far as getting the Frosties out of the cupboard, but the plan was derailed by the overwhelming thought of just how nice it would be to eat them. With all these things, they say it's the thought that counts and I did think about them getting as far as The Boss, it just didn't happen.

Monday 3rd April

This afternoon I'm going to see my Mum and Sister. There's so much to tell them. I know my Mum has been to Switzerland, but my Sister hasn't. She will be so jealous. It isn't that I particularly liked it there, but I shan't tell her that bit. If you can't try to impress your Sister, then who can you impress? Last time I saw my Sister she kept pouncing on me and rolling me over in the mud. I've been 'working out' since then, so hopefully I'm now strong enough to hold my ground and just maybe give her a run for her money.

Tuesday 4th April

What an afternoon it was seeing my Mum and Sister yesterday. I didn't get to spend too much time with my Mum; it was all rather strange. They told me she was 'on heat'. I presume that's like when I push the button on the dashboard and the car seat gets warm. But why would that mean she didn't want to see me? I saw her for a little while but she tried to bite me and I ran and hid behind The Boss.

We got stuck in traffic on the way home, so The Boss tried to get the clever GPS thing, to find us another route. Well all I can say is, now she can't complain so much about my map reading. If a machine can get it so badly wrong, then how can she expect a puppy to work it out?

The Boss let slip that I have to go to the vet this afternoon. When she realised what she'd said, she tried to make light of it, saying it was just to pick up my blood test results for my passport, but I don't trust her. I'm planning to hide somewhere just in case.

Wednesday 5th April

I was right to be alarmed. The vet didn't just stamp my passport. Oh no. Not to put too fine a point on it, he put his hands on parts of me that, whilst it's ok for me to lick, even in public, I don't expect to have prodded and poked by a man in a white coat. Now being a young puppy, and not having that much experience of life, I'm not absolutely certain which bits I'm expecting to find in which places. The vet and The Boss seem to be concerned about me, which is leading the vet to prod and poke in a most embarrassing way.

An alarming trend seems to have developed on the bird table. The birds are eating too much. No sooner have I been out and hung up some more containers of food, than I turn round and the food has gone. I haven't noticed that they're getting fat from over eating, so I'm guessing they have moved to a shift system to ensure that more birds can get a stint at the table. Perhaps that is what all the early morning singing has been about, the birds sorting out the 'sittings' for the day. I wonder if I fix a little bell on the end of the table, if I can get them to ring when they're ready for me to bring out their pudding.

I got a bit muddy today, but I have to say I have become a little vain. I rather like the contrast of the rich brown and white bits with the rest of my black fur and work very hard to keep them looking good. Although The Boss wiped my paws for me, I had the rest sorted in about half an hour. Doing it myself has the extra advantage of stringing out all the tastes from the walk, as I get to rediscover them matted deep into my coat. I think the taboos for humans are such a shame; they really do miss an awful lot of fun. Mind you, from observation, humans do rather let themselves go and very few can reach to lick all the necessary places by the time they're an adult.

Thursday 6th April
The Boss asked if I would like a 'flutter' on the Grand National. I'm sure the answer I was expected to give was a simple yes or no, however I started with 'What's a flutter?' whilst visualising something for birds, rather than dogs. Apparently, this means gambling. OK so 'what's gambling?' It seems to be where I risk my hard earned cash, on an event that probably won't happen. My next question was 'what's the Grand National?' It turns out that a lot of horses jump over some very big fences, whilst lots of humans watch them and try to guess who will fall off. At least I think that's what she said the humans are guessing. By the time she'd started to explain 'each way betting' and I found it didn't mean you were covered even if the horse turned round and ran in the opposite direction and that spread betting didn't come in a choice of cheese or meat flavours, I was completely confused. Maybe if I watch the race on Saturday it will make more sense to me. It turns out that there are people called bookmakers, who don't make books, but who are willing to take my money. I decided that all things considered, I'm happy to hang on to my own money if it's all the same to them.

Friday 7th April
I have a new favourite toy. My Master bought it for me last week. It's a squidgy pink rhinoceros that squeaks. You would have to put your mouth round it and squeeze it, to understand completely what I mean. It does have such a satisfying feel to it. Obviously, it can't completely replace Miffy, but I have to say she really isn't looking herself anymore. There's just a bit too much leg and ear missing

on the left paw side.

Saturday 8th April
I've been reading 'Three men in a boat', and quite like the idea of being taken for a long trip on a river. I could be captain and bark orders to my crew. I would offer to row, but I can't imagine having to sit on two legs all day; it seems such a waste when I can sit on all four. I do find using all four so much more comfortable and I'm uncertain how I would hold the oar. If truth be known, I'm lazy, but what's the harm in that? I suppose I could get a little motorised boat.

Sunday 9th April
I think it's brilliant. On a Sunday, the human supermarket is closed, but the one for my food is open. I've been very disappointed that they've been out of stock of the coconut shells I buy for the birds. They're filled with fat and seeds and the birds love them. The birds were threatening to go on strike and stop visiting the garden if I couldn't get any more. I've tried but to no avail. I can't imagine they will carry out their threat, they do still get lots of other food. My supermarket also seems to sell a very good range of plants for me to nibble and power tools that My Master finds very exciting. At times like this, I don't think I understand people at all. Why would you get excited about something you plug into the electricity that makes a hole? I can do that with my paws and as for the idea of a lawn mower, by the time I've peed everywhere we really won't need one.

Tuesday 11th April
I'm starting to suspect that a number of people are

reading my private diary. My conclusions are drawn from the number of people that start a conversation with me as though they already know me and I haven't a clue who they are. It's either that or I have a particularly bad memory for faces. Of course, if I'm allowed to sniff all their appropriate places, I can soon work out if I've met them before, but for some reason The Boss tells me that's not acceptable practice. It's perfectly ok in the dog world to sniff any bits you want, I can't think why humans are so boring.

I went to see Mackensey and it turns out she is on heat too, as well as my mum that is. She was behaving very oddly and really wanted to play with me. She doesn't normally want to play, so I asked why sitting on a warm car seat should have that effect and she laughed at me. I was really quite upset, but then even worse, she explained to me what it really meant. Oh diary, I just didn't know what to do, I was so embarrassed. I put my paws over my ears and ran round barking to block out hearing any more. I'm not even five months old yet; I really shouldn't need to hear things like that. Then she went on to explain why the vet was prodding and poking me and what I should be like when I'm fully grown. Oh diary, I don't think I can ever face her again, I just wanted to run and hide behind The Boss and get her to tell me that none of it was true.

6
I'M GETTING RATHER BIG

Wednesday 12th April

Life is so unfair. My Master and The Boss sat us all down and told us they're getting married. It's so exciting and we all thought it was great. There are four of us, one gets to be bridesmaid, one gets to be ring bearer, one gets to be page boy and then there's me. I don't even get to go. Me, their only dog and I don't even go to their wedding. I'm distressed, wounded, forlorn. Oh woe is me. I would have looked good with a little barrel round my neck carrying the rings. I could carry the back of the dress in my mouth, to keep it off the ground. I could hold the bouquet. I could even do all three if they asked nicely. How can they think to leave me out? So my passport will not be valid for England, they could delay the wedding and wait for me.

The other seriously worrying thing that has happened is that the woodpecker has discovered the bird table. Now whilst I'm more than happy to welcome him to join the early breakfast sitting, being one of the few meal times with spare places, he seems intent on chopping the bird table down and is pecking away at the centre pole that supports it. I'm starting to wonder whether he has had a disagreement with the other garden birds and is now trying to spoil it for all of them.

I'm used to having one nice long walk each day. At the age of nearly five months old, I'm quite content to walk three or four kilometres after lunch. Unfortunately, one of my companions for the week despite being four whole years old can't walk nearly so far. I'm really annoyed that I didn't think of the 'I want a carry' line when I was tired, rather than faithfully plod on next to The Boss. It would have saved so much effort. It's a bit late now that The Boss

knows I can walk that far and besides which, I've got too heavy for her to carry me. There are times it seems I still have so much to learn. Clearly, my lesson today is that if you are too helpful, then people take advantage of your good nature.

Thursday 13th April

Now I know you may think if I can write a diary then almost anything is possible, but this week has involved a four year old playing 'I spy' with lots of words starting with silent letters, that no one else knew were there. Then we've had his 'piece de resistance'- playing Scrabble when he can't even spell. For most people I realise that isn't a real handicap and they just look for words in the 'Official Scrabble Dictionary', but when you're four you can't even do that. If you can't read the words yet, it's a little bit difficult to find them in the dictionary, but never let it be said that Andrew lets that hold him back. I sat by, trying to make suggestions of ways he could change the order of the letters to improve his score, but frankly at the end of the day whether 'fdhis' scores more than 'sdhif' is somewhat immaterial.

My week also involved being encouraged to sit in front of a roaring fire, even though it's 25 degrees centigrade in the lounge. I don't even have a zip to undo my coat. Why do boys have to set fire to things? Why aren't they as keen to do the jobs that actually need doing, like throwing my ball for me to fetch and getting my dog treats out of the cupboard? I spend my evenings on 'Twiglet watch'. My Master would never be so careless as to drop one of his precious Twiglets on the floor, but the great thing about having a four year old around, is that he drops food everywhere and when he doesn't drop it accidentally, he does it deliberately. I even managed to 'con' The Boss last night into rescuing one I couldn't reach from under the settee. I told her it was my dog-chew and I needed it, as otherwise I might start chewing my toys again. How gullible was she? She actually fell for my ruse. Sometimes having innocent big brown eyes can be so useful.

Sunday 16th April

I don't really understand why, but today we had an Easter Egg Hunt. Ok, I get the bit about it being Easter and that being about Jesus and celebrating, but I don't get where the chocolate eggs came into the story. Don't get me wrong, I'm happy for it to be appropriate on any day of the year to chase round the garden looking for, finding and eating chocolate eggs, but why do it on this day in particular? Was Jesus particularly fond of chocolate eggs?

Monday 17th April

There I was at the park, when I realised that people came along with bags of food to feed the goats and deer in the pen. The animals in the pen all line up along the fence and wait patiently to be given scraps of food. What's a hungry puppy to do? I joined the end of the line. I was hoping the people with the food wouldn't realise that I was on the same side of the fence as they were and that I was in fact a dog. I was working with the 'I'm cute and furry, with big brown eyes and you're going to fall for me' routine. Try as I might there really was no fooling the adults; however, I did have a little more success with the children.

It's really good for dogs that children don't like vegetables. I would however prefer it if they didn't like steak, or chops either. I don't get enough of the biscuits or cakes come to that.

I've been wondering. Why don't modern children understand the importance of 'Lassie' in cultural terms, or the film 'Beethoven' come to that? It's so important to the independence of dogs that they should be able to secure the lead roles in films; there need to be more films written with the acting dog in mind. 'Scooby Doo' isn't bad but I really don't feel that they have given him enough lines.

Tuesday 18th April

How lovely to have a quiet day. I stayed in bed for ages. Well when I say stayed in bed that is not absolutely accurate. I got out of bed to get my Frostie and then went back to bed again. I was having a fantastic time, dreaming of chasing ducks. In my dreams, they don't take off and fly quite as early as they do in real life and I at least get to pull out a tail feather before they're in the air. Anyway, there I was dreaming away, when I heard The Boss on the phone to the vet. When can she take me to see him? How often do I have to say it? Never would be good in my diary. Unfortunately, The Boss seems to see things rather differently and wants me to go this afternoon. I'm five months old, exactly how much prodding does a puppy need? After that, the gloss had gone off staying in bed and I felt obliged to get up and try to show I was perfectly healthy and didn't need to see the vet. I didn't sneeze or cough once.

Wednesday 19th April

Ok enough already. I'm through with vets. The Boss told me I was just going for a blood test result. I thought 'right, nothing to worry about'. I bounced in and said hello to the vet, after all, he's quite a nice bloke, when he isn't doing unspeakable things to me. How could I be so naive? First he looked at my teeth, which have almost all come through now and I told him that the little bit of blood on my gum was nothing. I just chew on The Boss's arm when my teeth are feeling uncomfortable. Then he started prodding and poking my rear end again. I'm starting to think he has a bit of a thing for me. Then horror of horrors, he started talking about operations because bits aren't all where they should be. Whatever he has in mind, I'm definitely out that day. Then just as I started to relax, he explained to me that my blood test hadn't shown enough antibodies and I have to have it all again. Look, if it's this much trouble, I'm prepared to give up my right to travel the world. I can be like most other dogs and just stay home. Really, I can! Despite my urgent protestations, he stuck another needle into me and then booked me in for another blood test in a month's time. Why me? I'm just your average wimp. I can do without all this excitement.

In the meantime, I'm thinking very seriously of setting up in business in some form of activity involving weddings. It seems to work that whatever you would charge normally, as soon as someone mentions the word 'wedding' you are allowed to add an extra '0' on the end of the price. How can a cake cost THAT much money? Is it gold plated? My Master had even managed to find one The Boss liked, which was pretty good going on his part and his pleas of loving fruit cake had not fallen on deaf ears. Well if nothing else, it might help her to feel a bit less guilty about the cost of her dress. Now I know I can't go to the wedding, but I really hope they aren't thinking of leaving me out of the honeymoon as well. How many chances does a dog get to go on honeymoon after all?

Thursday 20th April

It seems that the car has shrunk. The Boss's car wasn't large, but we did both fit in it. I could sit facing forwards or sideways quite comfortably. Now it's shrunk, I can't lie facing forwards as I fall off the seat and my seatbelt is a bit restrictive for sitting up. There's nothing else for it but to lie sideways, which involves having my right front paw round the gear stick and my head on the handbrake. It wouldn't be too uncomfortable if The Boss could learn to drive without changing gear. I've offered to do it for her, but she says she would rather do it herself. Some people are so ungrateful. Don't say I didn't offer.

I'm feeling a bit tired and emotional after my injection the other day, or it may be the stress of worrying about my operation. Either way, I'm planning a lazy day with not too much running round, although I can't resist going slightly mad every time I spot pink rhino lying somewhere. I think it's the combination of his colour and soft squidgy shape. It really is very attractive to a puppy. I mistakenly tried to play with the orange furry turtle, but it turned out that wasn't for me and nearly caused a few tears. How was I to know? It looked quite like my furry squeaky toy from a distance. Admittedly, it was on Andy's bed and not mine but it was a simple mistake and I didn't do any harm.

Saturday 22nd April

I'm one happy spoilt dog. I have a new rubber rabbit. Ever since The Boss gave it to me I've done nothing but squeak it. Oh the sheer joy and pleasure. I wonder if it will last any longer than the last one. Rabbits really aren't built to last. On the downside, The Boss also bought me a harness. "Larger collar", I said, but no, she wanted it to match my lead and they didn't have any collars. Which bit of 'I don't want that thing round my body' do you think she didn't understand? To be fair it's quite comfortable but I just didn't see myself wearing something like that. I think she's got a bit too familiar with the notion of my being a cart dog. I'm expecting her to hook a skateboard up behind me some time soon, so that she doesn't have to put quite so much effort into walking me.

Tuesday 25th April
Spring is in the air. The plants are coming into bloom and the Boss is behaving very strangely. She seems to think that it's a good idea to put the roof down on the car and have fresh air coming in. It seemed a bit odd to begin with, but then I found the switch to wind my window down and sat up with the wind in my hair and my ears flapping back. It wasn't long before I realised that this really is THE LIFE. However, the point at which she pumped up the tyres of her bike and started pedalling down the drive, I was just hoping she wasn't expecting me to join in. I ran alongside for a while but I got bored and went to chew a stick until she came to her senses. I hope this isn't going to become a habit. She seemed to be making the suggestion that this is how we could go for a walk. Is she seriously expecting me to keep running along rather than walking in a leisurely fashion. I like to be able to stop and sniff at every opportunity? Can you imagine her pedalling along with me running and then suddenly stopping and shooting her over the handlebars? Now I start to visualise it, I quite fancy the idea.

Thursday 27th April
Some of the wedding planning has got a bit much. I'm not

sure what I'm supposed to do. I get confused by this boy / girl thing. What do you do when a girl cries? If it was me in tears, I'd just want to be left alone with my grief, not of course that you would ever catch me in tears. I heard the boss talking to my Master about it once. She tried explaining that girls are different, but I really didn't get it. I did try talking to my Master, but he said 'It beats me.' and that was the end of the conversation. Now I'm stuck not knowing if I should intervene.

Friday 28th April

The mole guerrilla army seems to have retreated from their reconnaissance mission to the back gate. I don't know whether that means they have decided our garden is a bad place to attack and have gone off to find some other poor unsuspecting family, or whether this is the quiet before the storm. They may have gone off to get reinforcements with a view to completing a 'spring offensive'. I've decided to set up a sentry position by the hedge to watch out for them, whilst dozing in the sunshine. They will never get past here without me noticing.

Saturday 29th April

I spoke too soon about the moles. There's a new garrison just inside the back gate. They have actually broken through the perimeter defences and are moving in on us. I'm not sure about their numbers but I really don't like their style of warfare. I think that my best approach is probably to start digging from above to see if I can get them out into the open. The biggest problem now is to start digging without The Boss catching me. I don't want to find myself being held responsible for the piles of earth appearing in the garden. I may also have to learn how to use a scrubbing brush to get the telltale signs of dirt from under my claws. The other option is to try camouflage. If I could find a way of disguising myself as a piece of lawn with mossy patches on it and a few bare bits of earth, I would blend in beautifully.

Monday 1st May
The problem with my regularity of queuing up outside the biscuit cupboard is that The Boss has got wise to it and only ever gives me half a biscuit at a time; something to do with keeping my waistline trim. Unfortunately, I don't seem to get much say in it. I really must learn to open the cupboards myself. The other bad news is that The Boss has shown my Master how to get me to sit, by only pretending to have a biscuit in her hand. Although he has adopted the technique with me, he is worried in case The Boss tries a similar approach with him.

Tuesday 2nd May
Yesterday was the sort of day you decide to reorganise your bone cupboard, if only I had one! I mooched around the house getting under The Boss's feet and generally making a nuisance of myself. Every so often, I'd go and get hold of the end of my rope or rubber rabbit and take it to her, trying to persuade her to get hold of the other end and play with me, just as any normal puppy would. Of course, as far as she's concerned, I am a normal puppy. Little does she know what I get up to in my spare time. Anyway, I got bored after a while and went and sat looking out of the window daydreaming. I might have looked as though I was watching the back gate and I even woofed at appropriate intervals as people went past, but

in my head, I'd caught a train. Not just any train, after watching Michael Palin the other night, in his version of 'Around the world in 80 days', I was on the Orient Express speeding my way to Venice. There were people waiting on me paw and foot, providing for my every need. I didn't need to rearrange the bone cupboard, there was someone to do it for me. They even played 'tug' with me when I presented my rope. What a blissful couple of hours I spent on my dream journey. Then I was being swept along in a gondola on the canals of Venice. I was annoyed when The Boss, who had been feeling guilty for not playing with me, disturbed my nap to bring me pink rhino to play fetch. Has she no sensitivity towards a daydreaming puppy?

Wednesday 3rd May
I went out the other day and the grass was quite long and when I came back it was short and smelt different. I did wonder if it was actually different grass, but it still had the same patches of moss, so if someone had swapped it, they'd gone to a lot of trouble. I also seem to have been losing a lot of hair. I was all ready to discuss with the vet whether I might be suffering from stress, but The Boss told me not to be such a hypochondriac and I was just moulting because of the improved weather. This led to me looking up the meaning of both hypochondriac and moulting, before going off in a huff that she should even suggest such a thing. Next time she says there's something wrong, I shall just say the same to her. The hypochondriac thing anyway, I can't see her complaining of moulting.

Friday 5th May
After the sort of day I'd had, I was worn out and needed

something to cheer me up. In the evening The Boss caught me upstairs carrying a tree branch. She explained that I had my indoor toys for in the house and it was best that I left the trees outside, so that they would still be there for me to play with when I went out. Several hours later, when she was sitting on the settee, she spotted the rest of the tree that I'd left on the other rug. By this time, I had chopped it into small pieces to make it particularly difficult for her to put outside. Strangely, she didn't seem to find it very funny, but it was just the sort of light relief I needed.

Tuesday 9th May

I'm quite looking forward to going to dog training tomorrow. I wonder if I'm old enough to start doing anything more exciting than walk round a ring and put up with The Boss pretending to be an aeroplane? The Boss did explain to me that it would help if I'd actually behave and do all the things on command that I can do at home. Oh yes, that might get me to do other things, but it would so spoil the fun of showing her up. You see all these goody two shoes (or possibly four shoes) dogs, doing everything their owners tell them and thinking they look really cool, but how can it be cool not to have a mind of your own and not to be able to make your own choices in life? How would it have been cool to sit in a large pool of water, when it had been raining, except in the literal sense of cool? Every week I set out thinking 'Alfie lad, this week you're going to behave.' Then every week it's like the 'fun gremlins' get me and I just can't resist being naughty.

Wednesday 10th May

For reasons known only to herself, The Boss has once

again washed my bed. Every time I get it just dirty enough to be acceptable in dog circles, she insists on spoiling it. I actually found the extra layer of dog hair and dirt helped to keep me warm. Not that it's particularly cold, but it's nice to stay cosy.

For the most part, I'm fairly quiet. But I've discovered that if I nip outside and give one howl, I can set the local dogs off and then run back inside and pretend it wasn't me. It's a fun game, but I don't think The Boss has been completely fooled by my behaviour.

Now that I have nearly grown up (in dog terms 6 months is almost old enough to be considered responsible), I have asked if I can have a puppy of my own, as a pet. I'd look after it and take it for walks and make sure I cleaned up after it. Sadly, The Boss doesn't seem to think I can do all those things for myself yet, so I guess I'll have to keep asking. I did think I could ask for a rabbit or a hamster, but that wouldn't be so much fun.

Thursday 11th May 2006.
I fell asleep through the football last night. I only had the mood my Master was in afterwards to work out what the result was. Strangely he seemed in good spirits and was consoling himself that they hadn't lost as badly as they had to other teams this season. I guess it's always good to see the positives. Apparently, even when they were four nil down with only four minutes to go my Master was still convinced they could score five and win. So, if you score no goals in 86 minutes, how likely is it that you'll score 5 in 4 minutes? Fiction is so much better than reality.

Today is one of the days that you circle on the calendar and remember to tell your children, although from what the vet said, I don't suppose I'll be having any children.

What you might ask was so special about this morning? I managed to cock my leg when I peed, without falling over. That is a very important step forward, or standing still as the case may be, for a male puppy. I now feel that I have grown up.

7
SIX MONTHS OLD

Friday 12th May
Have you ever noticed that butterflies never quite come close enough to touch your nose? They dangle themselves between your eyes and once they've caught your attention and made you lose interest in the stick you were playing with, they flit off so you can't catch them.

We went out in the car for what should have been a short drive. However, in Belgium there is a tendency to undertake roadworks, which close off whole roads and which involve very long diversions. Most of the time there are sign posts for these. When it's a really big road they're closing, it's as though they give up trying to work out the best route round and just leave you to it. That's ok if you know your way, or have sat-nav. Neither of those is true of The Boss. Her alternative is blundering through, convinced that if she just goes a bit further along, then it must come out where she wanted. Unfortunately, she doesn't carry a compass and doesn't have a perfect sense of direction. We get there in the end but it's not always the end I was planning on getting to.

I thought I was going to be in trouble yesterday. I had one of those 'it wasn't me' moments. I was playing with rubber rabbit, swinging him round in my mouth, which makes a very satisfying noise as well as feeling good, when I accidentally knocked something off the coffee table with the end. Well I dropped rubber rabbit on the spot and ran to a different bit of the room. The Boss immediately got up to see what had happened. I gave her the innocent big brown-eyed look, but she knew I was guilty. She tried explaining to me that it was much better to own up than pretend I hadn't done it, particularly when there was no one else in the house to play with rubber rabbit. Fair point, but I wonder if she would have been as understanding if I'd actually broken something. As it turned out, it was only a plastic dinosaur out of the cereal packet, but I'm giving rubber rabbit a wide berth for a while so that he doesn't get me into any more trouble.

Saturday 13th May

I'm so excited. Today I'm going to see my family. I don't know how many will be there, but I haven't seen 2 of my sisters and my brother since I was about 8 or 9 weeks old. I might also meet some of my half brothers and sisters and they can tell me some more about what the next stage of growing up will be like. We don't all live in Belgium, or all have English owners, so I'm not sure whether I'm going to have some problems with the language, but some things are the same in any language. I have a lovely new collar with bones on it that I've asked The Boss if I can wear and I've been getting my coat looking it's best, especially for the occasion. Of course, that plan was slightly spoilt by The Boss applying tick treatment to me. She had promised I didn't have to have it until after the visit, but I went and got a tick and ended up at the vet having an antibiotic injection, so The Boss had to apply the treatment early.

I do hope my family remember me and want to play. I wonder if they will be impressed that I can now cock my leg?

I'm called 'Alfie' because The Boss liked it and my Master conceded that travelling round Europe, being called 'Wellington' might work less well. I do use Dog as my surname, as I couldn't choose between The Boss's and my Master's names. My Mum called me 'Einstein' originally so I hope she doesn't get confused.

Sunday 14th May

Yesterday has to have been the most exciting day since… well, probably the most exciting day ever. My mum, my three sisters, my brother and two of my half-brothers were there. There was so much to catch up on.

I realised I'm going to grow quite a lot more, if my half-brothers are anything to go by, which is worrying as I only just fit on the car seat now. My brother was sharing his stories of being prodded and poked by the vet and we compared notes. I don't think I stopped running round all afternoon. I was so tired that when we got in, despite it being tea time, I went straight off to sleep again and forgot I hadn't had any food, though I had been eating treats all afternoon as bribery to get me to do things.

Well we've finally watched the end of Michael Palin's 'Around the World in 80 days' and I was pleased to see he made it. They really saved the best bit until near the end. There was a whole pack of huskies and some of them were pulling a sled and they were howling. Well I just watched transfixed. I'm prepared to reconsider being a cart dog; it looked brilliant fun, particularly if there could be a whole group of us doing it together.

Monday 15th May

It's been fun watching the water droplets roll down the window and working out which will get to the bottom first. I was getting quite expert at working out what would happen after staring at them for a few hours. Annoyingly, The Boss has resorted to doing a jigsaw and try as I might I can't persuade her to run round throwing balls for me. I've trained her to throw lots of toys for me to fetch and as long as I take them back to her, I can keep the game going for quite a while. I've found the Frisbee more of a challenge than other toys; it's not as easy to get my teeth underneath to pick it up.

Tuesday 16th May

The Boss has had the 'sense' (her word not mine) to do the jigsaw on the dining table this time, so that I can't reach to help, which really isn't fair. I have tried jumping up to look at the picture, but she keeps making me get down. The best I can hope for is waiting for the times she drops a bit and then leap in, pick it up and dart off with it to the other side of the room. I can then have a good look at it, to see if I can work out what the picture is.

I'm really getting the hang of this top-down motoring. I sit and watch where we're going and wave to the little children when they wave to me. I'm trying to persuade The Boss to get me some sunglasses so that I can look cool when we see other dogs. I could do with a little sunhat but maybe that wouldn't look quite so cool. I wonder if I could get a doggy sized baseball cap?

I've discovered that if I get all my squeaky toys together, at least those that The Boss has not put through the wash, and then squeeze one after another, I can make quite a good tune. It now seems a real shame that the squeak has gone from so many of my toys. I've also discovered that if I do the same one repeatedly, I can be really annoying. Now let me think, which would I rather be – musical or annoying?

Wednesday 17th May

I've discovered some rather tasty plant roots in the garden. I've tried suggesting to The Boss that she might like to try them, but she doesn't seem so keen. If I chew on them for a while, they really do seem to be very mellowing.

Thursday 18th May

Tragedy has occurred. Rubber Rabbit the Second has fallen apart. There we were playing 'fetch', where on command I make The Boss throw an object repeatedly for me. One minute there was one rubber rabbit and the next minute there were three. Well a body and two separate legs, if we're being strictly accurate, but what are a few body parts between friends? That is now two rubber rabbits that The Boss has managed to destroy. I really don't know how she does it. What is she thinking of, tugging the end she's holding, when I clearly have it in my teeth? She really must learn to let go rather than break my toys.

The Boss seems to think I have some hormones kicking in as well. I don't really understand what she's on about, but she says it would explain why I suddenly feel the need to raise my leg and pee on every tree we walk past. It's a very odd change to find overnight you move from peeing for the sake of necessity, to peeing for some deep seated urge to tell the world you're around. I also started running off in to fields along our walk just for the fun of it and The Boss doesn't seem too thrilled about it. I just feel the call of the wild. The Boss has responded to this by trying to explain to me how she wants me to behave. Yeah right! Why in heavens name would I want to walk to heel, when there are more exciting places to run? However, when she makes me stop and sit down every time I try to tug away, the walk gets very frustrating. After a while you start thinking, 'ok then, if that's the way it has to be'. For all the love and rewards I get along the way, I suppose I can't really complain.

I had a very disturbing evening. A pheasant moved into our garden. I was stuck on the inside and it was strutting up and down outside the window. All I could do was bark as it waved its tail feathers at me at every pass. In the end, The Boss got up and closed the curtains to stop the pheasant upsetting me. I said I'd rather go out and chase it but she didn't seem to think that was the solution.

Friday 19th May
My owners have concluded that I'm not cut out to be a guard dog, which is good as I never saw myself in a rough, tough 'heavy' sort of role. Apparently, it would be normal practice to, at least, give a little bark when someone walks past, but I prefer to wag my tail and see if they'll tell me what a lovely puppy I am. You may think I'm being shallow and vain, but I'm a bloke, what more do you expect? The best bit of our trip to Bruges was all the people stopping and patting me and saying how beautiful I was, it almost made up for my Master accidentally standing on my paw on three occasions. Once is an accident, twice is clumsy, but by the third time I was starting to get a little annoyed. How would he like it if I kept standing on his feet? I've found a way to get my own back. When we go walking, I've found that if I climb down into the ditches they are no longer full of nice clean water, they're full of thick black mud. When I say black I

mean 'very black' and when I say mud I mean the type that after I've put my paws knee deep in, makes the most fantastic paw prints on clean trousers. The only problem is that it then takes me hours to get them sparkling white again, my paws, not the trousers.

The Boss has finally repaired my cushion. It was so good to have it back that I spent ages just chewing it and trying to rip it apart. It really is a very satisfying feeling; I can't think why The Boss is so unimpressed. I then proceeded to swing it round and round, but I accidentally let go and it flew up in the air and came down knocking a cd off the side. Fortunately, it was only the cd case that was broken but the worst of it is that my cushion has now been confiscated, so our reunion has been short lived.

Saturday 20th May
It turns out that deciding to use my raised leg to scratch, part way through cocking it to pee, has disastrous consequences. Basically, I fall over in a quite undignified fashion. All well and good for The Boss to stand there laughing at me, but hurt pride is no laughing matter. She's also stepped up her attempts at training me. She has resolved to spend half an hour a day trying to get me to work the way she wants. "Heel Alfie", "Sit Alfie", "Down Alfie", "Fetch Alfie" - it really is too much. I'm even finding myself accidentally complying because it's easier than objecting. I can at least still pride myself on ignoring my Master's commands, with the added advantage that it really winds him up if I do what The Boss says and not what he says.

Monday 22nd May
It turned out that the car washing yesterday was more fun

than I thought. It involved running and splashing in lots of water, with little white bubbles everywhere. Then it moved on to chasing round with the cloth in my mouth with my Master coming after me, to get it back. We should play this game more often.

I've discovered the delights of an upset stomach. The Boss is not being sympathetic as she seems to think one of the many things I eat and drink, when we're out, is to blame. For some reason she does not seem to think that eating horse dung and drinking from the putrid remains of water at the bottom of the ditch is a good thing, but I'm a dog. Things like that come naturally. However, I currently feel like it's the end of the world as I know it and if this doesn't stop soon, I may just have to conclude that The Boss isn't as stupid as she looks.

Thursday 25th May
I'm proud to say I've learnt a number of new things over the last few days. Some of them even seem to be the things The Boss wanted me to learn. That cannot be said for discovering that if she closes the stair gate at the top of the stairs, I can squeeze through the banister rails and then by jumping just a couple of stairs, I can still get down. Apparently, this is dangerous and I could end up having a serious accident. The good news is, that rather than assume that I will take any notice of this 'little talk' The Boss has told my Master that she thinks the safest thing is to stop closing the stair gate, once again victory to the dog. I've also learnt that if I push a door with my nose, then it will open. This makes it much harder for The Boss to shut me in, or out as the case may be. This would be victory to the dog, except I have to remember to do it really gently as head butting a door that has a catch can be quite

painful, as can head butting the glass doors in the lounge.

The habit that I was supposed to learn, was that if I want a cuddle, I have to ask nicely rather than jump up. I was worried at first that if I just went and sat next to them they might not notice me, or wouldn't know what I wanted, but all I have to do is gently tap them with my paw and look all sweet and it works every time. It's great being an irresistible puppy with big brown eyes. I wonder if it will still work when I get older.

Saturday 27th May
I had a bit of a mishap whilst out walking yesterday. Personally, I blame the duck. How was it my fault when the duck ran under some barbed wire? Somehow, I managed to run in between the rows of wire on the way out. All well and good had I not run into the barbs on the way back. Ouch I thought. I don't want to do that again in a hurry. The only problem was, that The Boss was on the other side of the fence and that is where I needed to be. I stood and looked pathetic, which all things considered I thought was the best approach. The Boss tried to get me to come towards her by offering me a biscuit. Who was she kidding, the fence had teeth. I started to get the scale of the problem when she explained that there was no way she was going to be able to climb over to my side of the fence and one way or another I had to get back. I suggested she could come through the stream, as there was no fence there, but then she pointed out I was going to have to come back and as she couldn't carry me, I would have to come back through the stream. That didn't seem quite so attractive. I admit it, for the first time that I can remember, I was scared. The Boss got a stick and got me to hold the end of it, as I do when I'm getting her to

play and then she carefully guided me through the rows of wire. I have to say she didn't do a bad job and she cut her finger in the process. For at least the next couple of hundred metres I walked close to her and I promised not to do it again. Then seeing another bird, I went chasing after it, back to my old self again.

Sunday 28th May

I'm waiting for next month's pocket money to buy a new Frisbee. My existing one is rather jagged round the edges, where I grab it with my teeth. I need some new tennis balls too. The ones I found in our garden were great, but they all seem to have broken into two pieces now. I don't know how it happens. I suppose it's like The Boss not being able to get the top off the lemonade bottle after my Master has done it up. She says he just doesn't know his own strength; I think I take after him

Sunday 4th June 2006.

I'm looking forward to a day of being a normal puppy and going to play with other puppies on the walk today. When I say 'normal' that is in the sense of planning to misbehave, pull on my lead and generally show the other dogs that in our house, I'm the boss. Of course, the fact that The Boss is a big softy and whilst my Master was away for a couple of days let me snuggle up on their bed, just about proves the point. My Master put his foot down in a most unconvincing fashion when he came home, so I think it's only a question of a few cute looks and I will have him completely under control.

Well after careful consideration, you should disregard everything I said about dog food and how human food should be more like it. What did I know? I was just a young puppy. On reflection, I want Parma ham as well. The strawberries The Boss was eating smelt quite good too. Does she share any of these bits with me? I don't think so. The best I can hope for is my morning Frostie, singular, and the odd plain crisp. I'm seriously considering taking action. I pretended to be on hunger strike and refused to eat my food, but once The Boss left the room, I wolfed it down anyway. As I don't get to do the clearing up she knew I'd had it. I tried to tell her it was the 'rubbish fairy' but she explained that wasn't real and it's just how she explains to my Master how the rubbish gets out to the bin, without his assistance. Bother, I really need to learn which make believe character each of them has invented. I should have said it was the purple worm, as that was the character invented by my Master when he felt left out at not seeing all the woodland animals.

Monday 5th June
What a day out it was yesterday. To my surprise it turns out I'm quite a small dog compared to other Swiss Mountain Dogs. Have you seen a Great Swiss? Compared to me they are huge. None of them have as much energy as me, but then I guess if they bounced on people there wouldn't be much more 'people' left to bounce on. My mum was there, but none of my brothers and sisters, which was a shame. There were simply lots of Bernese mountain dogs, all beautiful and fluffy. I was glad my coat was shiny, otherwise I would have been quite envious. The other thing I noticed was that the bit of me the vet keeps prodding, all the other boys seem to have two of them, and in the case of the Great Swiss they are rather large as well. I still only have one and it turns out that isn't normal. I wonder where the other one has gone

and if there is anything I can do about it? The Boss told me I was 'special' when I asked her about it on the way home, but I think she may be covering something up.

Every so often in life, you discover a new pleasure and yesterday was one of those days. I haven't had so much fun in ages and for once in my life, far from getting into trouble for it, The Boss was actually part of the fun. It turns out that her chair in the office is on wheels. Now that I'm bigger, my weight is enough to make it move, even with her sitting on it. There we were, me standing on my hind legs with my front paws on The Boss's knees, whilst she was sitting on the chair, going round and round the office in fits of laughter. Every so often, we would run into the wall and she would have to move the chair round a bit, but then we'd carry on. All would have been well, if my Master had not been trying to talk to someone on the phone at the time and he did get just a touch cross with us. When he finished I persuaded him to have a go and he cheered up quite quickly as I wheeled him round. The only disappointment was that when I said it was my turn to sit on the chair whilst one of them pushed, neither of them seemed quite so keen. It would be good to try it somewhere with a bit more room, or even with The Boss on her bicycle, or better still a skateboard. It might be wise for her to check out where the local hospital is first.

Tuesday 6th June 2006.
Now I realise that to a dog this seems ridiculous, but maybe in human circles it's normal. As a matter of norm my Master does all the ironing and in general The Boss does all the clothes washing. Don't get me wrong he's by no means one of your 'new men', but The Boss offered a

deal whereby she would cook dinner every night if he would do the ironing. Well I've told you about how he set fire to the oven gloves, so it seemed like a good deal to him. However, every so often, the pile of ironing is huge and despite his best endeavours it doesn't disappear. Then The Boss started saying that she won't do any more washing until the ironing basket is empty and there he is replying that he bets he can go longer without the washing being done than she can. And there you have it, two adults in the middle of a bet about how long they can go without the washing being done. The ground rules of the bet state that they have to change their clothes with the same frequency, but it says nothing about just how odd the combination of clothes they wear can be. I ask you, when would you ever find a dog being as ridiculous as that?

8
GROWING UP FAST

Thursday 8th June

I discovered that with a little help, and some rather odd manoeuvring, I can actually get into the hammock with The Boss. She has to counterbalance my weight as I get in and all my subsequent shifting about once I'm there, but it turns out it's rather fun. I'm ok as long as The Boss keeps hold of me so that I don't accidentally roll out, or for that matter roll her out. We had one nasty moment when I forgot where I was and seeing someone going past our gate, I leapt out to bark at them. Well the poor Boss had to react very quickly to grab hold of the frame to stop herself from being rotated out of the hammock onto the floor. Realising what I'd done, I went back and apologised and said I would try to remember not to do that again, but please would she let me have another go sometime. She's said that she'll see. It wasn't a 'no', so I'm taking that as a good sign.

Friday 9th June 2006.

One of my favourite household chores has been taken away from me. It's all my own fault really. It was my job to get the post from the post box at the bottom of the drive. Unfortunately, I've been getting these urges recently. No, not what you're thinking. I just can't stop myself from running off into next door's garden to see if I can find Matilda. As cats go, she's a bit of a recluse, which just adds to the challenge of trying to find her. Now it means I'll be left shut behind the garden gate whilst The Boss goes down on her own. It's very disappointing.

I'm keeping out of The Boss's way for a while. She's having one of those days. Firstly, she trapped her finger in the drawer and bruised it really badly. Then as though that wasn't enough, she ran over my foot with a door. On balance, I think keeping out of the way is by far the safest option.

Now I'm really not sure what my Master and The Boss were trying to prove, but all three of us tried going out in The Boss's car. By rights it's a two seater car and by my reckoning there were three of us. My Master drove, whilst The Boss sat in the passenger seat and had this strange notion that I might be happy to sit in the footwell. Doh! Does she really think I'm going to sit where I can't see out of the window? I started with my back legs on the floor and my front paws on her legs, but that wasn't very stable, so I hauled myself up onto her lap. I may be 22kg but I can still be a lap dog. As it turned out, I was very comfortable and quite liked the arrangement. What I couldn't understand was that The Boss wasn't so keen and said she thought perhaps we wouldn't try it again. Shame. I was somewhat bemused that the journey ended with window shopping up and down the high street. Why go when the shops are shut? What is the point in that? I was also a bit fed up as my Master made me stop to look in the men's clothes shop windows and The Boss made me stop at the women's, but did they even take my down the road where the pet shop is? No! Was I given the chance to gaze longingly at new collars and toys? No! They took no notice of my protests, however much I tried pulling in that direction.

Saturday 10th June

I'd almost forgotten the wedding. The Boss and my Master were trying to decide what the menu was going to be the other day, it made me even more disappointed that I won't be going. To be honest, I quite fancied the children's menu, but with additional scraps from the main one. I'm not above a bit of begging if it's going to get me extra food. I'm actually learning to beg really nicely and in a way that seems to be almost irresistible, with The Boss anyway. My Master refuses point-blank to share any of his Twiglets with me.

Monday 12th June

The Boss has suggested I should have some water-wings for the pool. She says they're things that have air in, so that they float and I would put them on my legs. I'm just trying to imagine whether that means I will in effect be standing out of the water or whether my legs will be splayed out in all directions, floating, whilst my body sags in an odd direction in the middle. I'm led to believe that dogs can swim naturally, but it's one of those confidence things, you don't know until you try and the thought of trying is a bit daunting. Seeing The Boss disappearing into the water can be a little disconcerting. I've barked at her and run round to the other side, to see where she's gone but it's as though part of her has vanished.

I have become an expert at using a foot stool to bounce up onto the hammock. It only seems to work when there's already someone in it, and admittedly they do get a bit of a shock, but it's usually The Boss and she's used to me. I do feel a little bit guilty about the paw shaped bruises that she has on her leg, where I used her as a springboard to jump off the other day.

Wed 14th June

The Boss has been very negative about banks, so I thought I'd ask her whether there was a good reason. She asked me how many I'd like. The most recent she said, was a couple of weeks ago when she received a cheque for €10 and paid it into her account, which is a euro bank account. She was a little surprised to find just 32 cents credited to her account and €9.68 deducted by the bank for the privilege of cashing the cheque, because it was drawn on a bank in a different country. I think I'm starting to get the picture.

Friday 16th June

I realise that I can't go as my passport isn't valid yet, but that shouldn't have stopped them inviting me to the wedding. I could have tried to buy a fake identity on the internet so that I could travel. I've read in books that you can do that. Mind you, I wouldn't know how to go about buying a fake I.D. I'm presuming you don't just type in 'fake I.D. for a dog' on Google and find the relevant site immediately. Just hang on I'll try it.

Wow, I've lived a sheltered life. Apart from news items about fake I.Ds, I can find sites telling me how to make a fake human I.D. and sites telling me changing their I.D. is the sort of thing people think of doing whilst intoxicated. The strangest I've found, but probably the most useful, given my medical problems, is that I can buy fake 'dog testicles' for neutered dogs. Now you wouldn't think that was the first thing you were going to find when searching for an I.D. Unfortunately, they don't actually work, so I'm still back at square one with regard to career options, with 'stud dog' well and truly off the agenda. The Boss doesn't seem to think I'll make a guard dog either, something about being too nice. I've befriended everyone who has set foot in the garden so far, even when I'd never met them before. I bound up, wagging my tail politely and introduce myself, in the hope of getting some fuss. Alternatively, I rush straight up to them with my ball or my Frisbee in the hope that they'll throw it for me. Most people will if you ask nicely.

It seems to be a week for strange things. I was at the airport the other day meeting one of The Boss's friends and there was a girl waiting to meet someone from another flight who had obviously gone for the "I'll be the one wearing a flower in my lapel" joke. Sure enough, she was wearing a flower. It was a four foot long, fake, pink sunflower with a face about a foot wide. I could immediately relate to her sense of humour.

Saturday 17th June
I was listening to the radio and half heard a piece where they were talking about some sport and referring to the 'Open men's semi-final'. I was wondering why they would have a competition especially for 'open men'. Is it for men that aren't afraid to show their emotion? Is it one of those things that means it's ok for them to cry if they lose? Is there also a competition for 'closed men'?

I still haven't put a toe in the water on the swimming front. I'm not pretending I'm not tempted, when the children are throwing a ball from one end to the other and one of these days I might just go after it and forget there's nothing underneath me except wet. If that happens I can imagine it being a bit like one of those cartoons, where the animal runs off the cliff and gets quite a long way before looking down and realising there's nothing below them and only then falling to the ground. In my case, it would be when I looked down that you would hear a great splash. It would be a bit like the other day when I jumped to catch the Frisbee and forgot to put my legs down to land and sort of 'thudded' onto the ground. At least if I land on water it might be a slightly softer landing, but probably just as much of a shock. There's always the possibility that I would like it, but I'm not that keen to find out, not unless some mud is added first.

Sunday 18th June

We had an incident yesterday. A bad case of concussion, and it wasn't my fault. A young bird flew into the lounge through the open French window and then tried to fly back out through the closed one. I rushed to the scene to see how I could help and also to see if licking the bird would make it recover, but for some reason The Boss thought it would be better if I were out of the way. Then she opened the other French window and after enough recovery time, the little bird flew out. I chased round the garden to see if I could find it, but to no avail. My Master asked if we had written it in the 'Accident Book', but I think he was only joking. In this house, we would need a whole series of books rather than just the one. Perhaps we should have accident books covering different subjects such as 'Accidents caused by The Boss to herself, without any help from anyone else' this would be the biggest volume, although it would be a close contest with 'Accidents caused to anyone by Alfie'. Then there would be one smaller volume for 'All other accidents'. All other accidents would principally comprise birds flying into the windows. Why? Why do they do it? Don't they learn from each other? Admittedly when the glass doors to the lounge are closed, I have once or twice run straight into them, but in my defence so has The Boss. In her case, it was more that she walked into them rather than ran. If she had run, it would have been more of a mess. Perhaps we should put tape across all the windows at dog, Boss and bird 'eye height', to stop it happening.

If we're going to start the accident books, I could put the distress caused to my Master when I jumped up him yesterday morning. It was just after he'd got out of the shower and had no clothes on. Apparently, that bit of him is quite delicate and didn't want my claw on it, or for that matter he didn't want me leaving a line of claw marks down his thigh. Humans really are a bit soft when compared to dogs. I banged my head really hard on the underside of the dining table on Friday and it had absolutely no effect at all. Although The Boss said that's questionable.

Monday 19th June
Well I'm thoroughly fed up and it isn't made any better knowing that the circumstances that have led to this situation are all my own fault. How was I to know that when we all went in The Boss's car, it was a test to see if it was possible to take me with them if they went out for the day in it? It seemed obvious to me that I wanted to sit on The Boss's knee so that I could have a cuddle and look out of the window. So what happens? Yesterday they went out without me. I argued with my Master that I'm the one who usually goes in the passenger seat of that car and that he should be the one that went to the dog sitter for the day, but he took no notice of me at all. I actually had this little illusion that in some way it was my car and I loved it. How can he do that to me? Oh they had a great time and in fairness I had fun playing with my doggy friends,

but that isn't the point. Who wants to be reasonable when they've missed out on having fun? All that after I got my Master a Father's Day card as well. I'm building up credit in case there's a 'Dog's day' at some point in the year. He loved the way I'd signed the Father's day card with a paw print, I got the idea from seeing what a lovely shape it makes if I run across the wet grass, then across the garden soil and then before it dries, quickly run into the lounge and across the rug. It makes a lovely pattern.

I find it hard to understand why 22 men would run round for 90 minutes, watched by thousands of people and be happy to end up with a score of 0-0. Surely there is little point in bothering, they could have called it quits at the start and saved some energy for something useful.

Tuesday 20th June

I've enjoyed writing my diary so much that The Boss said why didn't I have a go at writing a book. I don't know if I could, but then you never do know until you try. Perhaps I could be the dog equivalent of J K Rowling. I could be interviewed on television and in all the best Sunday magazines. If you're reading this, I may already be part way there. I would even let The Boss come along occasionally as long as she promised not to embarrass me. You don't want to be in the middle of a photo shoot with someone telling you it's time for 'walkies' now do you?

The Boss let me sleep in her room the other night as my Master was away. I'm not sure he knows about it, but I'm guessing the dog hair might have been a bit of a giveaway. How was I supposed to know that the deal did not include sleeping in his place? Fine, so The Boss took my bed upstairs and told me that was where I was to sleep, but I thought she was only joking. I waited for her to go to sleep and then climbed in next to her. Strangely, my wriggling into position along her spine with my head on her hip seemed to wake her and she made me get down and go back into my own bed. Once she was asleep, I tried again. Don't some humans wake up easily! This time as she turned me out, she threatened that if I repeated this behaviour she would never let me sleep in there again. She seemed to mean it, so I went back to my own bed, which somehow didn't seem quite so comfortable anymore.

Thursday 22nd June

Strangely, it seems my Master doesn't like having my saliva covered, rubber rabbit wrapped all round his legs when he's wearing shorts. I would've thought he would appreciate being invited to play with me a little more than that. I tried suggesting he should wear long trousers, but he didn't seem keen in the warm weather. I took his criticism on board and decided I would try to wash rubber rabbit and then see if he'd play, my Master, not rubber rabbit. Rubber rabbit is always willing to play; I bit his legs off to stop him running away. I got as far as throwing rubber rabbit in the air and landing him in the bath, but then realised, I couldn't turn the taps on, or reach over the side of the bath to wash him. When The Boss fished him out of the bath, I explained what I was trying to do and she gently explained that she didn't think that would actually make a difference, so I've given up.

I'm not sure if this tells you more about my Master and The Boss than it does about me, it's probably a close run thing; anyway, in our office there is a waste paper bin that cheers whenever you throw something in it. My Master likes it best, The Boss says the novelty has worn thin. Not thin enough to actually remove it, but thin enough to let it annoy her when my Master keeps throwing things at it that are supposed to go into the recycling waste. I found it rather annoying too, until recently. I used to find that I would just be in the middle of a nice dream, chasing ducks or rabbits, when I would be rudely awoken by a mechanised cheer. In reality, it only sounds like a cheer if you know that's what it's supposed to be. Now however I've found that the bin can be my ally in causing trouble. If I stand in the right position and wag my tail gently, just hitting the bin, I can make it cheer repeatedly and that annoys everyone. It also annoys everyone when I forget to do it gently and hit the bin so hard it falls over. The down side of that, is it usually makes me jump in the process and scaring myself is never the object of the exercise.

The Boss described me as 'Dog enough not to be human and human enough to be a pet' earlier. I've been trying to work out whether or not that's a compliment.

Friday 23rd June
Some while ago The Boss went to see a comedian who obviously likes spiders about as much as she does. He talked about categorising them into three types with the largest being sufficient justification to move house. In our house the categories work a little more as follows: Category one, insignificant spiders that The Boss will tolerate sharing the house with unless they come too close or grow. Category two, medium sized spiders that are permitted to stay as long as they are in out of the way places; alternatively, if they can be reached I eat them. Category three, spiders that are of sufficient size that they are not permitted to stay in the house, which my Master removes by hand, I eat or The Boss manages to remove

with a glass. Category four, these require removal by my Master or me, failing which they will be killed by The Boss. Category five and over The Boss is likely to scream if they move, not want to allow them out of someone's sight until removed, in case they hide and which involve calling in any emergency service if my Master or I are unavailable, or if I fail to deal with the problem to her satisfaction. In this instance, her emergency services have ranged from a neighbour to an estate agent. Just don't ask.

I had totally forgotten how satisfying it is to chew Miffy's ears. Unfortunately, unless someone buys me another Miffy I'm not going to be able to do that anymore. I have two Miffy toys and not an ear between them. The last bits were removed a couple of days ago. It's amazing just how far round the lounge you can distribute the filling, if you really try hard enough.

From observation, turquoise is 'in' this season. I guess I'm destined to be out of fashion until black, brown and white are back. At least with my colours you don't stop and think you can have too much of a good thing. The Boss says she likes turquoise and told me that many years ago, when it was the 'in colour', in her younger day, she had a turquoise jump suit. Personally I think that just goes to prove my point, that you can have too much of a good thing.

Saturday 24th June
I've been wondering whether to change my name when my Master and The Boss get married. I started by thinking I could be Peregrine or Archibold, but then when I talked to The Boss about it, she explained it was my last name that I would change and that it was normal to change it to the same as the rest of the family. I felt a bit crestfallen,

I'm quite attached to the surname Dog, it's been passed down through generations. I feel it says something about me, something of which I'm quite proud. She said I could always keep it as my professional name and only change it for the purpose of the family. I said I'd think about it. It's all so complicated with having to get my passport changed and all the other paperwork. You don't think it would mean that I had to have my jabs all over again do you?

The Boss has been reading a book called 'A Clockwork Orange', it seems very odd, with a lot of made up language in it. She has found it hard work trying to understand what some of it means. It's a bit like talking to teenagers but worse. I was wondering if I could invent my own language. Start a trend by using a completely new word for something, to see if it would catch on. I wonder how long it would take a new word to go full circle. From when I first used it, how long would it be before someone completely different and unconnected would use that word back to me without knowing I invented it? The only problem is, that I can't think of a word to invent. All the ones that come to mind have already been taken.

Sunday 25th June

My Master has been fixing one or two things that The Boss has broken. Well she claims some of them weren't her, but I have my doubts. Firstly, the head had fallen off a fridge magnet. As it turned out, this was broken for the second time. Then there was the spoon rest that The Boss dropped a bowl on, the bowl is past repair but the spoon rest has lived to tell the tale and then there was the magnet from the shopping list blackboard. It's a particularly nice board, with chalk and then magnets made to look like vegetables. The garlic had lost its magnet and as my Master is very good at gluing things, The Boss had every confidence. However, it turns out there is something called polarity, and one way round a magnet will hold to something and one way round it won't. Guess which way my Master glued it back together. Unfortunately, the glue is a very strong, so now the choice is to use a hammer to separate it and then bin all the pieces, or stick the garlic to the side of the blackboard in an ornamental sort of way.

Do dogs get a sun tan or sun burn? I was wondering, if I lie in the sun, would my nose change colour? It's the only bit of me not covered in hair. It might just be that my hair will bleach and I will look as though I've had highlights put into my coat. I hope my white bits don't change colour, I rather like them as they are. I guess I might get sunstroke if I stay in the sun too long, unless I can find a hat that fits. So far, all the baseball hats I've tried on, look silly on me. The Boss explained they look silly on most people and I shouldn't be concerned. If I could only get some dark glasses to go with it, then at least no one would recognise me.

9
ALMOST THE WEDDING

Monday 26th June

I found a very big piece of wood just sitting in the garden. It's a piece of a tree trunk or something similar. It has a very satisfying chew to it. Well it was getting late and I'd had enough of being outside, my owners were busy so I didn't think they would notice if I brought it into the lounge to carry on chewing it in the comfort of my own chair. Unfortunately, The Boss seems to have developed the ability to spot what I'm doing, even when she is apparently doing something else and she stopped me right on the threshold of going in. She can be so mean.

There has been a strange screeching noise at nights recently. Clearly it's some animal, but we have no idea what. There have been suggestions of it being a mating call, but it sounds more as though the animal in question is concluding that the possible mates are extremely ugly and is none too happy with the choice. Surely, no other animal could be attracted by that sound? It's enough to make me cover my ears with my paws, not nearly as musical as my howling, although in fairness my howling is not a mating call. The Boss used to have a dog that would howl when it heard an ambulance or police siren. It seemed to think it was its 'pack leader' calling. It was all very well until she moved to live on the top of a valley above a hospital with a big accident and emergency department. They don't put things like that in the estate agents details when they're selling a house to you.

'Warning. Frequent sirens approaching the local hospital may upset your dog.' It's the sort of thing a dog should be able to get compensation for. The rate it's going, I'll be claiming compensation for distress from the animal doing the screeching, either that or persuade him to join a dating agency rather urgently.

This wedding thing is all getting too much for The Boss. She has started to have nightmares. The other night she dreamt that everything had gone wrong and she had to cycle to the church in her dress. Well I said to her she'd probably be better walking, if she cycled she'd get the dress caught in the wheels. She told me that wasn't an entirely helpful suggestion. I did think of trying to get her book of dreams down from the shelf to interpret it, but I'm guessing it's relatively straight forward to tell her she's getting married soon and she hasn't finished the planning and is worrying about it.

I had a very nasty experience the other day. I was out for a walk and squatted down to do my business, when I accidentally squatted on a thorny plant. Well I rushed out yelping and went to find another spot but it had given me quite a shock I can tell you. A dog should be able to do things like that in comfort not get prickled in places that shouldn't be prickled.

Tuesday 27th June

You have to laugh; well mainly when it's someone else's misfortune, when it's your own it's never quite so funny. Anyway, where we live they make you split all your rubbish into lots of different categories. There's the green bin, the grey bin, the red box, the blue bag, the cardboard, the bottles and so on. The green bin is for biodegradable waste and you have to pay for the number of times it's emptied. You can put it out every two weeks but the problem with that is, it's only partly full but you still pay the set amount to put out the bin. If you leave it longer, then everything starts to decompose, smell horrible and attract the flies. There is a solution to this problem, in theory. You can buy special biodegradable bags to put things inside. This is what The Boss has done. She puts the waste in the bag and the bag in the bin. She then ties a bag up and starts on the next one. However, you can get quite a lot in one bag so she doesn't tie it up immediately. She takes more rubbish out to it, lifts the bag out of the bin, puts the fresh lot of waste in and then puts it back in the bin. Bless her. She was undertaking this process the other day, whilst wearing open toed sandals. When she lifted the biodegradable bag out of the bin to put some more waste in, it had biodegraded and the bottom dropped out depositing well-rotted vegetables all over her feet. The moral of this story is, well I'm not sure, but I think it should be 'don't eat vegetables'. She seemed to think the decomposed banana skins were the worst.

I've found a way to make The Boss go all funny and make odd squeaking noises. There she was, sitting on her chair with her bare feet curled up under her. I think she was concentrating on something when I came up and started to lick the underside of her feet. I think what she said was something like 'stop that, it tickles' but through the laughter and squawks it was quite hard to work out the exact words. It was a shame because she had obviously walked through something that tasted interesting.

The Boss is convinced that the root I keep digging up and eating is the doggy equivalent of 'magic mushrooms'. Apparently, after I eat it I run round madly for half an hour. I think it just gives me a bit of energy but The Boss is less certain; she says if she could work out which root it was, she'd try to find out more about it, but does she really think I'm going to share that sort of a secret with her?

Wednesday 28th June

The Boss went to collect her dress yesterday. Now all she has to do is get it to England in one piece. 'Lay it across the back seat of the car' the shop said. Just a small problem, her car hasn't got a back seat. I suggested having the roof down and trailing it behind the car but she didn't think that was helpful.

I'm seriously worried about the levels of aggression being shown by the woodpeckers. The nut container ran out. That is no justification for throwing the thermometer, which communicates with the weather station, onto the floor. I said The Boss should simply refuse to feed them, and of course give me the nuts instead. She seemed to feel it might be better to meet their demands and refill the container immediately, before they set about taking any further action. It really isn't any good to cave in to the demands of these terrorists. You have to make a stand. I did ensure I ate all the nuts that fell around the bottom of the bird table as she refilled the container, as my mark of protest.

Thursday 29th June

Listening to The Boss trying to learn Dutch I can understand where the English expression 'double Dutch' comes from. Take 'time' as an example. What time is 'half two'? Now you would think that was an easy one wouldn't you. In England that would be 30 minutes after two, but if you arranged to meet a Dutch person at half two you'd be an hour late as in Dutch they express it as half before the hour. It's ok once you remember how it's done, but surely it's easier to call 'twenty to three' exactly that, rather than ' ten over half before three'? It's no wonder that England has such a problem fitting in to Europe.

Friday 30th June

The Boss doesn't seem to throw very much away. I've been going through a cupboard and discovered she still has all her school books, some of which look VERY old. The sad bit is, that when I asked her a few test questions, it turns out that she has a good forgetory as well as a good memory. There are an awful lot of things she must have known once that she doesn't seem to know now. I thought maybe I would like to study something. I could be an educated dog, maybe a philosopher. I'm seriously wondering if I could become a dog with a social conscience, although I don't fancy some of the implications of that, I rather enjoy being irresponsible. The Boss suggested I should read 'Animal Farm'.

I'm getting very worried about the bird table. I realise it's nice to bring your friends round, but it's always best if those friends know how to behave in someone else's house. The greater spotted woodpecker seems to have brought a pair of lesser spotted woodpeckers round and whilst eating the peanuts is fine, as long as we refill them regularly, it is the bird table itself I'm worried about. They seem to be pecking the trunk of it from 3 of the 4 sides. What's going to happen if they meet in the middle? Is the whole thing going to come toppling down? That sort of behaviour is really not all right. It would be like me chewing something that doesn't belong to me. Oh yes I might think about it every so often, but I don't actually do it. I've been out to talk to them about it, but the minute I turn my back and come inside they carry on as though they didn't hear me. It will be their loss if the bird table is broken and how precisely are they going to explain that to all the little birds?

I've been practising being a herding dog and have rounded up all my toys in one corner of the room. The problem is that once I've done it they stay where they are, so I don't get much practise. Every so often, I'll liberally redistribute them around the house, usually leaving them in the most inconvenient places and then I can start herding again. I do try herding anyone that comes for a walk with me, but generally, they don't appreciate my talents and just complain that I am trying to trip them up. They do say you're never appreciated in your home town, perhaps if I went to the next town and herded people there, they would appreciate it more. Either that or the boss could get me something that moves, like gerbils.

Saturday 1st July
The Boss assumes I have been eating more of the plant in the garden that seems to drive me crazy. In my defence, I'm just a boy and therefore have a lot of energy. I was tearing round the garden at a very fast pace and ran head-long into the back of The Boss's legs causing her to buckle. She only just managed to regain her balance in order to prevent herself going head first into the pool, which she was cleaning at the time. Clearly next time I need to hit her just that little bit harder. I said to her when she complained "Go on admit it, you would have laughed," but she didn't seem so convinced. She tried saying if I

didn't watch out she would throw me in, to see if I can swim. She's got a point, perhaps I need to be more careful. I'm sure I will go in one day, but I would like it to be in my own good time and that just hasn't come round yet.

I've found somewhere on the map called Dog Village, just outside Exeter and I really want to see what it's like. Do you think that dogs get special priority there? Perhaps people aren't allowed to go and I would have to go on my own. I've also found a place called Hound near Southampton, and there's an Alfieri in Italy, that really ought to be my sort of place.

I have been practising with some software that lets you change photographs. I'm assuming the exclusion of me from the 'engagement photo' was an oversight that my Master and The Boss would like me to correct. If I can get the hang of the software, I will also be able to use it on the wedding photos to make it look as though I was there after all. My attempts so far have put my head on a human body, which really does look strange, mainly because the style of clothes didn't suit me. Perhaps I would have been better trying a man's body. I've also managed one where I cut my ears off and that can never be a good thing. I can't ask The Boss for help as I want it to be a surprise.

Sunday 2nd July
The Boss just gets worse and worse. The way she was shouting at the players in the England football match yesterday, you'd think she thought that they could hear her. I've already walked behind the set several times to check there aren't really little men in it and if I can work out they're not really in our lounge, you'd like to think that this fact was not wasted on The Boss. However, her

team 'encouragement' seems to know no bounds. I was starting to get interested with the level of tension everyone was showing, but I still don't really get it. They play for 45 minutes and you think that's it, then they play for another 45 minutes. As if that is not enough they then play for two lots of fifteen minutes and all for no one to actually score a goal. What is the point? Then as if to make up for the fact they haven't scored any goals, they then score some special ones at the end, then they say that the other team has won. At no point did any of them pick it up with their mouths.

I've grown again. I know it isn't just my imagination as when I saw Mackensey the other day I had clean run over her, not, you will be pleased to hear, in the car, before I even saw she was there. To be strictly honest I caught one of my back legs on her on the way over and sort of landed in a heap. All very undignified and I don't think Mackensey was overly pleased either.

Monday 3rd July

Why is it that when the temperature hits 30 degrees, every Belgian seems to be obliged to get on their bike? There they are everywhere and I do mean everywhere. We went to the port or at least tried to. A policeman stopped us. "You can't go down there and won't be able to for another hour. I can't tell you any more than that. It's confidential." We drove away speculating on consignments of gold or diamonds being brought into the port. It seemed all rather exciting and somehow acceptable for us to have a wasted journey. Then as we drove down the road we found the real reason, a cycle race. No longer did it feel ok, now we felt cheated. We were being prevented from going where we needed to because of another bunch of Belgian cyclists.

What is the world coming to? On the way home, we found the entire Belgian population riding, in some places 8 abreast, making it impossible for cars to overtake, because there were also cyclists coming in the opposite direction. It looked like the 'Sunday cyclists' equivalent of a peleton (I had to look that up, it's the name for the pack of cyclists in a race). They looked as you might expect them to, after taking all the drugs out of cycling. There was a break-away group of a woman lagging behind a man in a rather unsightly white vest. It gives you a bit of an idea of the speed they were doing when I tell you there was a woman keeping up by jogging and I sure wouldn't want to have been around when she asked the question "Does my bum look big in this?" If I'd thought the cyclists were wobbling, that is nothing when compared to the jogger.

On a more domestic front, the herbs have died. Not as I feared 'The Herbs' that are the children's cartoon from when The Boss was young and of which she has a video. No, the herbs she bought, in a moment of culinary fantasy, to grow on the kitchen windowsill. She bought them in order to snip bits off when cooking. I'm not sure if snipping bits off when cooking is supposed to be a good luck thing or whether it serves any useful purpose. In any event, she may as well snip them all off now because they're dead. They are too far gone to join the intensive care unit, so sadly, for me, they are out of chewing range. I wonder how long it will take her to forget that she can't grow plants and get some more to kill?

Tuesday 4th July
Yesterday was far from being a good day. Now I know the wedding is in England and I understand that my passport doesn't let me go there yet, but I had sort of assumed I

would get to stay at home on my own. I know where the dog food is and as long as they leave the back door open, I could let myself out when I wanted to. Don't they trust me? Apparently, I have to go and stay with the dog sitter. I have visited a few times so it isn't completely unknown. The Boss reassured me that they would not be away long and would be home to me before I knew it. I just looked at her with my 'do you think I'm stupid?' look and walked off. How can they be so mean? Don't they realise I'll miss being in my own home, particularly if I haven't got them to play with? When The Boss managed to find me later she explained that I could take a favourite toy and I could ring them any time I wanted. How about if I call them right in the middle of the wedding? I bet they wouldn't talk to their dog then.

Wednesday 5th July
Yesterday was something called Independence Day or so it said on the calendar. What I don't understand is why only Americans have a day to be independent. What about the rest of us? I want to be independent. A day would be enough, I rather enjoy being looked after the rest of the year, but I don't see the harm in my having just the one day to be able to prove a point. What I'm not absolutely certain of, is what point I'm trying to prove.

Well rubber rabbit is now in more pieces than even I can count. It still gives quite a satisfying 'thwack' when I fling it about, but it's definitely past its best before date. What Matilda the cat will think I don't know, because her owners have bought me a rubber pig to play with, to console me for the loss of rubber rabbit. It isn't as long and floppy as rabbit but it fits comfortably in my mouth, with the added advantage of having convenient trotters that I can get The Boss to hold as we walk along. I have to say I'm quite taken with it and placed it carefully nose to nose with pink rhino so that they could get to know each other better.

Apparently, there are some little piglets in the pet shop. I was quite keen on the idea of getting one, until I heard someone say they're brighter than dogs and easier to train. I really don't think it would be a good idea for me to bring into this household another pet that could do my job, only better. If I did that The Boss and my Master might not want me anymore. Is it possible to make a dog redundant? "I'm sorry Alfie the position of pet is no longer available. You'll have to leave."

Thursday 6th July

Well I'm ready. I keep trying to think if there is anything I've forgotten. I've got my bed and the old sweater of The Boss's that I like to snuggle up to at night. I have my food and of course my collar and lead. Last but by no means least I have pink pig, a photo of my Master and The Boss in a little frame, my computer and my mobile phone. I think that's everything. I feel nervous but quite excited too. I've been away for odd nights before but never like this.

I went to get a mobile phone so I can ring my owners any time I want. I wanted one on a contract but The Boss refused to have it set up from her bank account. She seemed to think I might run up a big bill, but I've no idea where she got that idea from. It was amazing in the shop trying to decide what phone I wanted. They were telling me that the really small ones were popular and I said "What with these paws?" I wouldn't be able to press one button at once. There were ones that played music and ones with cameras. I said I just wanted one that made phone calls, but it seems there aren't really any that only do that, funny really for a phone. In the end, I chose one with a rubber cover that bounces every time I drop it. It's waterproof too, so when I hold it in my mouth the slobber doesn't stop it from working. I also like the fact that it has a little flashlight so I can see where to pee at night. By the time I got home, I was already looking through the leaflet at all the ones I didn't have and asking my Master if I could have a different one for my birthday. He said that it's still months to my birthday and I may have changed my mind by then.

When I got home, I went and hid under a bush to read the manual and learn how all the features work. It's even got some games, but they don't really compare with shaking Miffy. I rang The Boss from under the bush to see if she could bring me a dog biscuit but she didn't seem impressed and said "This is why I wouldn't get you one on a contract." She pointed out that if I carried on like that, all my money would be gone and I wasn't having any more until next month. There are times that she can be a real spoil sport, so I rang my Master but he said he was working and I would have to wait until he came home.

10
THE WEDDING

Friday 7th July

Perhaps being away for a while isn't going to be too bad. We went to a horse show, which was a real pleasure. Not only were there people, horses and dogs to play with, but there was quite a lot of horse dung to nibble. I do find it can be a real delicacy. I don't have to wear the car seat belt which is great. Ok I know it's safer wearing it, but it's so much more fun being in the boot of the car with the other dogs. When I say boot, I don't mean like a saloon car where it makes it all dark inside and you can't move. I mean one of those boots where there's a window and it's still a bit of the car.

It's difficult to find space and time to write my diary. Most of the other dogs haven't got computers of their own. In fact most of them have never used a computer at all. Every time I get it out to write anything, they all gather round saying "Can we have a look?" "Can we have a go?" "How do you make it do …?" It really can get very annoying. Then I sat down to a quiet game of solitaire and a little Westie came and bounced up and down trying to tell me what card to put where. Don't you just hate it when that happens? It's bad enough when they don't know what they're talking about, but when they're right it's so annoying. I'm going to have to find somewhere to try using it where none of them can find me, but that isn't all that easy while I'm staying here.

When my phone rang earlier I didn't realise it was

mine as it played some awful tune that I hadn't heard before. It was a Jack Russell that barked at me that he thought my phone was ringing and I suddenly felt very embarrassed. It was just The Boss telling me she'd arrived in England safely and checking I was ok. It was great to hear from her, but I do wish she would ring me at more convenient times, when I'm not in the middle of a game of chase with a Labrador. I asked if I could ring her back later but she said she was going out, so I broke off from my game for a minute. The other dogs laughed at me a bit, but I know The Boss misses me and likes to hear my voice.

Saturday 8th July

I've been trying to use the text facility on my mobile phone. I thought I'd just send a note to The Boss to say, "Hello it is your dog here. I just wanted to say that I am missing you. Love Alfie" Now I'd read in the manual that there's a thing called 'predictive text' which means it guesses the right words and you don't have to press the keys as many times. Unfortunately, I don't think that facility is turned on. What my message actually read was "gdjjm gt gp wmtp dmg gdpd. G jtpt wamtdd tm paw tgat g am mgppgmg wmt. Jmtd Ajdgd", so unless The Boss has a few hours to spare to work out the code, it seems a bit pointless. It's really hard with paws to push the right key, but to push the same one more than once is hopeless. I've got the phone numbers set up on speed dial settings so that I only have to hit one button. I've found that I'm better putting a stick in my mouth and using that to hit the keys, but then with texting I'm too slow and it's moved on to the next letter before I've got the last one right. Perhaps I should try to design a more suitable mobile phone for a dog.

After my phone playing such awful music when it rang yesterday, I set about changing it to something more personal. The Boss has hers playing her own voice telling her "Your phone's ringing, your phone's ringing", so I thought maybe I would record my voice for mine. The problem was that as soon as I started howling, all the other dogs joined in, so I ended up with a riotous cacophony of sound. Either way it's better than the tinny music it was playing, all artificially jolly and absolutely annoying. Now I just need it to ring again to see what happens.

It's no good. The first thing I need The Boss to sort when I get home is my bed. It just hasn't grown at the same rate that I have. When I was a young puppy I needed to gather my toys up in the other corner to make it feel less big and daunting. Now, not only is there no spare room for my toys, there doesn't seem to be entirely enough room for the odd leg, paw and tail either. I think I'd like one such as my owners have bought, where the mattress is specially designed to support all my little curves. I'm guessing given that I'm as happy curling up on the floor, the settee or for that matter The Boss's feet, that may be a little excessive, but a dog has to have standards.

Sunday 9th July

I think I'm homesick. I feel really lethargic and miserable and I keep thinking about the blue bowl with bones on that I have at home. Then I think about chasing the pheasants and about the remaining bits of my rubber rabbit. I miss my Frisbee too and much as I don't like to admit it, I miss my Master and The Boss. I'm never going to take them, or my home, for granted again. I couldn't face playing with the other dogs, I just found a quiet corner and moped. It does feel like they've been away forever.

I now know what happens when my phone rings. Not only do I get dogs howling as a ring tone, but then I get real dogs joining in as well. The other problem is that every time the dogs start howling I rush to answer the phone only to find it isn't for me. When it was my phone, I'd joined in the howling before I realised and ended up missing a call. It turned out that it was my Master telling me he's arrived in England too. Now you'd think that ought to be something to please me, but until now I hadn't realised that he was still in Belgium and therefore I could have been at home. Didn't he want me? Am I too much of a nuisance to him? I feel rather hurt as I really rather like being round him.

I probably forgot to mention that I had to be weighed for my new lot of tick treatment and it seems I now weigh 23kg. I was quite impressed until we got home and I discovered the grim reality of the situation. Not only does it now mean there is more tick treatment to squirt into my fur, but, tragically it means if you look at the chart on the sack of dog food and you find the line for my age and weight it means I should be eating a little less than I've been getting away with. Oh bother. Do you think if I promise to run it off and keep trim The Boss might agree to keep giving me a larger quantity?

Monday 10th July

I spent yesterday moping and feeling sorry for myself so I wrote to The Boss in the hope that would make me feel better.

"Dear Mum" That's what I call her at home. "It's quite

fun here, I get to play with a lot of other dogs and horses. When I say play with the horses, that is in the sense that I try to get them to chase me and they snort at me in disgust, but I still get some fun out of it. I'm bigger than many of the other dogs, so sometimes I have to remember not to be too rough, but most of them are ok. No one rubs my tummy and ears the way you do though and even if they try, they never do both at the same time. No one gives me my morning Frostie, lunchtime crisp and occasional (and by occasional I mean regular) bits of marzipan. It really isn't the same without you around. I've started to realise, you're a big softy and I miss snuggling up to you.

Marrying my Master won't make you less snuggly will it? You will still spoil me rotten won't you? I really hope you come home to me soon, I miss you. All my love Alfie."

I didn't actually feel better when I'd written it and then a Rottweiler puppy got hold of it and laughed at me for missing my Mum. Then he started calling me names. I went and hid in a corner until he'd gone to pick on another dog.

Tuesday 11th July

Yesterday wasn't so bad because the Rottweiler went home. The other dogs came and said they were sorry for what happened and they didn't really mean it, but they were frightened to disagree with the Rottweiler. It turns out that most of the dogs are frightened of him and generally go along with what he says rather than disagree. I can see why they do it, but surely if there is something wrong happening, whilst you might not always be able to stop it, it doesn't mean you have to join in and make it worse. Anyway, that was yesterday and today we all played together happily. I nipped the ear of a Westie a bit hard, but it was an accident and we were still friends afterwards.

We decided that it would be fun to organise a tug-of-war competition. A couple of the dogs brought with them some ropes as their favourite toys when they came to stay here. I'd wanted to bring all the bits of rubber rabbit but The Boss said I was likely to lose some of them, so I brought pig instead. We used some sticks to mark out lines in the garden and then put the rope in the middle. The idea was that we would get a couple of dogs on each side to balance the weight and then see who could tug the hardest. The contest didn't go according to plan and I'm probably not completely blameless. First of all the Jack Russell ran through at high speed whilst we were setting up and carried the rope off to the far end of the garden. The Westie and the Sheltie went off in hot pursuit and one or two of the others joined in. They'd been gone a few minutes when I completely forgot what we were doing and settled down to chew the sticks we'd put down to mark the pitch. Consequently, by the time the Westie came back, proudly carrying the rope, we had to start all over again to find some more sticks. Setting up the tug-of-war turned out to be a great game in itself and lasted for the best part of three hours. By the time we'd finished we all flopped down exhausted with no energy to pull a rope at all.

Wednesday 12th July

I was so happy this morning; I got a letter from The Boss. She misses me. I think I like being missed. It really cheered me up. I sat and thought about how lovely it is when I curl up on her knee, it's a bit of a feat as I don't really fit, but that doesn't stop me trying. She strokes me and tells me stories and rubs my tummy. Really, I think she probably spoils me a bit, I know my Master thinks so but he's a big softy too, even if he doesn't show it all the time. I really miss being tucked in at night and given a goodnight kiss before I go to sleep. It just isn't the same when you're staying with a whole load of dogs, it doesn't do to show your softer side too much. I think it's a dog thing, it may just be a male thing. Maybe the girl dogs feel differently about it.

I got bored with dog food so when the coast was clear I managed to nip out in search of the ubiquitous MacDonald's. I'm getting a little bit fed up with the number of times I go out craving 'two apple pies for 99p' and get to the counter to be told that this is just a mouth-watering theory. Although there are apple pies on the sign, and there is a machine behind the server to keep apple pies hot, the staff have not in fact put any apple pies into the machine, to be able to sell any to me. You build yourself up to a craving, the least they can do is to be ready to satisfy it. If you aren't careful you start to find yourself combing the streets in search of another MacDonald's and then another all of whom seem to think it's ok not to be able to sell you apple pies. I wonder what is the greatest lengths someone would go to in an attempt to be served an apple pie? I have contemplated taking the manager hostage, but I'm not absolutely certain a dog would be taken seriously, particularly one that looked as soft as I do.

Thursday 13th July
I've been having a few problems with my mobile phone.

It's so frustrating when you're in the middle of a call and you lose reception and have to start again. It's ok when you're talking to a friend, although admittedly a little rude. The biggest issue is when you're ringing a large faceless organisation. You have just got as far as outlining the problem that's led to your call, to the third successive department and then you lose signal and have to start again, only to be told you're number five in the queue and 'your call is important to us'. If my call is so important to you, why don't you answer the phone?

On a brighter note I do rather enjoy when I'm in the middle of a conversation that I've got a bit bored with, being able to say 'I'm going into a tunnel' and pretend to be cut off. I guess I can't have it both ways. The people that know me really well, will realise it isn't very likely that I'm going into a tunnel, but no one seems to be impudent enough to question my honesty. In some ways one of the greatest things about being a dog is that you really aren't held accountable for your actions. If you do something unacceptable people just say "Well he is only a dog". Of course, I object to the word only, but it's usually at a time that I'm not really in a position to argue with it. I caught my Master saying I was only a dog the other day and was really rather proud of The Boss for how upset she was and for sticking up for me. I would do the same for her if someone described her as 'only a human' but that's not a phrase you hear all that often. By contrast, I've heard my Master talking about being in 'the dog house'. What confuses me is that he says it as though it's a bad thing, when all things considered he should think it an honour to join me.

The other problem I'm having with my mobile, is that someone has left me a message. I realise that may be a good thing, but you're forgetting that I'm in Belgium and when I try to get it, some voice starts speaking Flemish to me and I don't know what buttons I need to press to listen to it. I might be missing out on something important, but to be honest I'm at a complete loss as to what to do. I might even resort to asking one of the other dogs for a bit of help, but I do so hate admitting I haven't got a clue.

Friday 14th July
I'm not happy. There's another dog staying here that has been saying that he went to his owners' wedding. That means I now know for certain that it is possible for a dog to go. Why didn't they wait to get married when I could travel? Failing that, why didn't they get married in a country that I can go to? I know The Boss muttered something about feeling it was important to be able to understand the words she was saying, but in all honesty, I think it's about time she got her priorities right. I'm their dog, their only dog. For that matter, I'm their only pet. Is it really more important to understand the words being said, or to have me there? I think there was a small matter of some of her family not having passports as well, but once again, who is more important?

I may have found one small way of making my presence felt. You know how dog hair can get everywhere… well, when my Master rang he said he had forgotten to take my blanket out before putting The Boss's dress in the car. He thinks that my hair has only got as far as the carrier that it's wrapped in, but I'm hoping there might still be a chance of it getting through.

Saturday 15th July
Well it's the wedding day today. I wonder if they're ok? I

think my Master's going to tell the story about when he and his flatmates all decided that The Boss was one of them. It's funny really, I don't know which of them it reflects on most. It turns out that on one occasion, when The Boss called round to their flat, they were all too lazy to answer the door. Instead of making a fuss, she simply climbed in through the kitchen window. I should perhaps point out that the flat was on the ground floor and it wasn't the window above the sink. After that she became an honorary flatmate and all because she didn't make a fuss at how lazy they all were. If it had been the window above the sink, she would have stood on a large pile of dirty washing-up and I don't think she would have been quite so happy about that.

Most of the other dogs that have been staying, since I arrived, have gone home now. There are other dogs here but after a while I start to miss being a household pet. Being a pack animal is great for a while, but new dogs arrive, full of excitement to be out of the household situation for a few days and ready to jockey for position. There are only so many times of being bounced on and having to extract myself from the bottom of the pile before I can say "I really don't need to be top dog", that I can take. It all gets a bit tedious. I want to go home.

Sunday 16th July
I have no idea how the wedding went, as my owners have been too busy to ring me. Anyway, I did send them a telegram, I hope they got it. This is what I wrote.

"Hello Mum and Dad, it's Alfie here your beloved, but rather left out dog. As I realised you wouldn't have chance to ring me today, I thought I would send you my best wishes by telegram. It's funny to think it's now seven months since you both came to meet me and my brother and sisters for the first time. It was obvious then that the way to Mum's heart was through Dad. I knew that if I made a fuss of him and he wanted to take me home then she would want that, just to make him happy. It's all worked out rather well really I know Mum thinks the world of him and he makes her really happy. He looks after her and she looks after me, not a bad set up for a puppy. Anyway, getting back to the point, my little suitcase is packed ready for you to pick me up for the honeymoon and please don't forget to bring me back a doggy bag from the reception. Oh and Dad just because Mum looks up to you and thinks you are the most wonderful bloke in the world, doesn't mean you come any higher in the pecking order as far as I'm concerned. I still expect to get the best seat in front of the fire and don't go getting any ideas about my fetching your slippers, it just isn't going to happen. All my love, your devoted puppy, Alfie."

I hope they liked it. I think I've packed everything. I have my sun cream and a little hat and some glasses, a bucket and spade and a beach towel. I've also packed the books I want to catch up with reading. I presume they're taking me on the honeymoon, but they haven't said. You don't think they would leave me behind do you? It wouldn't be the same without me.

Monday 17th July
Oh dairy I'm so excited. Today is the day my Master and The Boss drive back home. I've packed my little bag already and keep running to look out of the window to see if they're here yet. I hope they've brought me back a lovely big present. Obviously, the present isn't the most

important thing. If I keep saying that to myself over and over then maybe I will remember to say all the nice things like, "Hello, I've missed you" rather than rushing up to them and saying "Where's my present? Which bag is it in?" When you feel like this it's hard to concentrate on anything else.

One of the other dogs asked if I fancied a game of cards to pass the time whilst I was waiting. It was really nice of him, but I just couldn't concentrate. He had said snap every time before I noticed that the cards were even vaguely similar. He did try suggesting we should play something like Black Jack and play for money but in my state of mind I wasn't likely to win. My best bet is probably to spend the day running round the garden to tire myself out so that I can sleep for a while. The only problem with that is that I don't want to be asleep when they get here.

Yesterday was quite fun. One of the dogs suggested we organise our own little sports day. We set up an obstacle race and an agility course and a 'stick and stone race', it's like an egg and spoon race but without the egg and without the spoon. I wanted to do a sack race but we couldn't find any sacks at short notice. There was an elderly dog that said he would act as referee, as he really was a bit past taking part. This worked until he fell asleep half way through the 400 metres hurdles. We were just having an argument about whether the sheltie should be disqualified for running underneath and she was saying that as she only had little legs she didn't have much choice, then we turned to the referee for a decision and found him snoring. I would have won a couple of the races if I hadn't wasted time laughing at the other dogs. A St Bernard might be lovely, but they aren't built for agility and there was a young puppy that reminded me of me a few months ago, not yet being able to corner, he ran straight into a flower bed and got all tangled in some ivy. It's a shame we can't do it all again today to pass the time, but we caused too much damage yesterday.

11
A MISUNDERSTANDING

Tuesday 18th July

Diary, I am beside myself with grief. My Master and The Boss didn't pick me up yesterday. It turns out that I had completely misunderstood them. When they said they were coming back on the Monday after the wedding, what else was I to think than they were coming to pick me up to take me with them? It turns out they have now gone away for a few days on their own, without me. I felt so stupid last night when I rang them to say 'where are you?' and they asked me what I meant. Then I had to face the embarrassment of unpacking my bag, with the other dogs laughing at me. I had tears rolling down my face, so I just went to find a quiet corner of the garden to hide. Why is it that people, or in this case dogs, can be so cruel when a dog is hurting? Whatever happened to sensitivity? They wouldn't like it if I made fun of them. Some of them have short legs and may not be as effective in their cleaning regimes, but do I make fun of them? I might walk over them by mistake, if they're small, but it's only because I'm not looking where I'm going. Anyway, with my Master and The Boss it turns out it was all a bit of a misunderstanding, but that doesn't make me feel any better. Well it wouldn't would it? It may not have been said exactly, that I was going with them, but I thought it was the right thing to assume. Now I'm faced with realising they actually didn't want to take me. Oh it isn't like the bit when they were in England. I understood my passport wasn't valid yet and I couldn't go, but I can travel round other parts of Europe and I'm willing to try flying. Perhaps it's because I haven't been good. Perhaps if I behaved better and didn't jump up, they would have taken me. Do you think if I ring them and say I'll try really hard to be good they would come back to get me?

Wednesday 19th July

You don't suppose they've left me do you? They said I'm being picked up on Sunday, but maybe they're only saying that. What if I'm not? What if now they're married they don't love me anymore? I can't ring them again either. I've run out of credit on my phone and until they get back I can't go and top it up. They can still ring me, but I don't suppose they'll bother. I did try ringing the number I've got for topping up the phone with more credit, but the woman explained to me that I would need a credit card to do it. I said I know the number of The Boss's credit card, but apparently, that isn't OK and I'm not supposed to use it without her permission, but I really am sure she wouldn't mind. I've memorised all her security questions so that I know all the right answers, but I'm told that would be something called 'fraud' and it's not good. I had better stop ordering books on the internet, before she realises it's me.

The Boss did say that if I'd read the document she'd issued with all the details of who has to be where and when, I would have known that I would be collected on Sunday, but why should I read it? My Master didn't. When I said that to The Boss, she got a bit cross and said she makes all that effort so that everyone knows what's happening and no one appreciates it. I have a feeling she may not just be talking about me.

On a brighter note, The Boss was laughing about the things that happen when you travel in England in a car with foreign number plates. There she was sitting in her car, reading a book in a park, with the roof down, when a bloke came to talk to her about her car and started by very slowly and clearly saying, " Excuse _ me _. Do _ you _ speak _ English?" She was tempted to reply in Flemish to say she didn't understand but was, for once, far too polite and laughed and said she was English. In the end this chap wouldn't go away and she really wished she'd gone with the Flemish option.

I tried going to the sales in an attempt to cheer myself up, but came back having bought nothing and concluding that sales are nothing short of fraud. You see big posters in the windows saying things like 'up to 70% off' with the 'up to' in little letters and the 70 in very big ones. When you look round there are a few things that no one would want to buy, for large discounts and then everything that is really nice is close to full price.

Thursday 20th July

Well yesterday suddenly got interesting. A new dog arrived. When I say dog, she is actually a girl but describing her in proper terms just doesn't really do her justice. She has the most beautiful long hair that flows when she moves. I said it was a sort of grey colour but apparently it's described as blue, frankly if she wanted to call it beetroot I would support it and agree. She has such a gentle personality, but is always up to mischief and as for jumping, well I've never seen anything like it. I just sat in the garden watching her bounce and was in complete awe of her bounds and leaps.

I wanted to go up and introduce myself, as you do

when you're a dog, but I suddenly felt all strange and wondered whether my coat was glossy and then felt nervous. It was as though someone had tied my tummy in a knot. In the end she bounced in my general direction and I opened my mouth to say hello but nothing much more than a squeak came out. I eventually managed to say "Hi I'm Alfie and you're beautiful," then wondered why I'd said something so stupid and embarrassing. Fortunately Chloe, as I found she was called, didn't seem to mind and came and sniffed me in an approving manner. I've seen a picture on our wall at home of a dog that looks quite like her, so I asked if she was a bearded collie and she said she was. It gave us something to start the conversation, as I told her that the dog The Boss had before me was a bearded collie, so I've heard a little bit about them. Well that was it then, we spent the whole day together and it was amazing. Suddenly I didn't mind that my owners had gone away without me and I was walking round as though I was on a cotton wool cloud.

Friday 21st July
Once Chloe had got some bouncing out of her system yesterday, we spent the day playing together. She asked if I'd won any awards, as I was clearly a very good looking dog. I think I blushed. I said I hadn't tried to enter any and I was only eight months old. I was worried that might put her off and had wondered about lying about my age, but she would have found out in the end. Fortunately, she didn't seem to mind that I was younger than her, so I asked if she'd won any awards herself. She says she isn't really keen on obedience, as there isn't enough bouncing involved, but she does enjoy agility and has done quite well in that. I told her about the rosette The Boss has from

the Denbury May Fair. She won 'Dog most like its owner', which when you win it with a bearded collie tells you quite a bit about The Boss. We both laughed about it with me describing The Boss to her and Chloe trying to think what type of dog her owners were most like. I tried to think what sort my Master was most like but it wasn't easy.

My Master was given some burn proof gloves by the best man. It means I will be able to take things out of the oven without finding holes in the oven gloves where my Master set fire to them.

Saturday 22nd July

I spent all of yesterday with Chloe. We were inseparable. She's going home this morning and I really don't want her to go. We've exchanged phone numbers, but I had to explain that I'd run out of credit, so I wouldn't be able to ring her for at least a couple of days.

My owners have rung and confirmed they're picking me up tomorrow night, I do hope they don't forget me, as I wouldn't want to get all excited and then feel all let down and abandoned again.

Sunday 23rd July

Once Chloe left yesterday, I just moped around. I felt absolutely lost, even though she'd only been here for a couple of days. Every so often I would find one of her hairs on something and sigh. Her hair really does get everywhere. I didn't even feel hungry, which is quite unlike me. She'd taken a photo of me using her phone and we'd got one of the other dogs to take a picture of the two of us together. I do hope she emails them to me. I tried to spend the time focussing on the good things and thinking about the fact that if all goes according to plan, I'm going home today. I wish Chloe were here to meet The Boss I think they would like each other. My Master was never quite so keen on the bounciness of The Boss's bearded collie. Apparently, when he was a puppy, (the bearded collie not my Master) my Master was trying to eat a Chinese takeaway, when Sweep (that was The Boss's bearded collie's name), decided it was a good time to bounce onto his lap and bounced straight into his plate of food. I can't imagine my Master would have taken that very well, even from a little fluffy bundle of puppy.

I wasn't sure whether to pack my things up early this time. I really can't face the disappointment of my owners not coming to pick me up again. I could see all the other dogs watching me as I trotted past the window, just to have a look, I really don't want them all to make fun of me. Perhaps I should pretend I don't care, then at least no one will see that I'm hurting. It really is only natural for a dog to want to see his owners. I ought to be able to get excited without the worry of what the other dogs will think of me. I suppose it's the fear of looking stupid, no one likes to be made to look stupid. I'm almost certain they said that they would definitely be here for me today and I know that they said it would be evening, but you can't blame me for holding out a hope that they might surprise me and come early.

Monday 24th July

Well diary I'm happy to say I'm home. My owners picked me up yesterday evening, after what was for me a very long day of worry. I'd told myself that when I saw them I wasn't going to show my excitement; I was going to play it cool, but I'm a dog not a cat. I bounced all over them and The Boss wouldn't stop hugging me, she was so pleased to see me. It's funny thinking that I could have thought they didn't love me. I wonder how long it will take before she gets fed up with my not wanting to let her out of my sight. She actually seems to be rather enjoying it at the minute. I told her all the worries I'd had, that they didn't need me anymore and that they might not come back for me. She told me I must never think things like that. She said I would always be their dog and they loved me. I was wondering if I could use it to negotiate any increased pocket money or the occasional sleep on their bed, but maybe I'm pushing my luck.

Tuesday 25th July
Some new people have just moved into our road. I could tell they were new, as I hadn't smelt them before. I went straight up to the gate to say hello, when they were walking past. Isn't it great how people will say hello to a strange dog, or a child, but if it had been an adult, although they might have said "Hello" they wouldn't have come straight up to the gate to shake hands and introduce themselves. To be fair I don't shake hands yet. The Boss has talked to me about learning, but I'm not really socially adept enough to differentiate those times it's appropriate to shake hands and those times I can go up and sniff their bottom. The Boss has said that I should work on the basis that shaking hands is always acceptable, but sniffing bottoms is only ok with other dogs. "Where is the fun in that?" There is nothing quite like a good sniff to get to know someone.

I have evidence that honesty is not the best policy and in fact there are times when you're better to keep quiet. My Master came home and sheepishly announced that he had received another speeding fine. I saw an opportunity to tease him mercilessly. The Boss made the mistake of asking when exactly it was for and then admitting that it must have meant she was driving the car. She could have let him continue thinking it was him.

However, she can continue to tease him about setting fire to the oven gloves. The new oven gloves that replaced the ones he set fire to last time, now need to be replaced. It turns out he has set fire to that pair too. I can see a pattern developing here. Is it his carelessness when cooking, or is it a cry for help that he shouldn't really be left on his own for the weekend? Either way, if I see him heading for the kitchen I will be going out from now on.

Wednesday 26th July

Until now, The Boss has been able to put things on the work surface in the kitchen out of my reach. Not anymore. I have now discovered that I can stand on my back legs and put my front legs on the work surface. This enables me to get my nose and if necessary my mouth over the edge to investigate. Whilst The Boss has already caught me doing this, which will mean she is on her guard, I know what she's like when she's cooking and it's inevitable that she'll forget. It'll be a time such as when she's flustered, serving up lots of meals, but rest assured, I'm ready. I'm not fussy whether it's a pork chop or spaghetti bolognaise. I'll be there, ready to be food taster.

Whilst I was away, the bamboo in the garden has grown so much that I think the only solution is to invite a panda to move in. I wonder if we could get one on loan from the zoo, rather than it move in completely. It's not that I would mind having it live here, but from the pictures I've seen, I'm just a little bit concerned that it might look more cuddly than me and therefore get more fuss. Now don't get me wrong I'm not a jealous dog, I just feel a bit sensitive having been apart from my owners for a couple of weeks. Bamboo or no bamboo I don't think I'm quite ready to share them with a panda. We could do with a sheep for the grass too and maybe a giraffe to keep the hedges in order. At least if there were a number of other animals it would reduce the risk of one of them replacing me. Perhaps I could be in charge of managing their gardening activities. I could set up a gardening business "gardening the natural way", in which I took the animals round to do a clean-up operation of people's gardens.

Thursday 27th July

We went into Antwerp yesterday. To be honest I think The Boss was rather hoping I was going to stay at home, but there is only so much being left out a dog can take. In the car park, opposite to where we parked there were two glass doors. One was the ladies toilet and one was the men's. Well a glass door on a ladies loo is one thing, you only get to see them drying their hands, but it seems a bit odd on a blokes one – why build a separate room for it at all if you're going to have them on show to the whole world? Humans become more like dogs all the time.

The Boss is pleased that I haven't forgotten any of the things she'd taught me before she went away. I've learnt to sit on command. Now I realise that doesn't sound very impressive, but we have moved on from verbal commands. I now understand when The Boss tells me with just a finger movement, or a nod of the head. It's great that I can tell what she wants from some distance as long as I look at her. I will also go to her when beckoned. I get so much fuss and praise for getting it right that I have completely gone off the idea of disobeying.

I was mortified when the people I was staying with last week actually told my Master that I'd spent a lot of the time rolling around the garden with the other dogs and that it didn't matter how small the other dog was, I always ended up at the bottom of the pile. My Master said I was a wimp. I think that's a little unfair. I like to think of it more in terms of 'no one makes friends by pushing them around' and if you win all the time, then other dogs don't want to play with you. Of course winning once in a while might be considered acceptable, but I don't want to be too rough with the little dogs and besides, some of them really bark. I don't need to be top dog to prove I'm the best, I know The Boss thinks I'm lovely the way I am and she doesn't think I'm a wimp. Secretly, I think I'm above my Master in the pecking order, but it's best he doesn't realise I think that way.

Friday 28th July
Don't you just hate automated telephone answering services? "Please press one for new sales, press two for an enquiry for a previous sale and three if your enquiry is about something else". What it should really say is, "If you press one, because we still want your money, we will put you through to a human being. If you press two, your call may be answered, if you're lucky and only during normal hours. We already have your money and therefore don't need to be quite so keen to look after you. If you press three you will be put through to someone who can't help you. This is because our statistics show that you were clearly not planning to give us any money." If that isn't bad enough they put on 'soothing' music whilst you're waiting for no one to look after you, which is usually

something so irritating that if they did answer the phone you would struggle to resist the desperate urge to shout at them.

It wouldn't have been so bad, but I'd rung the wrong number and had waited forever, to get through to someone who had no idea what I was talking about. They gave me another number, also for someone that couldn't help. They in turn gave me another number and that person gave me the number of the person I'd rung first time, who said it wasn't anything to do with them. When I rang the second time the person that answered said it was them and they couldn't understand why I'd been told that it wasn't. By the end, I really wished I hadn't bothered in the first place.

There's nothing worse than someone visiting my house and saying 'oh I don't like dogs, can you shut him in another room?' I know The Boss doesn't like it either and has offered to come and sit in my room with me, or maybe that is to get out of having to look after visitors. Perhaps I should ask for a bigger room with one or two more things in it, including my computer, to make it easier and more fun if I'm confined to my quarters. You know, sometimes children don't seem to understand it's no different to them being 'grounded' when they haven't done anything wrong.

It turns out The Boss likes thunder storms even less than I do, which is saying something. She doesn't think she's afraid of many things. At least she didn't until my Master sat and listed the ones he was aware of. After that, she had to concede that in all probability she is a bit of a coward.

Sunday 30th July

My Master received a reminder letter saying a speeding fine hadn't been paid. He rang The Boss to get her to check that the money had left their bank and gone to the right place, which it had. In these circumstances my Master's usual approach is to screw up the letter and throw it in the bin, assuming it has crossed with the payment, rather than check there is no problem. He is then surprised when he receives a letter inviting him to go to court. He is however discovering from The Boss that there is a different approach. There she was, on the phone to him saying, "Could you unscrew the piece of paper and ring them to confirm?" He laughed nervously and asked how she knew he'd screwed it up. He retrieved the piece of paper from the bin. If he hadn't done, he would never have known just how inefficient the police payment system in Belgium is. Would you believe the man in charge of sending reminders said he had no way of checking and in the event that we should get a letter from the 'district attorney' or whatever it's called, could we please send copies of the bank paperwork to them so that they could cross us off the list. He was very apologetic but said most people paid in the post office and were given a stamp that acted as their proof. The police weren't yet able to cope with the bank reconciliation involved in direct payments into their bank account. All this despite putting their bank details on the form, to enable you to pay that way. It made me wonder whether there was any point in paying at all or whether in fact they would simply not notice if you didn't. What exactly did they think I was paying money into the police bank account for? Maybe they though it was a bribe.

12
ELVIS IS ALIVE

Monday 31st July

I made a new friend last week. His name is Elvis, which has already led to my Master trying to make wisecrack jokes that no one understood until he explained. I always find if you have to explain a joke, it may not really have worked. Anyway, Elvis is quite small but has bundles of energy. He's as soft as I am, so we can roll around and tumble without either of us thinking it's about who's in charge. It always confuses me when I'm having a simple game and then I find out that the dog I'm playing with, thinks it's something else completely and he's really trying to prove he's boss. It would be so much easier if the other dogs told me that at the start, as I would just roll over and save him the bother.

It turns out that Elvis had the same problem as me, of having only one testicle and had to have the operation I need to have. He came through it ok, which is a relief. He goes to the same vet, which is even better. My Master said perhaps we should change vet, but I said the problem wasn't the vet's fault. Elvis had to have a funny collar thing on for a while to stop him taking his stitches out. He was saying he forgot he had it on and used to run into things and get a bit of a shock. Apparently, he ran into the garage and it fell off, (the collar not the garage) but by then he was healing so it didn't matter so much.

Tuesday 1st August

Well my owners have finally brought their wedding presents back to Belgium. The outdoor dominoes are relatively easy to understand, but I'm having a bit more difficulty with the chess set. I've sort of understood that my pawns move forwards, except when they move diagonally and that they move one space, except when they move two. What I don't get are the little horses that can't make up their minds if they're going forwards or diagonally and seem to do both at once every turn, except when my opponent knocks them off the board. It's odd that the queen is more useful than the king in the way it moves, but it's still the king that means you lose.

In my experience, of playing games with children, you just make up the rules as you go along and as long as it makes sense to some of you and everyone is happy, it's fine. It only becomes a problem when adults come and get involved and tell you that you're doing it incorrectly. How can it be wrong if you've made up your own rules and you are enjoying playing? I see it more as 'evolution', after all how would games like rugby have been invented, if adults had simply come along and said 'you can't do it like that'?

I'm even more excited by the bar-b-q. My reasoning is that from observation, this type of cooking involves more food being dropped, which can only be a good thing for a dog.

Wednesday 2nd August

It seems I'm becoming more agile. It wasn't that I wanted to be clumsy before, it was just that bits of me didn't yet work in quite the way I might have liked them too. I still have a way to go on cornering. There seems to be a problem of my going too fast in the first place and therefore not being able to slow down at exactly the point I wanted in order to change direction. Where I have made an enormous amount of progress is in being a little more nimble. Now that my back legs are stronger and I can put all my weight on them, I can raise my front legs and gently put them on The Boss's knee, rather than cause such a wide range of bruises. I even managed to jump on top of her on the settee without causing quite as much pain as normal, which has to be an improvement. Sometimes I just forget she isn't a dog and is more sensitive. Then in my enthusiasm, I cause some superb bruises. I know she bruises easily, but there are times that her legs are almost rainbow coloured and it's mainly my fault. If she didn't walk into things it would help. Perhaps now I'm getting the hang of it, I should start trying to teach her to be more agile and nimble herself.

Thursday 3rd August

I've developed a new bedtime ritual. At first my owners thought I was being difficult and not wanting to go to bed, then they caught me in the act so I had to confess. When they put me to bed at night, I have to go outside to do anything I need to do first. The backdoor goes straight out from my room so it is fairly easy, but very often whilst I'm out there they leave the door open and the light on. This means that a few insects get it into their heads that they want to move in to my room, which is not something I'm happy with. Most of them are ok but I find the noise of the mosquitoes buzzing past my ear puts me off sleeping. I've started a little nightly game of seeing how many I can catch and eat before I get into bed. Swatting them is ok until you get one that is full of blood and are left wondering if it's yours.

Friday 4th August

The way things are run in Belgium sure beats me. The post lady rang the bell yesterday and The Boss went down the drive to see her. The Boss asked if she could help and the post lady said she had now put it in the letterbox. As The Boss went to the letter box the post lady drove off. In the letter box was a card saying that they'd tried to deliver a parcel which the post lady despite talking to The Boss had now driven off with, back to the post office. Somewhere I think the logic might be flawed. Why didn't she give The Boss the parcel or did she prefer the thought that after someone had paid for delivery The Boss now had to complete an hour round trip to go and collect it, having waved it off down the road with the post lady. The end result was that The Boss was not in a good mood.

Now I'm not one to cause alarm, but I think there's something alive in the bottom of the swimming pool. It isn't exactly the Loch Ness Monster but when The Boss tried to clean the 'dirt' off the bottom, some of it swam off. After it had done this two or three times, she started to think it may not be a coincidence. I suggested that if she would like to provide me with a little rod and line, I would sit there for a while to see if it would bite. The Boss thought that using the net might be more effective but it's right at the bottom and seems to move very fast, besides which I find holding the net a bit clumsy with my paws. Maybe it's a tiny piranha and it'll get bigger as it eats people in the pool.

Saturday 5th August

It's really funny listening to The Boss. This whole getting

married thing is clearly very confusing for her. She doesn't seem to know what her name is. She answers the phone with the wrong name almost every time, resulting in a lengthy explanation, or fits of laughter depending on who's on the other end. I caught her trying to work out how to write and sign her name the other day. She'd start writing one thing and half way through it would become something else completely. I said she should do something completely different from her current signature to reduce confusion. My Master said, if it were a signature why not leave it the same as it was, most peoples' signatures can't be read, so what would it matter if it actually said a different name from the one she would write. Being stubborn she just ignored both of us and carried on trying.

There is an altogether new experience going on in the house. The Boss is busy doing some decorating. They are painting a room in a funny pink colour, that's not at all to my liking. The Boss was at pains to explain it was not for her. I offered to help and suggested we could do a fancy paw print pattern around the edge. The Boss asked me as gently as possible if I could please keep my paws out of the paint. Apparently, you are supposed to apply the paint with brushes and avoid getting it over everywhere else. Where's the fun in that? Sometimes The Boss really needs to let her hair down.

Monday 7th August

It's most unfair. Having not let me paint, The Boss has put all the brushes in my room to dry and told me not to play with them. As if the thought would have crossed my mind. However, I may need to go and get some kitchen roll to clean off the pattern I've made on the floor with the drips, which are still a pinky colour, before she notices.

My owners used their new bar b q for the first time last night. What I really don't understand is why men who don't know one end of a spatula from the other and who are not safe to be left alone in a kitchen, suddenly become 'experts' when there is fire and charcoal involved. Spontaneously, they think they look good in an apron and there is no question that any women around should be let anywhere near the cooking. Strange that the very women who have to cook every other day of the week and without whom the men resort to takeaways, or beer as their main course, are suddenly deemed to know nothing about cooking if there is a bar b q involved. It may of course be that no one makes fun of men if they set fire to the food on the bar b q, that is 'normal', when they do it in the kitchen that is 'dangerous'.

Some of the wedding presents that my owners got are magic lights. They're amazing. The Boss has tried to explain that they are solar powered, but I think they're just magic. My main disappointment is that the lights have been put round the bits of the garden that my owners use, rather than the bits I need to use at night to do my business. When I complained to The Boss, she pointed out that if I got married then I could always get people to buy some for me, to which I answered "it may have escaped your notice but I'm a dog." Duh! Well in fairness I actually said the "Duh!" as well and got told off for being cheeky, but I'm only copying those around me, admittedly the younger ones of those around me, but copying none the less.

Friday 11th August
Well the moles have been undertaking what I can only

think is their equivalent of 'the Olympics'. There are lines where they've tried the 100 metres, the 200 metres and holes for the long jump, triple jump and high jump. I don't know who the winners were but it certainly wasn't us.

Don't you just hate it when people start to realise just how shallow you are? Until now, I have maintained the impression with The Boss that I'm quite bright and that I think quite a bit about what goes on. I think about my food, her food, my Master's food and basically any food dropped in an accessible place, either deliberately or accidentally. I think a lot about plates left in places I can reach them and I think about going to the supermarket. I think about my bowl when it's full and think about it sadly when it's empty. Unfortunately, The Boss has started to work out that that is the extent of my thinking. She thought I was musing on the state of the economy, world peace and the importance of education and health. Who is she kidding? Food! That is basically the long and short of it. I'm a dog and I'm male, what more did she expect? Maybe beer, football and sex, but they aren't so much dog things, well the sex is, but I'm a bit young.

If I'm quite honest, I'm at a bit of a loose end without everyone around. I tried playing with the giant dominoes and the giant chess pieces on my own, but I kept losing, so that wasn't much fun.

Saturday 12th August

I'm very concerned that the moles may have come an awfully long way to get to our garden. I always thought they were supposed to be nocturnal animals, but it seems ours make holes during the day. I have therefore concluded that we have Antipodean moles. It's either that or they are young moles having difficulty in understanding how to set a 24 hour clock. There was a classic moment where The Boss went round and trod all the earth down, then sat on the patio with her back towards the holes. When she turned round, the earth was all piled up and they had been digging again just as soon as she wasn't looking. If they keep going like this, the whole garden will be undermined.

I fear I may be growing again. I seem to be having a very sleepy few days. It may of course simply be my Master's influence rubbing off on me and I'm sure he's not growing. He thinks his is brought on by doing DIY.

Sunday 13th August

Personally, (or should it be dogally?) I'm rather concerned. One of the wedding presents is a Flemish cookbook. Apparently, there's a tradition that when a girl gets married, in this part of Belgium, her mother gives her this particular cookery book, which has been updated over many, many years. A friend of The Boss bought it for her. A lovely idea you might think, so why am I so concerned? Well it's not just Flemish recipes, it's all written in Flemish too. The Boss does know a fair few words, but what happens when she steams something that should have been roasted or sautés something that should have been frozen? I suppose on the bright side, I might stand to benefit if some of the dishes go wrong, but if they go very wrong even I might refuse to eat them. In fairness, they would have to turn out very inedible before my Master would turn them away. The Boss has promised to refer to her dictionary for any of the words she doesn't know, but I'm still a little anxious. I think the friends in question realise there may be some mistakes, as they also gave them some fairly large bottles of strong Belgian beer, which I can only assume are to be consumed on those occasions that the taste of the cooking needs to be 'overwhelmed'.

Mole hills are so 'last year'. We've moved on to 'mole mountains'. I'm starting to doubt the sense in the saying 'don't make a mountain out of a mole hill' being used to reduce concern with regard to a situation. I'm actually starting to think 'a mole hill' should describe a complete crisis in anybody's book. Maybe if things are really bad we should say 'I've got a real mole hill situation here.' Or maybe when you want to express the state of something that is about to go very wrong you should say 'the moles are about to move in on this one'.

Monday 14th August
There's been some 'discussion' about travel arrangements when we go on holiday on Friday. It seems that seven people, one dog and a lot of luggage will not all fit in one vehicle. The Boss said she is taking her car as well, but that only seats two people, or more to the point one people and a dog. A dispute has broken out because there are other people wanting to take the second seat in the 'fun' car. A different dispute has broken out about who gets to sit with me. When I'm in my Master's car I don't generally take up just one seat, I take at least two and three if I can get away with it. The Boss is therefore using this to support her point that I'm going in her car, which of course I see as my car too and I've said that as long as we can have the roof down I'm happy with that. Now we just need to get all the luggage in. Apparently, my bed and food seem to take up a disproportionate amount of space. I said, "leave my food, I'm happy to eat steak this

week as a sacrifice" but it fell on deaf ears.

Tuesday 15th August

Ok, I admit it. I have resorted to direct action with the moles. I have started peeing on the mole hills to see if that will put them off. If I'm going to pee on all the hills I may have to start drinking rather more, but at least it's a start.

I've been thinking about this whole decorating thing and I want my room done. I've been saying I'd like a new bed for ages as 'cosy' has long since stopped being a suitable euphemism for small. In fairness if I curl up, I do still fit in it quite nicely with just enough room for my pig, but when I start chasing rabbits in my sleep, there really is no hope of all of me staying inside the bed. I do now have a picture in my room and a clock, although the clock needs a new battery, so it permanently says bedtime, but I can live with that.

Wednesday 16th August

Sometimes you see the strangest things when you're driving along the road. We passed a lorry that had some giant teacups and saucers on the back. I presumed they were either being delivered to a giant, or to someone who gets very thirsty. My other suggestion was that it might be for some workmen to save them brewing up quite as often. The Boss explained they were part of a fair and that was actually a ride. Now I'm even more confused. Why would anyone want to go round and round in a teacup? Is it a way of stirring the drink if you haven't got a spoon handy or is it some bizarre ritual that is operated in some parts of the world? You would think for one journey that was quite enough excitement for me, but further along the traffic was going really slowly and it turned out there was a train on the back of a lorry. Now correct me if I'm wrong, but I thought the whole point of trains was that they run on rails and not on the road, otherwise all those miles of train track seem to be a bit of a waste of effort. The Boss thought they may be delivering the train somewhere, or taking it to a place that the railway didn't get to very easily. I have my own theories. I think it might have broken down, in which case it's not a very good advert for travelling by train. Failing that I think it was a sinister plot to slow all the road traffic down and make more people think it would be quicker to travel by train and rush out and buy some tickets. Although you would think that they would do that in disguise, unless the train was supposed to be a subliminal message.

Thursday 17th August
Isn't it funny how every country seems to use words and names from other languages and cultures to make things sound exotic? In England, you get food shops with French names and restaurants with Italian names. Kitchen designs are called after regions of other countries and even paint colours can have foreign words for names to make them sound special. Then you go to those other countries that sound so exotic to the English and what do you find? Can you buy a kitchen design called 'Provence' or dine in a restaurant called 'Bella Italiano'? No you can buy a 'Cotswold' kitchen and dine in 'The Pelican Station'. Everyone thinks that everyone else seems more exciting and exotic than they are. I wonder if any country thinks enough of itself to use its own places and language to celebrate everything that they consider special.

It gets a bit annoying when the family spend too much time playing outdoor dominoes and chess and insist on playing to the real rules, which rather prevents my playing, as I cannot remember for the life of me what I should do with my rook. Whilst I realise that it's not absolutely critical in the game of dominoes to know what to do with a rook, they have normally finished the game whilst I'm still moving the dominoes pieces diagonally and trying to take some off the board. They have now invested in a croquet set and I've been made to promise faithfully that I won't run off with one of the wooden balls. They have forgotten to tell me not to chew it, so I may still be able to contribute to the fun. Be honest, which is more fun – chewing a wooden ball or trying to knock it through a series of ridiculously small hoops with a wooden mallet, whilst everyone else tries to knock you out of the way?

Friday 18th August
Well the count down to the holiday is over and we're all packed up ready to go. I didn't realise just how many fights can break out trying to get ready to do something nice, let alone how difficult it is to get everyone out of the door and into the car. It makes the fuss I make about climbing into my Master's car, or rather wanting to be lifted up, seem relatively mild. I shall perhaps point that out to him next time he's complaining that I should be doing it for myself.

All I know of our destination is that it's in Belgium, but as I'm already in Belgium I wonder if we're just driving round the block and coming back and pretending we've gone away. While you might convince a four year old of that one, particularly if someone moved the furniture round while we were out, I can't see the adults or the dog being taken in.

I just need to practice all those essential holiday words and phrases. "Can I have another sweet?" "Where's my ball?" "Will you play with me?" "I'm bored" "Are we nearly there yet?" "I need the toilet" "I think I'm going to be sick". I think that's probably most of them.

13
THE END OF THE SUMMER

Saturday 19th August

I'm having too much fun to spend long writing. It turns out that I'm in a place called the Ardennes. I'm now thoroughly confused as I thought that was a type of pate. The Boss has tried to explain that it's a place where the type of pate comes from; a bit like Champagne. I told her not to be silly; pate is not a bit like Champagne. After I'd thought about it for a while I said, "I thought Champagne came from the rack in the garage?" but she said I was just being difficult and she knew I understood what she meant really. Some people just have no sense of humour.

Sunday 20th August

I've been thinking about motorway food. Why when you drive round continental Europe are the service stations not as busy as the ones in England, but the food is so much better and usually cheaper? I don't understand why the ones in England are so bad. Even supermarkets manage to keep hot food nice and fresh, by putting the chickens in bags or on a spit roast machine, so why do English motorway services and airports use hotplates that just dry the food out and make it all leathery whilst keeping it only luke warm? Jacket potatoes are the worst. How difficult would it be for them to keep their jacket potatoes in those special little ovens? Do you think somewhere in England there is an award they're all competing for, which is given to 'the worst food you can possibly serve'? Maybe they are in league with the fast food outlets to ensure that the fast food is compared with something that makes it seem positively 'fine cuisine'.

Monday 21st August

Did I mention the journey here? I think for our transport arrangements the logic may have been a tiny bit flawed. The car with sat-nav, followed the car with the dog navigating from the map. That would be me. I've always thought that left and right are such overrated terms.

I've realised there is no door to my room, so I'm free to go upstairs. Last night The Boss put me to bed and went up to her room and whilst she was in the bathroom I went and joined her, so she put me to bed again. When everything was quiet, I went back upstairs to check they were ok and then came down of my own accord. The good thing was being able to go back up three times in the night and gently nuzzle The Boss and wake her up to check she was ok. Once I'd checked I went back to my own bed, content that in this strange place everything was normal.

Tuesday 22nd August

We've been playing mini-golf. It's great. You chase little balls through all sorts of obstacles. I think I was supposed to be doing it in turn and counting the number of goes I had, but there's a finite number I can count up to and I do hate losing. Some of the holes were really difficult to get round, they were not in straight lines and there were all sorts of things in the way. It was fun, but it did all seem a bit of a pointless exercise.

I do really want to have a go at archery but the bows aren't very suitable for dogs.

Wednesday 23rd August

Whatever you say, I refuse to accept that it was my fault. I was off the lead, but was it my fault that the Jack Russell growled? What does a dog do in that circumstance? His owners, to protect their 'little precious', scooped him up, so I jumped up to get him. Well his owners had such a go at the poor Boss and even when she went and apologised to them again later, they said they didn't accept her apology. I felt so sorry for her. I almost wished I hadn't tried to get him. I will sort it out if I see him again. I'm not having anyone speaking to The Boss like that.

Now I know I'm a dog and smelling is part of the package but I'm getting a bit concerned about the humans around me. It would seem that hot water is only available in limited quantities on a daily basis and those quantities may not be enough for every member of the party to be as clean as normal. Isn't it funny how given the least excuse a boy will decide he doesn't need a shower. What is wrong with cold water is what I say, even cold muddy water? However, it seems there is an expectation amongst humans that water for showering should be clean and hot. The Boss says the whole thing is a bit like indoor camping and as I know what she thinks of camping, I'm guessing she may not be overly impressed by the experience.

Lesson for self (well more lesson for The Boss really), only leave the bathroom window open when showering, when you're not on the ground floor immediately next to a footpath. I don't think she was too thrilled to get the opportunity to say good morning to a stranger, whilst completely naked!

Friday 25th August

Well we're back to the arguments of who sits where for

the journey home and of course how we get all the stuff in the car. Isn't it funny how your belongings can expand whilst you're away and don't fit in the suitcase on the way back? I've done my best to eat all the food I brought with me, so I've made a bit of space, but no one seems to be showing much gratitude for my efforts. I'm going to miss having extra time with The Boss. It's been great. I have occasionally provided her with the perfect excuse not to join in. "Sorry I can't come, you can't take dogs in and I can't leave Alfie that long in a strange place." In reality she could leave me that long, I'm a very well behaved Alfie, although I would have been a bit lonely so I'm quite pleased.

Sunday 27th August

Most alarmingly, I was grounded earlier. The alarming bit is that it was The Boss who grounded me, and after my Master said The Boss thought I was perfect and she's too soft with me. Of course, I am perfect, but it seems that trying to dig up the moles is not acceptable. I'm not actually sure if it was just the digging up of the moles or traipsing the mud all through the lounge, but whichever it was, I was grounded.

The biggest problem with having had so many visitors staying, is the fact that the washing machine and tumble dryer are in my room. When will The Boss start to understand that putting it on when she goes to bed is most unfair on me? What dog wants to be woken by a hyperactive washing machine bouncing round the room? I've told it to stay in its own corner, but to no avail. The tumble dryer, whilst obeying the command sit, has a nasty habit of beeping at intervals to tell me it's finished. I can't get to sleep properly until it finally stops.

Monday 28th August

Now I'm a dog, and I'm expected to eat everything I can get my mouth round. In fairness, I do tend to be a bit more choosy than many of my species and I've never eaten anything I shouldn't eat, not that really mattered anyway. I eat the odd root, purely for medicinal purposes you understand and maybe the odd slug now and again. All this just adds to the fact that yesterday I was completely confused, as was almost everyone else as to why a four year old boy would choose to swallow a magnetic ball bearing. Fortunately, they are relatively small and round and highly unlikely to get stuck, but all in all you have to think it isn't the brightest idea. The Boss found a bit on the internet about the sort of things children swallow and when to seek medical advice, just to calm my Master down, and actually found it really made quite amusing reading. At the end of the day, you really do have to ask yourself the question why do humans swallow odd things? To be honest coming from a dog that may sound a bit rich, but I'm not just any dog.

Wednesday 30th August

Yesterday was brilliant. We had a bar b q for The Boss's birthday and, as a treat for me, she invited Elvis. Elvis the dog obviously, not the original Elvis, the latter would have been more for my Master than me. Quite an evening with nine children, seven adults and two dogs. To be honest the dogs were more like several extra children as we ran round getting in everyone's way, but it was fun.

You've got to laugh really. I've managed to convince a four year old that the rug by the side of The Boss's bed is a 'magic carpet' and that when I go to sleep on it, we fly away to far flung places. I've told him about some of the exciting adventures we have and the treasures we bring back. I've then quietly gone downstairs leaving him trying to get to sleep on the rug. Peace at last and at such a small price. The only concern is that I have told him the bamboo in the garden is like the magic beanstalk in 'Jack and the beanstalk' and that I can climb up and end up in a different place. I may need to tell him the truth when he wakes up, otherwise he might try climbing the bamboo and if it won't take my weight then it really won't take his. I found it wouldn't take my weight when I tried to climb up to see if I could find the magic kingdom that The Boss had told me about. You know, sometimes I really think she should know better than trying to play with the mind of an impressionable young dog.

Saturday 2nd September

I gave the game away earlier this week, of just how high I can jump. I was trying to keep it secret just in case it came in useful, but then when I was chasing Elvis, at one leap I cleared the settee, from back to front. Elvis got a bit of a shock, thinking he had found somewhere to hide, but The Boss was more shocked.

Everyone is trying to train me. It's a nightmare. Apparently, no one likes it when I jump up, particularly when I have muddy paws. I only get a "nice dog, good dog" and all the associated pats and strokes as long as I sit quietly in front of them. Now it isn't that I don't understand what they mean, and it isn't that I don't sympathise with the general idea, but how is a dog supposed to show his emotion if he can't jump up? There is only so hard I can wag my tail and I get told off for barking. All I want to say is that I'm really pleased to see you and I'm not taking for granted how lucky I am to have you around. Humans hug each other, why can't a dog try to hug a human? I'm only trying to follow the example you set. What should I be doing?

Sunday 3rd September
I sat daydreaming earlier. There I was dreaming about sunshine and running through fields of rabbits, it was all going very well until the rabbits started to develop mole faces. Then they all started digging in unison and I couldn't get back across the field. I couldn't get home. To be honest I may have fallen asleep altogether. I usually get to rummage through the food cupboard and help myself to anything I fancy in a daydream.

I had a poorly tummy last week, and it has left me with a bit of a wind problem. When I say 'a bit' of a wind problem, what I actually mean is that I don't want to be in the same room as my rear end. It's times like these you really wish you didn't have such an acute sense of smell. I've tried pretending it isn't me, but as the smell goes wherever I do, no one is fooled. I've been sent to my room several times, which is so unfair. I didn't want to be with me, so I couldn't really take it that personally that the humans didn't want me around, but would they not think to open a window in there for me?.

Tuesday 5th September 2006
Out of the blue, The Boss asked whether I'd thought any more about careers. 'Well frankly' I said 'No.' To be honest I thought that had all been forgotten and maybe I could get away without one. Unfortunately, it seems I was barking up the wrong tree and I still need to work out what I want to do. I mulled over 'mole catcher' for a brief time, but realised I've been wholly unsuccessful in that

capacity in the last few weeks and at the end of the day it is more a cat's work than a dog's.

Wednesday 6th September

Nature really isn't nice to dogs. Is it our fault we feel compelled to eat everything? It's such a high price to pay. We get the upset stomachs every so often and then, worse still, we get the worming tablets. I reminded The Boss how poorly they made me last time, but she said that was no excuse, I was a big dog now and the vet would give me the right thing. Vet! Did she say vet? It's bad enough having to take medicine, but he is the one that prods and pokes me in places that make me blush. Unfortunately, The Boss says there is no getting out of it and besides she wants to talk to the vet about when I should have my operation. It really goes from bad to worse. The only consolation is that after the operation there should be less need to prod and poke me, at least there anyway.

The day had got off to a particularly nasty start when The Boss said my tick treatment was due. Now I'm not one to grumble about a bit of liquid squirted into my fur, but it was what she said next that caused alarm. "You smell a bit, I think I'll give you a bath first." The bit about smelling had felt like a compliment until the threat of clean water was introduced. Oh I see, just because the children have gone back and she can't make James have a shower, she has started on me. I think she has a problem. I'm not so small as I was the last time I had a bath and I didn't want to co-operate. Well she only went and did that thing where they get you by the scruff of the neck and you become all submissive, because if reminds you of when you were a little puppy and your mum did it to move you around. What can a poor puppy do faced with that? So a bath it was. A very wet bath. If you're going to be forced to get into the bath, the least you can do is insist on sharing it with a friend, even if they don't get into the actual bath itself. The Boss was soaked. At least that gave me some cause for a laugh and believe me it was the sort of day when I needed one.

Thursday 7th September
My Master is away, which seems to be an excuse for The Boss to spend the whole evening playing on the Playstation. "Get a life," I said to her. "You could at least come downstairs and watch a movie with me." I do find the games she's playing very confusing to keep track of. Who is this Harry Potter anyway? Quite apart from that, I'd forgotten how boring The Boss can be. There's me saying 'lets go out and play' and there she is wanting to sit behind a desk all day writing. I kept going and tapping her and saying it's sunny outside and she just left the back door open so I could go out when I wanted to. That really wasn't the point I was making.

At least now that some of the leaves have fallen off the hedge I can watch the world go by more easily. I had almost forgotten that I used to be able to see people go past. I'm even learning where acorns come from. They seem to drop out of the sky when I'm walking in the woods. I'm guessing there is an acorn god throwing them down in a 'feeding the birds' sort of way.

Friday 8th September
If you're relaying slabs, and you break a few in taking the old ones up, you could work out that the ones you have left are not going to meet in the middle, when you put them back down. Surprisingly enough, when the

workmen in our garden put the slabs back down, the 'slab fairy' hadn't been with a special delivery to magically make it all fit and, yes, it was going to be necessary for them to order some more. Frustratingly when you don't speak much of the same language, it's very hard to get cross. But then, this is Belgium and everyone seems to smile and shrug and regard such inconveniences as inevitable.

This whole 'training the dog' thing is going too far. Now it seems I have to learn to sit quietly at meal times and not beg. For once, I want my Master to say 'he's only a dog'. Yes, I'm a dog, and what do dogs do when there's food around? They beg. This sit quietly stuff is for budgies or cats or even hamsters, but I'm a dog and we expect to beg.

I'm now nearly ten months old, so in human terms that makes me nearly six. I'm past the tantrum stage (theoretically – although judging by The Boss you're allowed to never completely get past them.) I have to wait to be a teenager to completely rebel. I guess I shall just have to learn to be a good doggie for another year and then I can break out. I'm thinking of shaving my head and having my ear pierced, that will dampen the 'cute' image. Behind this soft exterior there's a fully developed 'bad dog' just waiting to break out. In the meantime, I'll just lie quietly by The Boss's side and plan my campaign.

Saturday 9th September

I think the books The Boss reads should be censored. It isn't that they're full of bad language and violence, it's just that she's driving me nuts. My Master recently bought Terry Pratchett 'Thud' as an audio book, read by Tony Robinson and The Boss is completely hooked. It's bad enough when my Master starts pretending to be a troll and The Boss does the vampire voice, but now my walk is being affected and I think it ought to stop. There is a bit in the book that is one character reading a children's book to his son. We were walking down the track by the woods, when The Boss suddenly said 'Where's my cow.' Then added 'That's not my cow, it goes baa, it is a sheep.' Now if this had happened once I could have forgiven her, but two days running. It isn't as though we had seen any sheep.

Listening in on conversations is never a good thing. I overheard The Boss booking my operation and now I have a couple of weeks to worry about it. I did hear her say I will not need long to recover, but the worst of it is that I also heard her say I'm not allowed any breakfast that day. Not only that, but apparently, they said I may not feel much like eating for the rest of the day either. It must be really serious if it will be enough to put me off my food. In my experience, it's only long car journeys, to strange places, that do that and I wouldn't recommend those to anyone. It doesn't help that I have to travel for an hour and a half each way to get to the vet doing my operation. For all that trouble they'd better be good.

Sunday 10th September

I presumed that the purpose of shedding my coat was to reduce its thickness for the summer months. I don't understand why I'm losing so much of my coat before the winter. Everywhere I turn there's dog hair. I shake and there's dog hair, I scratch and there's lots of dog hair. I seem to be leaving a special Alfie made carpet all around the house. The Boss has even resorted to brushing me regularly, so that I can lose it in a controlled manner, but I prefer to hang on to it, so that I can lose it at more inconvenient times. What was the point in The Boss being bought a cushion that says 'no outfit is complete without added dog hair' if I can't be the one to add the dog hair?

Monday 11th September

My own fault I know, but we nearly didn't go to the seaside yesterday. The day was all planned out and my Master decided to wash the car before we went. As The Boss was busy, I thought I'd help him. Unfortunately, it was a lovely day and I could smell freedom on the breeze. Don't get me wrong, I love going out with my owners, but it was one of those times you just want to go for a walk on your own. The garage door was open, the gate at the end of the drive was open and I could hear the call of the wild, well the open road anyway. Off I went. I just went for a little run to the top of the road and round a few neighbours' gardens, nothing too exciting; at least that's everything I'm telling The Boss about.

When The Boss got out of the shower, she came downstairs and asked my Master where I was. "I don't know he said, he won't have gone off anywhere." So she looked inside. She looked in the garden. She called me, she looked in the garden again. She looked inside again. It was by this time clear I may have gone out. She went round the path at the side of the road calling me and a man with a little girl asked if she was looking for a black and brown dog, which he'd last seen outside number 11. The Boss thanked him and ran up the road calling me. I'd left number 11 long since when I heard her and was in the garden of number 23. Her relief at finding me seemed excessive. My Master on the other hand felt a bit sheepish and said he'd be more careful in future. This means that next time I want to go off on my own, I may have to be a bit more imaginative about how I get out. The long and the short of it was that The Boss didn't feel much like going out after that, but in the end my Master said it would do her good.

14
SANDCASTLES

Tuesday 12th September

You'll be pleased to know that with my Master at work and no one to leave the gate open, yesterday was uneventful. Sunday and my trip to the seaside was a little different. Apart from the sandcastle exhibition, the funniest bit of the afternoon was a bit later on. I'd found it all fairly stressful with the crowds and more especially the loud noises being played through the speakers. It's really odd suddenly having wolves howl at you, without being able to see any bodies and as for crying babies, well I just couldn't understand why no one went to give them a lick.

Then we went to find a nice pavement café, or in my case to leave a trail of nervousness on a section of pavement. My Master was heroic in his attempts to clean up after me with the little poop scoop and then was desperately looking for a bin to deposit it in. We passed a house with a bin bag outside and he put it in before The Boss asked 'Are you sure that's a rubbish bag and not a charity clothes collection?' Oh, can you imagine the horror of emptying out a bag of clothes to find my little addition in there. Wouldn't it be awful. Once we found that there were some more and they were definitely rubbish we all rocked with laughter, and relief.

The café we found was pretty good, they had a special 'bar' for dogs. It was more a tap and a water bowl, but the point was the same.

Wednesday 13th September

Ok, I admit it, I knocked the flowers over. In my defence, they were dead already and it wasn't being out of water that dealt the final blow. This is what happens if you put them in the fireplace and I wag my tail. There's a lot of tail to wag. Accidents are, on occasions, going to happen and it was just one of those times. I am however, passing the blame on to my Master. He put me to bed last night. How does that make it his fault? Well my room has two doors and he put me to bed and went out of and closed 'one' of the doors. He left the other one wide open. I got up and had a bit of a wander round in the dark and to be honest I just didn't see the flowers. All things considered, I was very good, I stayed downstairs and only went and knocked on my owners' door when it really was time for breakfast and I was hungry.

Thursday 14th September

There has been an ongoing saga relating to a wishing well in our garden. I won't bore you with the details so far, except to say that there is a reason they provide you with the dimensions of what you are ordering from the internet. Finding out how big it is when it is delivered is not normally the best plan. Anyway, it has now been filled with water and within two days 'things' have started to grow. Odd things, I prefer to describe it as 'primordial gloop'. I know gloop isn't a real word but it does describe it rather well. They're odd white creatures with long tails and seem to have appeared from nowhere. If that is what can grow in two days, I'd give them a couple of weeks to go through several stages of evolution. I'm fully expecting them to be walking out on two legs, the week after next, and I'm worried. This could mean a whole change in world order as we know it. Maybe being 'man's best friend' I'm backing the wrong horse, so to speak.

Friday 15th September

When I read about the seasons I thought it said summer was warmest and winter was coolest with spring and autumn somewhere in between. I can only go on the experience I'm having, this being my first year, but it doesn't seem to work the way the book said. That is unless this is another of those Belgian things. It could be a bit like shops being open on days you expect them to be closed and closed at times they say they're open and with bank holidays in the middle of the week and bridge days that no one can tell you whether they're actually a holiday or not.

Saturday 16th September

Correct me if I'm wrong, but I thought when you paint something, the idea is to get the paint on the thing being painted. I'm clearly wrong, unless The Boss was intending to paint her hands, arm, leg, trousers and foot and was only using the bench as an incidental prop. I thought about going up to her and pointing to her elbow and saying you've missed a bit, but I thought better of it.

When we last went to the airport, I noticed that instead of saying 'departures' and 'arrivals' on the signs for the 'pick up' and 'set down' parking they have pictures of aeroplanes either going up or coming down. I presume they must think this makes it obvious in any language, but as The Boss pointed out if you are departing you want an aeroplane that has just landed. I'm not sure how she gets to the aeroplane 'going up' for the arrivals though.

Sunday 17th September

It seems the whole of the local wildlife wants to get in on the act of being annoying, or at least that's my assumption. Whilst we were walking, we were hit by a large number of falling acorns. The Boss said that it's because in autumn they fall off the trees and I shouldn't take it personally. However, my theory is that it's a gang of adolescent squirrels looking for kicks.

We had a bit of an incident earlier. It was an accident. I didn't mean to hurt her. It was a crazy thing to have been doing anyway. The Boss was leaning precariously into an alcove which has a window, trying to get a mobile phone signal, as you do. Then I decided it was a good moment to jump up and give her a hug. I didn't mean to crack her head against the wall. I didn't know she was that off balance and besides she ought to be used to me by now. I suppose I ought to go and apologise, but that sort of thing doesn't come naturally, I am a boy after all. Perhaps I'd better swallow my pride. I think I hurt her quite a lot. It resulted in my being shut outside the office so I couldn't make things worse and it isn't often that happens.

Monday 18th September

Well it's time to pack my little suitcase and visit my doggy friends for a while. Once again my mobile phone has credit on it, until I waste it texting my friends and have none left to speak to my owners when I need to.

It's cruel having to see my owners packing right in front of me. I don't want to know they're going where they'll need swimming costumes and sun cream. I wonder if they'll send me a postcard this time. It would be very hypocritical to send one that said something like 'having a lovely time, wish you were here'. If they really wished I was there, they'd have gone somewhere they could take me. I'm under no illusions.

I've been thinking about 'the call of the wild'. Is there definitely only one 'wild' in which case it is 'the Wild' or is there more than one? In which case it should be 'a wild'. How do you know that 'the wild' that calls you to nip off down the road on your own, is the same 'wild' as the one that runs 'the jungle'? It's all very complicated.

Wednesday 20th September

So now I'm worried. I was talking to one of the other dogs about the fact that I am going to England later in the year. If I'm being honest, it might be fair to say I was boasting just a tiny bit. He asked me how I was travelling and quite frankly I didn't know the answer. He laughed and said if I was going by plane, he hoped I didn't bruise too easily. He was trying to get me to believe that I'd be treated like a suitcase and put on the scales, probably incurring excess baggage costs, before being sent off down the conveyer belt with all the other suitcases. Would they treat a dog as roughly as they treat suitcases? Do you think The Boss would really allow something like that to happen to me? More worrying is the thought of all the stories you hear where the person goes to one place and their suitcase goes somewhere else. By the time he'd finished laughing at me, I was feeling all knotted up inside and worried. I sent The Boss a text message to ask how we were getting there, but I'm guessing with the time difference it may be a while before I get a reply. She tried to explain how the time difference thing works, but it sure beats me. How can she be having breakfast when it's past lunchtime?

I was looking at the map of where England is and wondered why the piece of water is called the 'English

Channel'. How come the English have managed to lay claim to naming it rather than the French, or for that matter the Belgians? I think we should rename it the 'Belgian Channel' or at least the 'Partly Belgian Channel'.

Thursday 21st September

Panic over, The Boss rang me back. We're going by Channel Tunnel. I suppose that's the 'English Channel Tunnel'. Apparently that'll be the best way for me to travel, as I can sit next to The Boss in the car and don't have to be alone at all. The other piece of good news is that she's missing me. To be honest it serves her right for going without me, but it would have been awful if she hadn't really noticed I wasn't there. What she actually said was 'It's strange not having muddy paw prints all over my clothes' and I'm taking that to mean she misses me.

Friday 22nd September

I still don't get this whole time changing thing. Why isn't it the same time everywhere? It isn't actually a different point in time anywhere in the world as you are reading this, so why call it something different? I'm presuming my owners haven't discovered some means of time travel, whereby they have actually gone back six hours in time, but if they have, how did they manage to speak to me on the phone? I don't suppose there are also special phones that allow you to do that. Why are humans so unable to cope with the concept that in some countries you get up when it's dark and go to bed when it's light? Then we could call it the same time everywhere and business would all operate at the same times all over the world and you wouldn't get jet lag. Teenagers manage to do it, why can't adults? You wouldn't have any more problems if someone was travelling, of calling them on the phone and having to start the conversation with "Oh sorry, did I wake you? Here? Well it's lunchtime!" "No, ok. I'll ring back later when you're more yourself." Mind you from what The Boss says that can happen at any time of day when she rings my Master, even if he's in the same country.

Saturday 23rd September

Well I wasn't expecting that. Chloe arrived last night, all smiles and flowing hair. I found myself absolutely tongue tied and that doesn't happen often. "Well aren't you going to give me a hug?" She said as I stood there with my mouth open. Well of course I was, but I was so overwhelmed. I fell over her suitcase as I bounded up and we both ended up in fits of laughter. It's taken my mind off thinking how much I'm missing out. I can live without sunbathing, beaches and warm sea. I don't mind that I've been left behind. Ok so I do mind, but I don't want them thinking that. At least Chloe's owners have only gone to a city for a couple of days and although it would have lots of exciting lamp posts to sniff, by and large from a dog's perspective, cities are vastly overrated. You don't get to let your owner off their lead. You have to make sure they're ready before you pull them across the road, they always seem so reluctant to run for it when there's a gap in the traffic. Worst of all they seem to think it's unacceptable to answer the call of nature. No, cities are not places for dogs.

Sunday 24th September

Well yesterday was fantastic. Chloe and I spent the day

alternating between running after each other playing tag and resting under a bush to get our breath back. On the other paw, my owners probably shouldn't be allowed out on their own. Apparently, they got the hotel shuttle to the capital of the island and then tried to get transport to visit the distillery. In general, I don't think visiting any place serving alcohol is a good idea for them, quite apart from a whole distillery of it. They couldn't work out which bus went where and queued up for ages at what they thought was the 'Bus Ticket Office'. Once they got to the front of the queue the poor lady hadn't a clue what they were talking about, but could have sold them stamps for the postcards they hadn't yet bought to send to me! Then they wandered round in the wrong direction, before eventually giving up and deciding to go back to their hotel.

As always, when they gave up, that was the point they found a taxi. Now of course, if I had been with them, the first thing I'd have said to them would have been 'Have you thought about how you're getting back?' I wasn't there and basically they hadn't. And that was before they'd sampled any of the produce of the distillery. Sometimes humans just can't be trusted to be sensible. They didn't know exactly which direction they'd come from, in order to catch a bus and being rather out of the city there were no taxi ranks. What happens? They only ended up being taken back by a pizza delivery truck! You can see it now the driver getting out and shouting "Anyone ordered two people?" Even with Chloe around it makes my day seem uneventful.

Monday 25th September
Well I'm back to moping. Chloe went home yesterday and I'm back to thinking of all the places I'd like to be. It was

funny saying goodbye, I felt as though I had a lump in my throat. I thought I was going to cry, but as a dog that really wouldn't be acceptable.

Tuesday 26th September

I've been thinking about what 'normal' is. I've concluded that it can't possibly exist. As dogs go, I think I'm normal. It all started when a poodle asked if the clipping of his tail was straight. Well what do you say? I actually said "Get a life," but it didn't seem to go down too well. He seemed to think worrying about whether he had a hair out of place was 'normal'. I conducted a poll of all the other dogs and they thought worrying about their appearance to that extent might be normal for models and dogs going into the show ring, but that for any of the rest of us it was just pointless. The poodle however was convinced that he was normal and all the other dogs he knew would be just the same. It transpired all the other dogs he knew were poodles too. This led me to conclude that either this was normal behaviour for a poodle, or that all poodles are not normal. To be honest I tend toward the latter view.

Other than that, the day was a bit quiet really. I thought about causing trouble, but couldn't find the energy, so contented myself with just thinking about it, which is almost as good. Sometimes just knowing you could do something is as good as actually doing it, with the added advantage you don't have to face the consequences of your actions.

Wednesday 27th September

Now don't get me wrong, I'm really looking forward to going home today and seeing my owners. However, although all that seems very exciting I can't help thinking about the fact that tomorrow is 'The big day', the day I become less of a dog than I am today, my operation. Alas, oh woe is me. I'm worried about the whole thing really. I don't fancy the idea of a general anaesthetic, although being told it will be as though I'm drunk afterwards makes it sound a little bit fun. I don't fancy the idea of being cut and I certainly don't fancy the idea of being without the bits they're removing. What is the world coming to when a dog can't be a real dog? I know it's all for my own good and not just to stop me having puppies, but it really doesn't seem fair. I know I'm too young to think about having a family now, but what if I want one later? I might have made a good dad and everyone says I'm very good looking, it seems a shame not to pass these handsome features on to the next generation. Anyway I'd better pack my little case and settle down to wait to be picked up. It's never the same, playing, when I'm waiting to go home, I wish they'd collect me in a morning and not leave me until later in the day.

Thursday 28th September.
Today's the day. Not one that I'm looking forward to, but it is THE day. The day when I undergo an eye watering operation. The day when I'll become slightly less of a man, well dog. I've packed a bag of things to take, mainly my little comfort blanket to hang onto when I get scared. I thought of packing one or two dog biscuits, but to be honest I think I might not feel very hungry later. Now, on the other paw, I'm starving and all this talk about food is not doing me any good at all. It's funny isn't it, when you're hungry you start fantasising about all sorts of different types of food, including ones you wouldn't normally consider. At the moment even The Boss's

slippers look appetising. However, what I would give to get my paws on a nice juicy steak.

This operation really is for my own good, however awful it might sound, and believe me it does.

Friday 29th September

There are two ways of dealing with having an operation. My way was to be quietly nervous, whimper a bit when I saw the needle and mutter to myself as it took effect and I started to doze off. The Boss on the other hand spent her morning shaking and then while I had my operation went and cheered herself up with an endless stream of coffee, meaning she was bouncing of the ceiling by the time she picked me up. By the time I knew much about what was going on, it was the afternoon and I was home again. They told me I would feel a little bit like being drunk, which of course I had nothing to compare to. All I can say is, if that is what feeling drunk is like I don't know why people do it. I kept walking into things and felt all wobbly. It was a very odd sensation.

Now being a dog and a bloke at that, I've undertaken a very thorough investigation and it seems there really is now less of me than there was before. It all feels a bit strange to be honest.

Sunday 1st October

I'm stuck in a female dominated household, as one of the boss's friends is here. From my perspective female domination is never a good thing. On the bright side, it is kept tidy and I am spoilt, so it can't be all bad. What isn't so good is the sort of films that get watched. What's with all the sentimental stuff? Why not have a bit of action? Then my Master says he wonders why I miss him so much. Of course when it's just me and my Master I'm less spoilt and the meals aren't so good, so all in all I do prefer them both being around. Whilst men and women are really very different and struggle to understand each other, from a dog's point of view, life is a lot more balanced when you get a mix of both types of human.

Tuesday 3rd October

The Boss seems to have got it into her head, that until I have my stitches out, I should be careful and not be leaping about too much. I do have some bruising in some very delicate places, so she may be right. I keep giving everything a good lick, but I will be happier when the purple coloured bit returns to normal. I was alarmed when she told me she'll be the one removing my stitches. Since when has she had any type of medical qualification? Does she really think I'm going to let a complete novice remove stitches from such essential bits of me? She tried to reassure me that she has removed stitches from an animal before, but it turns out that was a female cat. Does she really think a cat would be an acceptable comparison? Thursday is the appointed day so we'll just have to wait and see.

It was sad taking The Boss's friend to the airport yesterday. She did say she wondered about trying to smuggle me out with her, but as she planned to put me in her luggage, rather than pay for a seat in first class, I wasn't all that keen. I don't suppose I would have got that far, as The Boss has taken charge of my passport. She said after my little outing the other week I couldn't be trusted and she didn't want to risk finding out that I'd gone by getting a post card from South America. Personally I think she's been reading too many crime novels. As if I'd head for South America. I was thinking more in terms of the Cayman Islands or Bermuda. It's a shame I've never got any pocket money left to deposit in an offshore account in readiness for my escape.

Thursday 5th October

I got out of the wrong side of bed this morning. Well to be honest it was more the right side but the wrong time. The Boss has gone to London for the day and insisted on waking me when she came down for breakfast at five. Why she felt the need to wake me she didn't say, but in the end she left, leaving me in the capable hands of my Master. To be fair he did remember to give me breakfast and to let me outside, so it isn't going too badly. On the good side it does delay the removal of my stitches by a few hours.

Why do people keep thinking I look like a beagle? I know I may be Swiss by origin and am living in Belgium where people may not be as familiar with my breed, but how many times do I have to tell them I'm an Entlebucher. I know it's hard to pronounce, if you're English speaking anyway, probably not if you speak Swiss German, but that is what I am. I'll agree that beagles look cute and I do like Snoopy. I also realise my nose is a very similar shape and I do like walking with my nose to the ground. I'm also the same three colours but mainly black. That is, however, where the similarities end. I've never smoked in my life and I don't go hunting. I say I'm mainly black, but I've been very alarmed to find three small patches of white hair on my back, since I lost my puppy hair. It's as though I'm starting to go grey already and I'm not even eleven months old. I keep checking to see if they're still there but sadly they seem to be permanent. I've suggested to The Boss she could dye them black to match the rest, but she just laughed at me and told me not to be so vain.

15

THE LAUNCH OF THE PET DOGS DEMOCRATIC PARTY (PDDP)

Saturday 7th October

I'm now without my stitches. It wasn't quite as straightforward as everyone had made out and I was a wimp. There were only two that needed removing and between them my Master and The Boss rolled me over and I wriggled and wriggled so much that The Boss couldn't get near enough and my Master lost patience. The Boss got cross with my Master and he got equally cross, so I felt a bit sheepish and when they came to try again I co-operated a bit more. Well as it turned out I might as well have co-operated the first time, as The Boss realised they were slightly infected and promptly called the vet. It explains why I have been so sleepy the last couple of days, I just put it down to the change in the weather. Anyway, off I went to the vet and he removed them with me standing on my back legs with my front paws on The Boss's shoulders. I did try to cover my eyes with my paws and feigned pain to get some sympathy, but actually it didn't really hurt at all. In fairness it's a lot easier to get sympathy out of my Master in those circumstances, than it is out of The Boss, but unfortunately The Boss took me to the vet. My internal stitches will dissolve on their own, which is a good job as there are certain parts of my anatomy that I really don't want The Boss removing stitches from.

Modern houses in the Western World have inside

toilets. Houses with outside toilets are thought to be in some way sub-standard. So why is it that even when it's raining I am expected to go outside when I need to go to the toilet? I think I should start campaigning for improved housing for dogs and an end to these near slum conditions.

Sunday 8th October

I've been thinking of setting up my own political party to campaign for dogs' rights. It makes sense to set it up in Belgium, rather than England, not least because with proportional representation I stand a much better chance of being elected. Besides that, in the UK, dogs aren't allowed in as many places, whereas here we are seen as an important part of the family and would get more sympathy. We will of course be able to lobby the European Parliament to have the laws changed to allow dogs into restaurants and other public places in the UK and end the outdated segregation which is so clearly dogist. There is no better time than a quiet Sunday to work out the ideals of a new political party and draw up an action plan. Dogs of the world unite, although you may need a little help from your owners to stop the ensuing chaos.

Monday 9th October

Well she actually went and did it. Voted that is. Admittedly on leaving the house The Boss seemed pretty nervous, but that was mainly at the prospect of it all being in Flemish and her only speaking a tiny bit. She'd undertaken painstaking research and reached a conclusion on who to vote for, based on more than mere guess work, but the actual process remained a mystery. It was still a bit of a mystery by the time she came back, due to the confusion over the fact that she could only vote at a local level and not in the provincial elections, but despite the language problems she thinks she has done it right. Somehow voting on a computer screen seemed quite different to marking an 'X' on a piece of paper. I suggested the word she was looking for was 'up to date' to which she pointed out that was in fact three words. I wonder if I ever make any progress in politics, if she would vote for me.

It took all of yesterday to think of a name for my political party. It's going to be the Pet Dogs Democratic Party or PDDP for short and is not to be confused with the 'Polish Debian Documentation Project' or the 'Participatory District Development Programme' whatever they may be. Trust me they're really things the letters PDDP stand for, I looked on 'Yahoo'. I suppose it might be better to change the name rather than having people get confused, but it took all of yesterday to come up with that. So far, the only definite policy is campaigning for inside toilets for dogs, to be available in bad weather. I quite enjoy going outside when it's dry, so wet weather toilets would be quite sufficient!

Tuesday 10th October
A new type of missile is being hurled at us from the trees as we go for a walk. The Boss says these are conkers or horse chestnuts. I'm not sure where the horses fit in, but they're definitely bigger than acorns and hurt if they hit you. The Boss showed me how to take their little prickly green coats off, to get to the nut inside. When she asked me what they were used for, I thought the answer she must be looking for was 'to eat'. However, it turns out

that their most important use is the game of 'Conkers' in which one is attached to a piece of string and then used to attack another person's conker until one of them breaks and comes off the string. She explained if you keep your conker until next year, it hardens and is therefore better. Apparently, you can cheat by putting them in the oven or by doing something with vinegar.

The biggest problem I can see is that to hold the string properly I would have to hold it in my mouth. Then when someone hit my conker it would come back and hit my head and I don't think that's such a good idea. Perhaps she could just play against my Master and I'll take bets on the outcome.

To add to our requirement for inside toilets the PDDP will campaign for all shops, bars and restaurants across Europe to welcome dogs and provide water bowls when requested. I was wondering about making it illegal to carry out any experiment on dogs without their written consent, but I don't want to be labelled extremist at this early stage. It would be good to see the legislation preventing selling cigarettes to humans under the age of 18, extended to dogs as well, although I don't suppose many buy their own.

Wednesday 11th October
I was talking to The Boss whilst we were out walking this morning and explained my idea of the PDDP. She asked if I'd thought about working dogs. After some consideration I reluctantly agreed that she may have a point. I am now in a complete dilemma as to whether it should be called the Pet Dogs' Democratic Party or the Pet and Working Dogs' Democratic Party which would make it the PAW DDP, which although appropriate is a bit of a mouthful.

After much consideration I've decided to keep the name PDDP, but allow both pet and working dog members. It actually made me think that every dog, working or otherwise, should have the right to be a pet. Dogs that work in teams for hunting or medical testing should still be able to go home to a cosy fireside for the evening and get all the fuss and attention that comes with being a pet. Of course the antisocial ones can stay in kennels if they prefer, but it should at least be a right.

Thursday 12th October

I'm still finding it difficult to understand how a trip, to a big shop called Ikea to buy a desk, could possibly lead to my owners bringing back a large plant for the lounge. If The Boss was any good at keeping plants it wouldn't be so bad, but to be a live plant in this house you have to thrive on neglect, so on the whole only cacti and succulents apply for the available positions. What is even more confusing, is that the Yucca was in fact my Master's choice and he has to be reminded to feed me, so a plant doesn't stand much chance at all, unless it drinks beer, in which case it may be ok. I'm also presupposing that this is not an immediate answer to my demands for an inside toilet and that I'm not supposed to be using it in that capacity.

The PDDP has had a completely independent election for its leadership and I'm proud to announce that I have been elected to the position with 100% of the votes. In fairness I'm still the only member of the party so it wasn't that difficult and thankfully I was unopposed. As leader I am ready to announce more of the policies of the party and these will include extending the laws on the minimum wage and the working time directive, to cover all dogs as well as humans. The only difference being that the minimum wage for dogs will apply in full from 6 months old and not 18 years of age, which would clearly be ridiculous as few dogs live that long. The introduction of these laws may increase the number of jobs for guide dogs and hearing dogs as they will need to work a shift system, so as not to be in breach of the working time directive and clearly a dog should never be pressurised to sign a waiver.

Friday 13th October
I'm disappointed that as yet I've not been contacted by any dogs wanting to join the PDDP. In fairness if I had been, I would have some work to do, which doesn't sound like a bright idea, but what is the point in being a political party and not having any members. I suppose it might help if I undertook some advertising so that it became more widely known, but I'm not really sure what the best means is to reach my target audience.

Saturday 14th October
I was watching the film 'Finding Neverland' last week. It's a great film but what I don't understand is why they have a part in a play for a dog and have it played by a human, dressed up as a dog. Why not give the part to a real dog? There really aren't enough jobs for dogs anyway, without ones that should be for dogs being taken by a human. Perhaps this is something the PDDP should take up. I've been thinking about the problem that when animals take acting parts, they don't receive their wages direct, but find them paid to their human owner. In reality this whole concept of having an owner is little more than slavery, particularly when they're made to work in this way, without receiving their own earnings. Now don't get me

wrong, I have quite a cushy little number here and don't particularly want my freedom, but dogs should be able to have their freedom if they want it. I think that should be our top priority, no more slavery for dogs, we want civil and human rights too. Is it possible for a dog to have a 'human' right?

Sunday 15th October
One thing that's made me laugh, has been looking at the internet to discover how people managed to find my diary. When I first wrote it, I called The Boss 'Mistress'. It turns out some people have searched for the words 'diary' 'of' 'a' 'mistress'. Well just imagine how disappointed they must be when all they find is my diary. I can't imagine it was what they were looking for when the person searched for 'humans eating acorns' either.

Monday 16th October
Now I'm worried. The first applicants interested in joining the PDDP are a cat and a working dog. I was just getting the outline of the Constitution written and now I don't know what to put. To be fair, the working dog doesn't actually work and he is my cousin on The Boss's side, but how does a cat join the Pet Dogs' Democratic Party? Isn't there a clue in the title? Frankly, apart from chasing them I don't know the first thing about cats. Matilda, next door, isn't so bad, but she thinks she's a cut above all us dogs. I wonder if I should allow Sally to join or let her down gently. More worrying to me is that if there are other members, they might not vote me in as leader and that would spoil all my fun. I'll have to think about it before getting back to Sally.

One thing I'm absolutely clear about is that all business

of the PDDP will be conducted in English. You only had to listen to The Boss trying to explain the rules of cricket to a German, in English, to realise that crossing language barriers would be completely impossible, cultural ones are hard enough. She got as far as explaining that not all games take five days and that some in fact are limited to fifty overs, when she found herself getting stuck on explaining what an over was. She was completely stumped, if you'll pardon the pun, when he asked why there are six balls in an over. Why indeed? It is one of those English things again, like there being fourteen pounds in a stone and 16 ounces in a pound and twelve inches in a foot and three feet in a yard. So basically the rule if you're going to do anything the English way is never to have a clear rule that explains why you do something and then make exceptions to that rule at every opportunity.

Tuesday 17th October
Earlier The Boss said she was 'just mad enough to stay sane'. Whilst I think I get the point she was trying to make, I think she may have lost the plot altogether, if she thinks she has stayed sane. At the point she said that having seen I was considering a cat for membership, she wondered if she might join the PDDP I was almost speechless. After I'd got over my first reaction which was to be angry that she had been reading my diary and my second reaction which was, in fact, much the same as the first, I started trying to work out how I was going to explain that in terms of the PDDP policies she represented the enemy. Obviously not her personally, she's really very nice to all pets and working animals, unless of course spiders fall into this category in which case, she may be

not quite so nice. Anyway, the whole point of the PDDP is to fight against the injustices brought upon animals by humans and whilst the name is the Pet Dogs' Democratic Party we shall welcome all animals regardless of creed as long as they are proud to wear the name dog for the purpose of any party political activities. Therefore, in my capacity as party leader I have decided that Sally and all other cats supportive of this noble cause will be eligible to join. The Boss, on the other hand, will not. Animals of the world unite, the future is ours. We will fight injustice in whatever shape it takes, right after our next nap.

Wednesday 18th October
Gone are the days of getting excited about going to an airport. Now you have to be prepared to be treated as a criminal and strip searched before they even let you near the aircraft. Ok, strip searched may be an exaggeration but coat, scarf, belt and shoes can feel a bit like that when you're at security. The Boss is threatening to take all her clothes off next time, just to see what reaction she gets. She's also wondering if she would still set off the buzzer that seems to go off for entirely random reasons.

It turns out that in fact my Master was lucky to get to the airport at all; his taxi set off with him in it, just before the taxi firm decided to go on strike. It's a good job that the driver didn't go on strike with him in the car, that could all have got very awkward.

Thursday 19th October
I don't think The Boss has quite got the hang of youth culture. She got a text from James in response to one she sent. The response said 'Hus dis', so pronouncing it exactly as it was written, she asked what it meant. To be

fair, even I didn't get that that translated as 'Who is this?' so maybe I'm just not a cool sort of a dog either.

I still think it's the squirrels throwing the acorns at me as I walk underneath their trees. The Boss says they fall on their own, but that all seems a bit ridiculous to me. You would have thought, having taken the trouble to spend all summer growing, they could at least have learnt how to keep their balance.

I had a note from Chloe. She's heard about the PDDP and thinks it's silly. Perhaps she should take more interest in politics, it affects her life as much as anyone else's. I couldn't bring myself to reply to her; to be honest I was a bit upset. I've been thinking the PDDP ought to have a logo and maybe a slogan, but all I've come up with so far is 'Best friends not subordinates' and although it sums it all up, it's a bit short on the 'snappy' front. Maybe something like, 'Never mind Christmas a dog needs rights' would be a bit more punchy.

Friday 20th October
There was The Boss getting dressed this morning and I noticed the big bruise on her leg that's now fading. 'That looks exactly the shape of a paw print', I said and laughed. I realised she hadn't joined in the laugh, so I asked if there was any chance it had been caused by a paw and she nodded. I then asked if there was any chance it was caused by a different dog than me and she shook her head, so I gave her a big hug and said sorry. I really must try to be less boisterous. I didn't like to ask how many of the other bruises I'd caused.

Where do dogs stand with regard to the Bible? I know where the Bible stands with regard to us, we are the lowest of the low, gathering crumbs under the table, but what are our thoughts on the Bible? I know we don't go in for all that marriage stuff, but I'm not sure where we stand on the whole God thing. You would think given the closeness of God to dog, as a word, that it would have been us he made in His image, but I suppose I'd better be careful not to cause offence to anyone. I was most concerned with regard to the whole 'coveting' thing. I'm not bothered about my neighbour's ass, but is it ok for me to covet The Boss's pork chop? If it isn't, then yesterday I sinned and need to repent. The day before it was the chicken and I am sure it will be something else again later. My flesh is weak, I'm only a puppy. I wonder what the punishment would be?

I think for my career, apart from running my political party, I would like to run a bookshop. I can only describe being surrounded by books as the equivalent of a hippopotamus wallowing in mud. It is wonderful to go and leaf through and see what you don't know. Just sniffing them is half the fun.

Saturday 21st October
Do humans really think that dogs can't spell? I write a diary for heaven's sake and yet The Boss still says things like 'We'll be going for a W.A.L.K. in about half an hour' to my grandparents in the vain hope that I won't get excited immediately. Firstly, I can spell and secondly I can get excited for no apparent reason. I really don't need the prospect of a walk for that. Sometimes my exuberance has unforeseen consequences. Yesterday Granny had dozed off in the chair when I suddenly thought, wouldn't it be fun to play tug with my rope, and who better to pull the other end than Granny. The Boss is less willing to play and Granddad was busy reading a book, so Granny was

the obvious choice. I ran up to her with the rope and launched myself at her. Well I can see now that being woken like that might come as a bit of a surprise and make someone less keen to play. I gave my most appealing look and nuzzled her a bit and she soon gave in. I shall be sorry when she goes home, she makes a great playmate.

They're all off to Gent today and I'm not sure yet whether I'm invited. I misbehaved a bit on my walk yesterday, so I may just be a tiny bit grounded. It wasn't really my fault, other than in an 'I was totally out of control' sort of way. I met a bloodhound and got extremely over excited. After that I would do absolutely nothing I was told and was pulling really badly. To be quite honest, I don't know what came over me but in my defence I am still a puppy.

Sunday 22nd October
I didn't get taken to Gent. I've been there anyway so I didn't really mind. Well not that much. I stayed at home contemplating my behaviour or so I told The Boss. In reality I was thinking about being a wolf in a pet dog's clothing and wondering how scary I could make myself for Halloween. All the children round here are going 'trick or treating' and they'll be calling at our house. I thought it might be fun to turn the tables and scare them witless when The Boss opens the door. I was thinking about making a 'ghost wolf' costume and perfecting my howl, then maybe making a pumpkin lantern and using the light of it to project really scary wolf shadows. If The Boss gets to find the plan I will probably get shut out of the way, so that I don't really frighten the younger ones, but what is the point of them coming to scare me, if I can't scare them

back?

I do however need The Boss to buy the pumpkin, unless I steal Matilda's that's sitting outside next door. I didn't think cats were into all that sort of thing, I thought they would consider it below them.

Being grounded was not the worst result of my misbehaviour. To be quite honest the good thing about my harness was that if I wanted to go in a different direction to the person holding my lead, I could really throw my weight into it. I have very well developed shoulder and chest muscles, I'm quite proud of them. Now to have the same effect I will have to develop my nose muscles, as I have a new lead that goes round my nose. Annoyingly it works, I can't pull against it. The best I can do is sit down and refuse to move but then I lose out.

16
NEARLY ONE YEAR OLD

Monday 23rd October
I am not keen on this new head-collar that I have to wear to go for a walk. All the fun has gone out of being able to win the battle of what direction we go in. Yesterday morning I just plonked my bottom firmly on the ground and refused to budge. The Boss cheated, she went off without me. I was so torn. Should I go running off after her and give in to the new device, or stay sat on the floor by my Master and potentially let her out of my sight and worse, miss my walk. She won. I trotted on like the good puppy I am and despite another little paddy further along I don't seem to have convinced them that this new way of walking me is a bad idea. Perhaps I'll try today when The Boss is walking me on her own.

We went to Brussels Midi Station yesterday. Where other than Belgium would they close off the main approach road to a station for a Sunday market? There are hundreds of roads in front of the European Parliament buildings or the embassies where no one seems to go on a Sunday, or there is the one that needs 24 hour access, 365 days a year. Now which one shall we close?

Tuesday 24th October
The Boss bought me a chew the other day to 'keep me quiet'. It's about a meter long and I can only just carry it, or drag it, round with me. I've made a bit of an impression on one end, but I will not be beaten. I can't carry it

upstairs, so I started chewing The Boss's arm to get her to fetch it for me. She had to go all the way downstairs and then when she came back I said I'd changed my mind and would have a nap instead. As soon as she sat down I started pacing round and said I needed to go out, so she had to get up and go downstairs again. I could make a game out of this all day if I tried.

She brought my birthday present home at the same time that she bought the chew, but I'm not supposed to know. It's hidden on the top bunk in Andy's room, where she thinks I can't see. It's a brand new bed that's big enough so that my head doesn't flop over the edge. I'm hoping she'll be getting some toys to go with it, otherwise it isn't going to be very exciting at all.

Thursday 26th October
Someone is getting the hang of this new-fangled lead and it's not me. I couldn't get my head out when we met another dog yesterday; the best I could do was plonk all my weight down on the ground and refuse to move. What made it funny was that the other dog did exactly the same thing. His owner suggested we could have a picnic whilst everyone was waiting for us. Mind you, if anyone had had a picnic on them they could have used it to entice me away, I'm a sucker for a bit of food.

The poor Boss is trying so hard to train me and to be fair, at home, without distraction, I'm doing just fine. All it needs is a leaf falling off a tree, let alone an acorn, squirrel, person or dog and my concentration goes completely. It's never that I don't understand, it's just that I choose not to do it. Without distraction I will walk at heel on or off the lead, sit and stay and come when called. I'm refusing to co-operate with the whole 'lying down' thing, particularly when I'm outdoors and risk getting my coat dirty, but I like to think I make up for it in other ways. I keep saying to The Boss, 'look on the bright side, I could be as badly behaved as the dogs in the books you're reading.' The worrying thing is that from one of them, about a sheepdog, she seems to be starting to understand some of the things that come naturally to me. Is it my fault I feel compelled to herd? To me a van is just an oversized cow and I need to chase it down, to get it under control. We've had a little talk about it and she has asked if, for my own safety, I would try to curb this tendency. I guess she has a point.

Friday 27th October
I've managed to slip out of my new lead. I got very excited when I saw another dog and well there you have it. I had worked out how to get my head out of it. Unfortunately, my Master and The Boss were one step ahead of me and had secured it to my collar, so although I could bark a lot and cause mayhem, I still couldn't get away.

I hear it's not all that uncommon, when you're younger, to have imaginary friends. The problem now looking back at early puppyhood is what was real and what was imagined all gets a bit blurred. You can actually convince yourself that something imaginary was completely real, The Boss seems to manage it nearly all the time. My Master asked her this morning to explain how the wireless connection on his laptop worked and she said 'That's easy. There's a little imp sitting in your machine that shouts to an imp sitting the other end of the connection and they send the information that way. Imp shouting is of course not in a human's hearing range.' My

Master asked why it didn't always work and apparently that's when one of the Imps has a cold and either has a croaky voice or has bunged up ears and they can't communicate so easily.

Saturday 28th October

I may not have the perfect slogan yet, but I do have a logo for the PDDP. It's a large paw print.

The PDDP should campaign for every car to have a built in dog ramp. At least they should be compulsory on every car that involves climbing more than a certain number of centimetres to get in.

Now that the weather has cooled down, I get the choice when The Boss goes out, of either going with her in the car, or staying home on my own. Apparently, in hot weather it would have been dangerous to leave me in the car, although with the number of gaps in the roof of The Boss's car, even when the roof is up, I suspect it would be a relatively low risk.

Anyway back to the original point. When we're in her car it's easy, one hop and I'm in. In exchange, I get a very bumpy ride, close to the ground. However, if we're in my Master's car I do get a nice soft ride, but I have a bit of a problem climbing in. It's hard to do it in two hops as the seat doesn't give room to jump on the floor very easily and when I try to jump straight onto the seat my towel tends to slip and I end up in a bit of a heap. There's a special doggy ramp in a catalogue, but it's quite expensive so I'm thinking of borrowing my Master's power tools and making my own. I wonder if he'll mind me using the drill? I can't see it would be useful for what I need to make, but it's always looked fun and he clearly enjoys playing working with it. I don't think he's got an electric saw. Perhaps I should suggest we have a little trip to the DIY store. However, this whole problem would disappear if car manufacturers took on board the needs of dogs.

Sunday 29th October

I'm beginning to think that I need to start chewing books. It seems to be the only way I can stop The Boss from reading them. I have no objection to her broadening her mind on harmless reading, but books that give her ideas on how to train me should be censored. I'm starting to think wistfully of the days at the dog training classes, when the worst I had to do was sit with my delicate little bottom in ten centimetres of muddy water. If I wanted to be understood, I would explain myself to her. I don't need her starting to understand dog psychology and second guess what I'm going to do, before I've even decided for myself. I'm consciously trying to be irrational to confuse her. It's the little things, like walking to heel out of choice when I'm off the lead, that really get her going. She doesn't expect that. I try to be as much a 'scenting hound' as a 'herding dog', but I guess at heart all I really want to be is a spoilt family pet with 'attitude'.

Monday 30th October

As I've noted before, the Belgian people are lovely, probably the most friendly in Europe, but I've observed that their administrative systems are not particularly efficient, with one possible exception, The Post Office. As I've already mentioned, they are the only efficient collector of speeding fines in Belgium, even though other methods are listed on the back of the fine. Then of course, there are times you make the mistake of ordering something from a country outside of Europe, or for that matter receive a gift from someone outside Europe. Once again there they are without a moment's hesitation, the Post Office, holding on to your parcel until you go and hand over the tax to them. It wouldn't be so bad if it was the nice man we normally see, but he isn't strictly speaking the Post Office for our area, he's just the nicest and you can park outside. We have to go to a Post Office 5 miles away from here, and you really aren't going to believe this, they don't even let dogs inside. How can I go to pay the tax on my parcel when they won't let me in? Just to make it even harder, you have to show your ID card to get your parcel and The Boss has real difficulty in pretending to be me. I said she would be better going in on 'all fours' but she didn't seem keen.

Tuesday 31st October
Humans have an expression 'being in the dog house', which to a dog is a very insulting term, as it stems from the presumption that a dog is lower down the pecking order than a human. Anyway, I'm guessing as a dog I should be using a term like 'I'm in the fish tank', to carry the same sort of meaning. You may of course be wondering why I'm in the fish tank. Can I help it that I'm an enthusiastic dog who misses The Boss whenever we're apart or that I'm always pleased to see her on her return? Is it my fault that I want to show her just how much I miss her, as I bound over to give her a big hug and as it turns out, chip her front tooth in the process? It isn't very badly chipped, but when you're scared witless by dentists, any chip is one too many. She's even wondered whether a bit of sandpaper would take the rough edge off it and prolong the time she can avoid the dentist for. Let's face it, she's had toothache on and off for about six months, is she

really going to rush and see him now, just because her tooth is sharp?

It wasn't really her weekend, seeing as the one night of the year that everyone gets an additional hour in bed, without getting up late, she woke up with a sore throat and decided to go and get a cup of coffee. This in itself wouldn't have been a problem if she'd been at home, but she was staying in someone else's house and didn't know they set the house alarm at night. So having crept downstairs, without disturbing anyone, she went into the kitchen and set off the alarm waking the whole street at 7.45 on a Sunday morning. Guilt is a wonderful thing. She was already feeling bad from reversing my Master's car into a post the day before. I think she needs a holiday, but in the meantime I am steering well clear.

Wednesday 1st November
So there you have it – 'Trick or Treat' becomes much more alarming when you're faced with a demented dog with a glow stick attached to his collar. I'm proud to say I cast quite a daunting shadow and would have made quite a frightening picture, if only I could have stopped my tail from wagging. I was reluctant to hand over all the chocolates, but having failed on the 'totally scary dog' front, I didn't fancy the 'trick' element.

I was sorry to have missed out last weekend on the scary train ride that my Master and The Boss went on. It was only a large model train but it ran round through the trees, with odd strategically placed coffins and cobwebs. A howling dog could have really added an edge of authenticity.

Thursday 2nd November

It was an odd sort of day yesterday; it was one of those Belgian midweek bank holidays. The sort of day when you expect things to happen and nothing does. No one drives past the end of the garden to work, the postman doesn't come, there's no point going to the shops and my Master worked from home so as not to get lonely.

I'm distraught. Do my Master and The Boss not love me? Have I done something wrong? Am I not their beloved puppy? What shall I do? You may wonder what is so dreadful that I'm so beside myself. In less than two weeks it will be my first birthday. I thought I would like to spend it being waited on paw and paw, showered with gifts and having my every whim pandered to. What I had not expected was to find that The Boss will be in London, my Master in Manchester and me staying with my dog-sitter. What have I done to deserve this? I can't imagine the other dogs will be prepared to spoil me on my birthday. The Boss says she will simply delay my birthday celebrations by a couple of days, but it really isn't acceptable, unless of course I'm getting lots of extra presents to make up for it.

Friday 3rd November

I've been thinking about global warming. It all started when I was listening to someone on the radio talking about carbon dioxide offset. Apparently, some very nice people have set themselves up to help me have less of an adverse impact on the environment. If I go on a flight, I can voluntarily give them some money and they will allocate me a tree to compensate for all my pollution. There is the problem, 'allocate'. I don't want a tree that another dog has already peed on. I want them to plant me a whole new tree of my own, that I can christen and visit at times of my choosing. Now don't get me wrong, if I do visit I will of course have another tree 'allocated' to me to cover the pollution caused by the first visit, but it's important to feel I have added a tree and not simply given them some money to maintain the status quo. They even give me a nice little calculator to work out how much pollution I create, but how do they know whether my plane is full and how much my luggage weighs? They tell me the tree will not be felled for 99 years, but what if it blows down? I live by a forest and there are always trees falling down. I wonder if my forest has been 'allocated' or whether I can save the middle man and claim that my journeys are already being offset?

Saturday 4th November

According to my dog-sitter, I'm an 'alpha dog' but without the aggression. I don't know what all that means and I'm quite happy to practice aggression if it would help, but I think I like the alpha bit. I'm happy that The Boss is pack leader at home, but I see my Master more as a litter mate than a leader. I miss him dreadfully when he isn't here to play with and am always pleased when we can cause trouble together. The Boss is threatening to try to train him using Twiglets, in the way she uses Marzipan with me. He's threatening to teach me all his bad habits, but there are so many, he may be faced with teaching an old dog new tricks before we're finished.

The Boss has been explaining an odd English tradition to me. Apparently on November the 5th it's 'normal' to make a pretend man, stuffed with straw and wearing old clothes, put him on the top of a big bonfire and set fire to him, then set off fireworks. This apparently heathen tradition, is to celebrate a man who tried to blow-up the Houses of Parliament. Now you can call me a dumb animal if you like, but wouldn't that be called a terrorist now? I sometimes fail to understand progress, or for that matter what makes a tradition acceptable. The best bit, as far as I can see, is that before burning these straw men, children sit with them on the pavement 'begging', asking for 'a penny for the Guy' and this is also thought acceptable, even by the same people that write to the national papers saying how dreadful it is to find beggars in every major town. The children are the ones that are onto a good thing, in one week they can go trick or treating, to be given free chocolate and go begging for money as well. If English children have acquired trick or treating from their American neighbours perhaps it's time for children elsewhere to start celebrating Guy Fawkes and the Gunpowder Plot. I wonder if I could make a Guy and do some begging here in Belgium?

Sunday 5th November
We now know that winter is on the way. We've had the annual 'please turn off your outside tap before it freezes' letter from our landlord. At least this year The Boss knows where the tap turns off, however it remains to be seen whether she is strong enough to do it, or whether, as last year, she will wimp out and get my Master involved.

To be quite honest I'm not overly impressed with the night time temperatures going below zero. I tried asking if I could come and snuggle up in bed with The Boss and my Master but they don't seem keen. On a brighter side, when I eventually dragged The Boss out for a walk it was amazing watching the steam rising off all the fields and trees. It looked as though the whole countryside was very gently on fire. Once I'd got The Boss outside she got it into her head it was such a beautiful day that she wanted to go for a long walk. That had not been part of my plan. What do you do? I did the only thing I could. I sat down and refused to move. She tried tricking me by coming for a cuddle, giving me a dog biscuit and then trying to carry on. How stupid does she think I am? Even my Master is starting to believe I understand a whole range of things, including sentences rather than just words. This revelation came about when I went up to The Boss for some love and she was drinking a hot cup of coffee and said could I go to my Master until she finished it, which is exactly what I did. How does he think I can write a diary if I can't understand something as simple as that?

Monday 6th November
I find it hard to understand how my Master gets away with staying in bed until lunchtime. More to the point, I really don't know how he can give his teenage daughter so much grief for not appearing until 1pm, when given half an opportunity that's exactly what he does. Fortunately for me, The Boss is more of a morning person. Not necessarily the sort that is all cheerful in a morning, more the sort that is grumpy because she simply is not programmed to be able to sleep in and resents being awake. However, whatever mood she's in, at least it means there is someone for me to bounce on.

Tuesday 7th November
You would be forgiven for thinking this story was apocryphal, (I found that word in the dictionary apparently it means 'made-up',) but believe me I couldn't make this up if I tried. Yesterday the new washing

machine was delivered. The old one didn't work very well. The Boss put that down to its age and the fact that it's designed to be 240v in England and not the 220v we get here. The old one was ten years old, which The Boss was able to recollect, not only because of the 'free flight offer' that never quite worked out, but because she gave the previous one to a friend, who promptly dropped it on someone's leg and they ended up at hospital. You may think that is enough history for one washing machine, but this particular machine is clearly programmed to cause trouble from start to finish. When The Boss came to unplug the old one she turned the hot water tap off and disconnected the hot water hose. At this point the hot water spraying all round my bedroom gave a bit of an indication that all was not well. She quickly reconnected the hose and presumed the washer on the tap was faulty. This was not the case. When she turned the tap back to the 'on' position and then disconnected the hose, no water came out. So in fact since it was installed here in Belgium, the hot water tap has been off and no hot water has been added to the washing cycle. It was amazing, when The Boss tried the machine with the hot water on, all the soap was taken from the soap dish in a way that hadn't taken place for twelve months and actually despite the voltage difference and its age, the machine works just fine. Now the problem seems to be, what do you say to the men who turn up with the new washing machine and who are expecting to be taking your old one away? It may be ten years old but it does seem an awful shame to be getting rid of a perfectly good washing machine. Maybe it can go in the garage with the spare microwave that only works in England.

Wednesday 8th November

I went for a walk in the dark. There seems to be a lot more 'dark' at the moment. It's appearing at times I'm really not expecting it. As you may imagine this particular walk involved my Master; The Boss did come along too but in fairness her presence only made me nervous. Isn't it funny how jumpy someone can be, just because of the absence of a bit of light. It was helpful that she came, as she was the only one with a torch, although as it was just the one that is part of her mobile phone it was not all that effective. However, having a torch did at least stop us treading in anything unpleasant. Mind you, if we had trodden in something, it would have been the same thing unpleasant that I had tried eating in the light the day before. After that episode, The Boss asked me if I could refrain from kissing her for a month and a half, but I have no idea why.

Where has all this dark come from? I know changed the clocks the other week, though in actual fact, the new ones look exactly the same as the ones we replaced. I'm guessing that in the process of changing the clocks, all the countries must have moved round a bit and we are now in a different time zone. I asked The Boss and she said it was the end of 'daylight saving' which has left me a bit confused, if we'd been saving all that daylight why isn't there any left? It turns out I'm going to have to go on most of my walks a bit earlier in the day, or wait for my Master to take me. I wonder if The Boss would cope better if I stopped going up behind her and going 'boo' every few minutes?

17
MY FIRST BIRTHDAY

Friday 10th November

The Boss wants me to publish some of my dairy. It all came up as we drove to the dog sitter yesterday. She casually asked if I had thought of putting any of it together as a book. I was mortified. I explained to her that it was private and she shouldn't have been reading it in the first place. She apologised for being away for my birthday and said she hadn't realised that I would be so upset. I started worrying about all the other things I might have written about her in the last ten months and started to get quite cross. In the end we had a big argument and I wasn't talking to her by the time I got out of the car. Now I realise how silly it all was and there isn't much I can do about it until I see her. I feel dreadful. Seeing her looking so sad as she drove away, when I wouldn't say goodbye, really got to me, but by then I was too late. I've sent her a text message, but I don't know whether she's had it or not. I did wonder looking back, whether anyone would be interested in publishing it. Perhaps I should find out. I wonder if The Boss would help me put it together.

My mobile phone beeped as I wrote that last paragraph. I'm so relieved I've had a text message back from The Boss saying 'I'm sorry too. I love you. Mum.' That's what I call her at home, I know she isn't my real mum but somehow calling her 'The Boss' would all be a bit formal. I'm so glad we've made up, but it's never quite the same if you can't have a cuddle as well, and I do so like being cuddled.

Saturday 11th November

Well the Pet Dogs' Democratic Party is going to have more work to do than I had envisaged. I decided to conduct a survey amongst the other dogs staying here, asking them about everything from what they're allowed to do at home, to what they enjoy doing in their spare time and what were their main concerns. I typed it all out on the computer and printed it out and then started going round the other dogs to ask them to fill it in. It turns out that many dogs can't actually read and write. I was shocked. It seems the first priority must be to have freely available education for all dogs, regardless of their ability to pay for it. Many had been to training schools, but despondently explained that all those had set out to do was teach them to obey, rather than provide them with any of the tools they needed to be able to think for themselves. It's no wonder so few have signed up for membership, they didn't know anything about it. In the end I held a little meeting and explained that the PDDP was there to work for better conditions for them, less social exclusion, equality and all the usual bits and pieces. One or two of them sloped off saying they weren't sure if their owners would like them being part of something so radical, but the others listened all the way through. I did get a little depressed when a Jack Russell wouldn't stop bouncing up and down, asking whether it would mean he would get free dog biscuits. A couple of the brighter ones seemed to get the point and said they'd like to work with me on it, so it wasn't all bad. We put the survey off until later today and I said I'd go round them individually and ask them the questions.

Sunday 12th November

I can now report that in a recent survey (yesterday in fact), 5 out of 8 dogs said they weren't allowed on the sofa and 7 out of 8 weren't allowed on the bed. It became clear, quite early on in the survey, that we were dealing with one very spoilt dog in the case of a certain Pekingese. 5 out of 8 of those surveyed refuse to stay when told to and 6 admitted to stealing food. I started to realise I wasn't as badly behaved as I thought I was. As to spare time activities, peeing on lamp-posts came very high up, as did playing fetch and being pampered. The most peculiar activity was one dog that likes going on his Master's motorbike. When asked what they thought they were best at, the answers ranged from begging to chasing rabbits. Unfortunately, the one chasing rabbits, used to share his home with three pet rabbits but one of them has recently come to an untimely end. It was sad realising none of them were able to read books, although one or two of them said they shared in the bedtime stories that were read to the children in their houses and I even found that one of them was a fellow Miffy fan.

In response to being asked about their biggest concerns, I was depressed that these were so parochial. Not being able to open the dog biscuit cupboard came highest, although on the whole they said they would rather open the fridge anyway. None of them talked about their lack of employment rights or the discrimination against dogs. Am I alone in caring about the big issues? It had never occurred to any of them that it was unreasonable for them to be left tied up outside the Post Office, or that being refused entry to an airport was unfair. It seems that there is more to education than just learning to read and write.

Monday 13th November

Happy birthday to me, happy birthday to me, happy birthday dear Alfie, happy birthday to me. I am finally one year old. I don't feel any different and for that matter I don't look much different than I did yesterday, but I'm now a whole year old. My Master and The Boss rang me first thing this morning and sang to me. To be honest I could have done without such a raucous start to my birthday, but they meant well. On the whole it has been a pretty good year and there isn't very much about it that I would have liked to have done differently. I'm sorry I can't see my birth-mum and brother and sisters today. I wonder how they're celebrating. I just wish I could have my presents now rather than waiting until Wednesday. I thought it might be best not to say too much to the other dogs, I didn't want them coming up with any ideas that I would not have appreciated. Do dogs do 'the bumps'?

Now I'm a year old I get adult food too. It tastes much the same as the puppy food did, but the pieces are bigger and need more crunching before I swallow them. I can still get it all down in a few seconds, so it hasn't added much to the time I need for meals. The worst part is that apparently I'm supposed to eat a little less than I have been doing and The Boss has given me a choice. Either I can cut down on the size of my dog food meals, or she will cut out all the little extras that I get through the course of the day. "Are you serious?" I asked. "Really?" I couldn't believe she would consider cutting my supply of marzipan, Frosties and crisps. Inevitably I plumped for less dog food, although I wasn't thrilled about that either.

Tuesday 14th November

Given that I had nothing better to do today, I decided to

try to teach some of the other dogs to read and write. I couldn't believe how frustrating it turned out to be. It wasn't really their fault, but I wasn't sure if I should be teaching them the names of the letters or the sounds they made. I eventually decided to start with phonetics and only then realised that I was assuming that they would all want to learn English and they didn't. It turns out that the phonetic sounds for the letters aren't the same in Flemish as they are in English and the letter 'g' is particularly odd. So we ended up having a disagreement about whether there was a right and a wrong way to do things and one of the brighter ones said that he had heard that even in English there were some letters and sets of letters that sounded different when used in the same word. At this point I conceded that he had a point and we agreed that maybe I wasn't cut out to be a teacher. One of them tried suggesting that if you could say things in different ways then it wasn't possible to ever actually be wrong and whilst I thought this approach had some merit it would be very hard to communicate if we all had that attitude. I concluded that teaching may not be as easy as it had first appeared and that I would be far better leaving it to the experts.

Wednesday 15th November
It's odd thinking about the difference between dog ages and human ages. I could almost feel cheated out of the six birthdays I would have had in the last year on top of the actual one I had if I really equate to seven years old in human terms. I suppose it's a bit like people whose birthdays fall on February 29th only getting a proper birthday every leap year.

It doesn't seem fair that humans live so much longer

than dogs do, or do I mean it isn't fair that dogs live so much less time than humans? I look after myself, I eat healthily and get lots of exercise. What more do you think I would have to do to live to be seventy plus in real years? When you're a dog there doesn't seem much incentive to avoid drinking heavily and smoking, either way I only get to live for ten years or so. I suppose there would be little harm in taking up some dangerous sports, although I think The Boss might have something to say about it.

Thursday 16th November
It might have been delayed but I had a lovely birthday. I had an amazing brand new bed. It's bigger than my old one and there's room for me to get one or two of my toys in with me. Best of all I got a new Miffy comfort blanket that I can take to bed with me and, as things stand, it still has both its ears. I also had a new special 'doggy frisby' that throws in the same way as my old one but doesn't have any sharp edges and is soft both for my mouth and the hand of the person throwing it. I also had the most enormous raw hide chew that will take me weeks to get through. I didn't know where to start so I bounced around everything for a while and then flopped down in my new bed exhausted.

A funny thing happened last night. We were all in the office at home and The Boss was leaning over my Master's shoulder helping him with something on his computer. I spotted the opportunity to make them both jump. I quietly crawled under my master's chair and pushed the lever that makes it go up and down so that all of a sudden the chair shot down really low with him sitting on it. It had the desired effect, but what I had not foreseen was that it would result in my being stuck underneath because it had come down on top of me, so we all ended up in a bit of a startled mess. It was worth it though.

Friday 17th November

Well whatever happened to normal? I may be back home but my food has been reduced again. Someone round here seems to think I am putting a little too much weight on. I think they're mistaken; I'm just a little cuddly. Then we went for a walk and there was a sign on a tree in Flemish that The Boss walked straight by. I told her I thought she should have tried to read it and she ignored me. I just had an uncomfortable feeling about it so I said please could we go home and have a walk later. On the way back she had a look at the notice and found it said 'Keep out – shooting'. I was very relieved that I'd made her go back and she even seemed to think I'd done the right thing. Now I'm worrying about what exactly they're shooting and come to that, who 'they' are. I like the deer and the rabbits and the buzzards, and the pheasants aren't all bad. If they have resorted to shooting moles then I'm willing to join them, but otherwise I'm not very happy, I am however, way too much of a coward to make any sort of protest.

I have never seen The Boss get as cross as she did yesterday and it wasn't at me. She is trying to change the address on something that is in my master's name. Firstly she rang the number on the internet, a premium rate number at that. She was then told to ring a different number, which being a National Rate number is still expensive to ring from Belgium. The person who answered asked her all the security questions and only then told her he couldn't help and she would have to ring another number. So she rang the third number and was on hold for twenty minutes waiting for her call to be answered with an overly bright voice saying at intervals 'Good news. You have moved forward in the queue'. Then when they did answer they told her they couldn't do it and that my Master would have to ring. Well you can imagine her reaction. At that point she said, no shouted, that they were lucky to have any customers and that it was unacceptable. Just another day really.

Sunday 19th November

What an exciting walk I had yesterday. I was busily going along, fascinated by a tree that was so rotten it had just bent over like wet cardboard and another that had roots that were so tired of holding onto the wet ground that they had given up altogether and the tree had toppled over. I almost missed the fact that a hedgehog had got itself stuck between the wires of the fence. At least, we think it was stuck. The Boss put together a rescue mission and used a stick to ease its tiny paws together and then lift its little body backwards, through the wire. Then she moved the stick to under its tummy and lifted it back to bring its head to the right side of the fence. By this time it was rolled up in a ball with all its spines out and I said "What if it hadn't been stuck and it was just having a breather before pushing through to the other side?" However The Boss seemed quite convinced that it was stuck. We checked up on the way back and it had unravelled itself, put its spines down and was happily ambling along the side of the fence looking a lot more in control than it had done earlier. I like days where we can do a good deed.

Last night was a little more eventful. Something went wrong with the log fire. When I say 'something went wrong' I mean in the sense that we ended up with a completely blackened chimney and smoke coming into the lounge and going upstairs. The Boss made my Master go and put the fire out which he wasn't too pleased about, but later did see the logic in the suggestion. I wonder if there is something stuck in the chimney. It seems to be a bit early for Santa Claus.

Tuesday 21st November

When we went for our walk yesterday I looked at the autumn colours and thought how much better they would look if they were not against a grey background. All those greens, yellows and browns would look lovely with a blue sky. It would be much better if everything changed colour in spring when you could really appreciate it. I was thinking it would make a good 'colour by numbers'.

I've been thinking about what The Boss said to me about getting my diary published. As I walked through the woods I started daydreaming that there might come a time when children the world over would know these trees as 'Alfie's Woods'. I realised I rather liked the idea, so maybe when I come back from my travels I'll try to do something. I wonder if publishers get many letters from dogs. The Boss has explained that as a writer you have to get used to rejection letters. I'm not sure how well I would deal with that, but she said if she can cope then she thinks that I would. I asked her what she did to cheer herself up when she gets one and she said she cuddles me. I suppose if we're both trying to get things published there could be an awful lot of cuddles.

Thursday 23rd November

Well this is it. I'm all packed and ready to go. We have the strangest assortment of things packed in the back of the car. We have all sorts of 'odds and ends' of rubbish that The Boss can't work out which bin they're supposed to go in here in Belgium, so she's taking them to throw away in England. It's an awfully long way to go just to go to the tip.

The vet wasn't too bad yesterday. He gave me some of the nasty worming stuff, but apart from that, he just signed my passport and told me to have a good trip. So now, it just remains to set off. I know The Boss is a bit concerned in case there is any problem with my passport. She doesn't want to have to drive all the way back here and leave me behind. I asked if that was likely, thinking she was joking. She said, as she had never done it before she really didn't know what to expect. And so, as with all good films, the intrepid heroes drive off into the sunset...

Friday 24ᵗʰ November

I wouldn't be me if I didn't start with a complaint. England smells much the same as Belgium. I don't know what exactly I imagined, or why I expected it to smell any different, but I have to say I'm disappointed. To be fair you don't pick up the smell of chocolate or beer quite as often and in fact both the beer and the chocolate do smell different but otherwise there are much the same trees and flowers and dogs roll in much the same things as they do back home.

We were asked some questions when we checked in at Eurotunnel and we had to show the nice man my passport, but although we were a bit anxious, everything seemed to go ok and here I am. The train itself was a bit odd. For one thing, it swallowed the car. It was a bit like a whale, but as far as I know it stayed on the train track rather than swimming through the Channel. We had to keep our windows open on the crossing, something to do with the change in air pressure but The Boss didn't explain it very well. It did all make my ears go a bit funny and I had to give them a good scratch. I was quite pleased when we came out the other side but I shan't mind doing it again. The Boss said that was a good job, or I wouldn't be able to get home.

There's lots more traffic on the roads in England than there is in Belgium. What really freaked me out though was that they drive on the other side of the road and I kept feeling I was a bit close to the oncoming traffic. What was fun was confusing the cars that went past by pretending that I was driving.

Saturday 25th November

This travelling lark is so busy. The brief stay at my grandparents was great. I spent the time running round the garden with my granddad showing me where The Boss's previous dog 'went through the greenhouse' in an exuberant game of chase with my grandparents' dog. I promised to try to be careful and if I wanted to go into the greenhouse to use the door.

Sunday 26th November

The worst bit so far about England is that there are lots more places that I'm not allowed to go into. The Boss went to the coffee shop to connect to the internet and despite asking ever so nicely if I could go too she explained they wouldn't let me in and I would have to sit outside in the car, which is never as much fun. She promised that I can go next time, but only because she has found out that if she goes when it's shut she can sit in the car in front of the shop and connect to the internet from there. It saves her having to go when everyone is Christmas shopping.

The other bit of the trip I was really not expecting was finding I have got to help with the packing for the house move. I thought I was coming for a holiday. What sort of a question is 'would you rather dismantle the bunk beds or the wardrobe'? Is it ok to answer 'neither, I'd rather go to the pictures with James'? As it turned out that answer was not ok and I found myself holding wardrobe panels whilst my Master undid the screws. He tends to be better with the screwdriver than me, although I'm not bad at it when he lets me near the electric one, having said that, he doesn't often let The Boss near the electric one. I'm waiting to see whether I can have a play with the electric drill, but I am guessing I might have to do that when everyone else goes out. I wonder what I could use it on so that they wouldn't notice it was me.

Monday 27th November
I've noticed one or two odd things about England. The Boss is surprised there are only one or two. It takes longer to get anywhere here. When I'm at home and I see a sign saying 50 to a place, we get there quite quickly. In England when I see a sign saying 50 it takes much longer. The Boss says this is because miles are longer than kilometres and because we aren't allowed to drive so fast. I think I prefer kilometres then, because the journey seems to go more quickly. I'm having much the same problem with money. My pocket money is less in pounds and although The Boss has tried to convince me I'm still getting the same amount I'm not entirely sure. I'd find it easier if I could carry a calculator around but it looks a bit daft round my neck and I haven't got any pockets.

It seems ironic that my Master wants to throw out some of the broken bits of my toys when we are moving so many of Andy's broken toys to the new house. It's the sort of typical 'double standards' I have come to expect. There is one rule for the humans and another for the dog.

18
FASHION

Tuesday 28th November

We went for a walk past the new house yesterday. I am now uncertain whether I'm looking forward to getting the keys later. It turns out there is a very big dog living over the road. He was the sort of dog you don't like to shout 'hello' too loudly to, just in case he doesn't like your tone of voice.

There are lots of things that are different about England as compared to Belgium. Whereas in Belgium shopping centres are nice places to go with not too many people, here it seems the national pastime is shopping. Everyone seems to do it pretty much all the time. It turns out that The Boss is odd by not really liking it. There only has to be a hint that the car park might be full and she stays at home. So far the dogs all seem pretty much the same but then 'dog fashion' doesn't usually vary as much as human fashion does. I suppose poodles might wear their hair a little differently but that's about it.

Wednesday 29th November

Well they sure know how to live. What is the first thing you do when you get the key to a new house? Did they go round and sniff in every room? Did they go round and pee on all the strategic points of the garden? Did they work out the best place to curl up and go to sleep, the point where the sun keeps you warm, but isn't so bright as to stop you sleeping. No. Although in fairness when I suggested that last one to my Master he could see the point. They spent their first afternoon cleaning and putting up curtain poles. It was left to me to sniff out the history of the place and investigate the garden in the traditional way.

I am getting to see different scenery and draw one or two conclusions about the English. They speak with an odd accent up here. In fact it is more than that, they say some words in a completely different way and use other words I've never heard of. In fact there are times I don't even realise they are speaking English. It's a bit like playing the game where you invent a secret code. It's almost as bad as the myth that Americans speak English, I wish they would start admitting to speaking the American language instead of hijacking someone else's, but the same may be true of the people who live in the North-east of England too.

Thursday 30th November
Whilst we were walking, a lady in a black Mini waved at The Boss and she waved back. "Who's that?" I asked and The Boss replied "I have absolutely no idea. I don't know anyone who lives round here and the last person I knew who drove a black Mini sold it in about 1988." The obvious question was 'why did you wave back?' but The Boss may have read my mind. "Not knowing anyone can feel pretty lonely, sometimes it's nice to pretend." Maybe she has a point. I've met quite a number of dogs since we came including a large boxer that came running over to ask if I wanted to go round and play. His owner was bemoaning the fact that he seemed totally out of control so I am assuming the invitation may not stand.

All in all The Boss is not having a brilliant week, once

again someone has tried to fraudulently use her credit card and impressively the card company have spotted it. In my observation, she has the oddest pattern of expenditure so how amongst all of that they can manage to spot the transactions she didn't undertake is quite a miracle. It seems to happen so often that she's thinking of putting their number on speed dial.

Friday 1st December
Have I mentioned how badly dressed people are in England? I now know where The Boss gets her 'dress sense' from. It seems that here the teenagers are very fashion conscious, then there are some middle aged people trying to look like teenagers (and failing). After that are a handful of stylish people and an awful lot that miss the mark or, as in The Boss's case, don't bother at all. In Belgium, each age seems to have its fashion and all of them involve being more refined than seems the case here. I don't think it's going to do The Boss good to stay around here too long, she might end up trying the 'looking like a teenager' thing.

I am now sporting a very attractive new design to my coat. My right ear has a lovely magnolia trim to it. How was I supposed to know that The Boss had just pained that bit of wall?

Saturday 2nd December.
We went to the 'Clothing Bank' to drop some clothes off earlier in the week. I was wondering if it was like a normal bank and whether they pay interest on deposits. Does it mean that the pair of trousers that The Boss dropped off she will then be able to go and collect with slightly longer legs or would she get additional small

items of clothing back from the bank? I tried asking my Master but he just started to wonder whether the same could be applied to the bottle bank. Perhaps I need to open an account so that I can find out how it all works. I wonder whether I need to take my passport as a form of I.D. and whether there are 'clothes laundering' regulations in the same way that ordinary banks have 'money laundering' regulations to comply with.

There's a stone heron in the garden. When I saw it the other day I froze, went down on my haunches and had a good bark at it. When The Boss said it wasn't real I said 'I knew that' and felt really stupid. I tried to walk over to it nonchalantly and cocked my leg, but I don't think she was fooled.

Sunday 3rd December

I learnt a lot yesterday. I learnt that if you put a screwdriver through the skin on your hand it bleeds a lot, and I learnt that if you don't work out exactly what you need from the shop then you go back three times. It all started with The Boss trying to repair a lamp for James. Apart from using a screwdriver there was no apparent way to prise the back off. Unfortunately in trying to use the screwdriver, rather than it having the desired effect, it slipped and went into The Boss's finger leaving blood dripping on the kitchen floor. The lamp is now her sworn enemy. Still that was not as bad as the washing machine. All that was needed, apart from larger muscles, was a bit to fit on the end of a pipe. Unfortunately, neither The Boss nor I knew what the 'bit' was called. The Boss measured the pipe and decided it was 5cm across and went to the DIY store in search of a suitable 'bit'. Now I don't like to question her ability to use a tape measure, but it turns out plumbing connections only come in 40mm or 32mm and not 50mm. How she had measured it as 50mm is beyond me, but then I can't hold the tape measure so I probably shouldn't criticise. After half an hour of looking along the shelves she found a packet that claimed it was for the very purpose of fitting a washing machine so she bought it and drove home. Going back to the subject of her ability to measure, it was 40mm and was too big. Work it out for yourself. So she drove back to the store to buy a smaller one. They don't come in smaller ones, so she decided to buy a special connector that reduces the size of a pipe. You have probably guessed but on coming home, she now had two pieces that didn't fit the hole and didn't fit each other. That last bit you would like to think she could have worked out in the shop. By this time it was 10pm so the washing machine connection has been delayed.

Monday 4th December

What a way to start the day. First take the bits, that don't fit the washing machine, back to the shop and get a refund because they don't have an alternative. Then go to the tip. Then go to another DIY shop. This time after half an hour looking on her own and no confidence that they had the right bits either The Boss had the sense to ask an assistant if they had something suitable. It turns out that if she had been looking in the right part of the store, she would have found they had exactly the right thing. When she got it home it only took ten minutes to fit. The trips to the DIY stores had by comparison taken several hours. To be quite honest I think this moving home thing is vastly overrated. She put a key rack up and the screw was so long it came out of the other side of the cupboard. I don't think I'm supposed to have mentioned that as she hasn't actually told my Master about it. I did think she was a bit more imaginative when she put the towel rail up and couldn't find a spirit level so used a golf ball instead.

Tuesday 5th December

There are so many places I am not allowed to go in England. So much for it being a nation of 'dog lovers'! I'm not even allowed to go into the motorway service stations, they pretend to be nice by putting a bowl of water at the entrance for dogs to drink from, but what about my burger and chips? I don't want to have to eat outside all the time. I'm not allowed in restaurants either. I think Belgium is much more tolerant than England, it makes me proud to be able to say I'm Belgian.

Thursday 7th December

Well we went to Bradgate Park yesterday. It's not bad. There's plenty of space to run around and oak trees with hollow insides that you can hide in. There were two things I didn't understand though. Firstly, there is a house that is derelict. The Boss says it is known as a ruin, but derelict seems a perfectly good word to me. I didn't get the point of it. Why not knock it down and grow some more trees? The Boss didn't seem to appreciate my suggestion. Secondly, there is a jug on a hill, or at least that is what it looked like to me. The Boss told me it's called 'Old John' and it's a folly. Now I can see why you might call it a folly, but I wondered if 'a pointless' might be a better description. It was fun climbing up to it though and there was a great view and more importantly a great smell of rabbits.

Friday 8th December

The biggest downside of The Boss spending time with friends that still work in normal businesses is that they were talking about having their appraisals. Now you may think there is nothing wrong in that, until you realise she came home suggesting that I should have one. Now that I have been with her for nearly a year we should sit down and discuss how I have performed my role. I said it was totally inappropriate and besides which she hadn't sat down with me and gone through my objectives at the start. How can I be appraised when I don't know what I'm supposed to have achieved, but she said that didn't usually stop people in business. I thought about it for a while and asked if my pocket money would be increased if I'd performed well, but she said that pocket money was not linked to the appraisal and would be dealt with separately. I then asked the obvious question as to whether it worked both ways and I could appraise her performance as The Boss in return. Surprisingly she didn't object to this idea. We have agreed to sit down on Tuesday when we're back in Belgium to discuss it properly. I've never had an appraisal, should I be worried? Having said that I'm pretty much the perfect puppy so I should be ok. I just need to think about how she has performed.

In the meantime it is back to doing DIY. How did she think I could reach up high enough to hold the bathroom cabinet for her to fix it. It's no good shouting at me because I let my end down a bit so it wasn't level, I was struggling to get my paw up that high. She said I had seemed to manage it when I wanted to open the lounge door at my grandparents and as she had a point I thought I'd stop complaining.

Saturday 9th December

The funniest thing happened whilst we were staying with my grandparents. My granddad said to The Boss "When are you going to take all your things with you?" She was very confused and said she thought she had. He said "What about the seat in the garage? I'm fed up of moving it every time I go in there." "What seat? She said. To which her mother chipped in "Your birthday present." It was at that point that The poor Boss was able to say "But you haven't even given it to me. I didn't know it was there." "Oh" said her mother "Happy birthday." Given that her birthday was several months ago it was pretty good going.

I'm finding the whole Christmas thing a bit confusing. I'm not absolutely sure what I'm supposed to be celebrating. I saw a little scene made up of a reindeer, a snowman, a Father Christmas, some robins and a baby in a shed. It seems to be one of those things that you can pick out the bits you like and put them all together. I'm thinking of setting up my own little Christmas scene. It will have some presents, an acorn, a few birds and a dog biscuit. I wonder if The Boss will let me put it on our front lawn with lights all round it as everyone else seems to have done. I am looking forward to getting to eat turkey for a month and a half and chasing round in empty wrapping paper. I think, so far, the worst bit about Christmas is hearing the same music everywhere I go. There is nothing like stating the obvious, just in case you managed to miss it 'so here it is merry Christmas...' I'm not sure yet if I want to be 'merry' or whether to be the one that goes round saying 'bah humbug'. Oddly my Master and The Boss seem to switch to merry, which leaves the whole position of 'bah humbug' wide open.

Sunday 10th December

This is one of those times when you aren't going to believe this but it's absolutely true. The Boss went round the garden clearing up all those little presents I had left when she was too lazy to walk me. She put it all in an old Tesco's bag, fortunately inside another bag and all tied up. Because she wasn't ready to go to the tip and didn't want to forget it, she put the carrier bag outside the garage doors on the drive. Unfortunately, when she came home after going to the shops, it had gone. First of all she thought someone had stolen it and that it probably served them right, but then when she went into the house there was a little thank you note through the door from a 'charity collection' that had been picking up bags of clothes to sell. It would seem they had mistaken the bag waiting for the tip for a bag waiting for them. How on earth was she supposed to know that was going to happen? She now feels really bad and presumes that they will think someone did it deliberately. She is also concerned that it's not safe to leave anything out as someone will presume it's for them.

The rest of the weekend seems to have involved drills, screwdrivers, picture hooks and holes. The holes haven't all been in absolutely the right place and progress can be slow when a four year old hides the blocks of wood you need and won't tell you where they've put them. Then of course are the things that are faulty when you try to put them up and the things whose instruction have clearly been translated from an obscure language by someone for whom English is not their first language.

Tuesday 12th December

I have been observing teenage behaviour ready for when I

reach the equivalent stage. So 'whatever!' 'Yeah' or is it just 'uh'? Actually, I think I'll make quite a good teenager, I can really 'do' attitude when I want to. I know I look soft, but it's just an act.

I am ready to settle down to a quiet day and prepare for my appraisal. I've been putting together a few notes on how I think The Boss has performed. Unfortunately my master is away so I shall have to wait to tell him where I think he could do with improving.

Wednesday 13th December

Well all things considered, my appraisal went quite well. We ran out of time for me to appraise The Boss, so that has been deferred until later today. The summary was that I am a perfect pet, a great companion and just wonderful to have around. I may of course be paraphrasing it a little bit, but I think that was the general gist. I did well on all the normal puppy problems. I have never chewed anything that wasn't mine and all I've ever broken was a cd case when I got a bit enthusiastic flinging my toys in the air and trying to catch them. I also did well on being so easy to house train and on keeping myself clean. So that all makes me just about perfect. I suppose it wouldn't be a real appraisal if I weren't given areas to improve on. It seems I am already making progress when it comes to jumping up people, in as much as I am starting to learn that I'm not supposed to do it. The Boss has given me a target of March to completely master it. I am also making good progress on walking to heel, but need to learn not to get distracted so easily. I've been given a bit longer to get that right and need to have the hang of it by the end of June. The day I decided to run away seems to have gone against me a little bit and The Boss has suggested it would be good if we didn't have a repeat of that. Apparently when I fetch things I'm supposed to be prepared to drop them, rather than run off with them. Now where is the fun in that? I am totally perfect at leaving things when told, unless it's another dog. It seems I am however, a miserable failure at security and being prepared to go for a walk in the rain. You can't win them all.

Thursday 14th December

So yesterday was the appraisal rematch. I'd got ready all the things I wasn't happy about, just in case I didn't like the way my appraisal went. It was going to be a sort of counter attack. I hadn't really prepared for the event that The Boss thought I was wonderful, I just assumed an appraisal was a bad thing. All things considered it seemed a little churlish to start complaining about the frequency that she washes my bed and the fact I really would like more food. If truth be known I'm probably one of the most spoilt dogs I know and complaining seems a little unfair. So I told her how much I appreciated that I am rarely left on my own and never for very long. I get lots of cuddles and she never really tells me off when I forget myself and put muddy paws all over her. I did explain that there is always room for more stroking, and will be until it gets to 24 hours a day. I like the amount of walks I have and appreciate that when I don't really want to go I'm not made to, but The Boss will always turn out for me whatever the weather if I do want to go. I like being allowed to sit on the settee. I have all the toys I need but would like The Boss and my Master to play with them with me more often. My only real complaint goes back to the early days when I was taken to dog training and The Boss really thought I was going to sit down in a muddy field. On balance I'm a very happy dog and know when I'm on to a good thing. After all who else would feed me little bits of marzipan when I ask for them?

Friday 15th December

She's only gone and invited the neighbours for mulled wine and mince pies. When she first said it I thought 'mulled wine' was a high pitched howl that you had thought about for a while. I was disappointed to find mince pies are not made from beef mince either. As long as she doesn't think I'm going to don a little waiter's outfit and go round serving people. I have my pride and whilst I am quite prepared to wear a Santa hat in exchange for the odd mince pie, I draw the line at being a waiter.

Alarmingly, there has been a cat visiting our garden. This is what happens when you go away, someone turns up that doesn't understand that this is my territory. Well it really was too much. I was sitting at the window whilst The Boss was on the phone and there it was as bold as anything. I wasn't in a position to rush outside so I had to content myself with whimpering, then growling and finally howling. I had quite forgotten The Boss was trying to talk to someone, she had to apologise to them for the noise I was making. Fortunately, they had a dog too so they understood.

Saturday 16th December

Why have they brought a tree into the house? Do you think it is in response to the Pet Dogs Democratic Party's demand for inside toilet facilities in bad weather? I had tentatively thought about trying it out to see what response I get but something is telling me that they wouldn't be putting tinsel and lights on it for my benefit.

I have discovered that I can use my paw to push my Halti off my noise when I want a really good bark at another dog. I discovered it by accident. My nose was itching so I scratched it and pushed the nose band off. When The Boss put it back on I did it again to make sure it hadn't been a fluke and sure enough I can take it off whenever I want.

I have heard of this person called Santa Claus or Father Christmas. I'm not sure why he has two names, perhaps he has debt problems and changes his name to stop them catching up with him. Anyway, I've heard that if you've been good he brings you presents at Christmas. That may of course be how his debt problems started. The bridleway behind our house would be a perfect dog-size rally track. Do you think Santa could bring me a rally car?

19
SO HERE IT IS MERRY CHRISTMAS

Sunday 17th December

I have been reading through a few Christmas carols and am a little put out that the Shepherds always seem to get a mention but not the sheepdogs. Where would the shepherds have been without their dogs? Who do you think was left minding the flocks so they could take a look at what the star was all about? I think the PDDP might need to campaign for the rewording of some Christmas carols to make them less discriminatory. Christmas should be a time of inclusion. Firstly we would like 'While Shepherds Watched' to read as follows:

While sheepdogs watched their flocks by night

All lying on the ground

The angel of the Lord came down

And glory shone around.

"Bark not," said he for there they were

All woofs and other sounds

"Glad tidings of great joy I bring

To you and other hounds."

The remaining verses are ok, so if that first one were changed I think we would be happy.

On a completely separate note I have been thinking about the term 'sunset'. Does it mean that the sun is like an ice cream and during the day it melts from its own heat and it has to be put away at night to 'set' again before the next day?

Monday 18th December

I have heard about an elderly lady in England who has lots of Corgi's and sends a Christmas message to the nation on Christmas Day. Not a bad idea I thought, so I have decided that on Christmas Day I will give a Christmas address on behalf of the Pet Dogs' Democratic Party to all dogs everywhere and of course one or two owners as well.

Is there really any point in appraising my Master? I'm sure I have already mentioned the excessive recycling system in operation in Belgium. There are almost as many categories as there are items of rubbish. After The Boss had to fish a yoghurt pot out of the badly decomposed green waste, because my Master somehow thought as he ate it with his banana at breakfast they must go in the same place, you would like to hope she had got the message across. Yesterday after he had finished off a container of shower plughole unblocker, The Boss asked where he had put the empty container. She was so pleased when he said it had gone in 'dangerous' waste that she gave him a big kiss. Unfortunately, his response to that was "if that's what happens, I'm going to put everything in 'dangerous' waste from now on." I think he may have missed the point. Maybe his recycling ability is like the fault in The Boss's computer. She says it's an intermittent fault because it only happens 95% of the time.

Thursday 21st December

I think my first new year's resolution is to find a girlfriend. I'm considering looking into whether there's internet dating for dogs. I do meet other dogs when I'm out, but these are mostly boys. There must be some nice girl dogs out there but they just don't walk in the places I go. I need someone that can cope with my lively, energetic and enthusiastic nature and the fact that I don't always know my own strength. I've given The Boss enough bruises to last a lifetime so it would be no good my finding a really soft sensitive type. I'm pretty much stuck if they want puppies, too. I suppose I could look for an older dog that has already had puppies, but I think I might be a little too energetic for that. To be honest a girl about my age might be best. I wonder how I should describe myself for an advert.

'Handsome, rugged and playful young dog. GSOH, enjoys travel, writing and politics, seeks fun loving bitch for possible long-term relationship.' I thought I would leave out the bit about being castrated, it might put some of the girls off replying. Now all I have to work out is where the best place to put the advert is. I could either put it on the internet or maybe in a magazine. I don't know if either *Horse & Hounds* or *Dogs Today* run personal ads. The problem would come if things go well and she wants to move in together. I'm certainly not leaving The Boss and I don't know whether she'd let me have another dog come and live here. In the short term, I suppose the bigger problem is the fact that I live in Belgium and I'm advertising in English.

Saturday 23rd December
My Master upset me the other day by saying I don't really count as a puppy anymore. I pointed out he wasn't still young either, but we all like something to hide behind. I'm staying a puppy for as long as I can get away with. Human children don't really stop being children until they're at least teenagers, so by my reckoning that gives me until about September time.

Following on from the appraisal a week or two ago, The Boss has now suggested introducing Team Briefs to raise morale and make me feel more included. Apparently, once a month she'll sit me down and tell me what's going on and I get a chance to ask questions. She clearly doesn't realise I go through everything on her desk when I sit down to use the computer and already know more of her personal things than she would appreciate. It's a good job that I'm not by nature the blackmailing type really.

Sunday 24th December
Now run this Santa business past me again. If I've understood this correctly, sometime when I'm asleep tonight, a bloke on a sleigh pulled by reindeer, is going to drive through the sky to bring presents to all of us and gain entry to our houses down the chimney. Not surprisingly I have a few questions. Firstly, how does he know where to find me? Secondly, who decides whether I have been good this year? Was that what my appraisal was all about? Thirdly, obviously I want to know how on earth he can visit all of us in person in that space of time? But I would also like answers to some more obscure questions; such as can all reindeer fly? And why did The Boss bring me to England to a house with no chimney and not leave me in Belgium where we have a lovely chimney? Is there a risk if I haven't got a chimney that he won't be able to get in? Finally, why does no one take action against Santa for trespass?

Monday 25th December
My Owners and I would like to bring you all Christmas greetings, wherever you are this Christmas Day. We bring

you these greetings from the comfort of my trusty old travelling bed where I am snuggled up after a large Christmas lunch.

It is important at this time that we remember those dogs who give their lives in service to their country. Many dogs work tirelessly throughout the year, keeping our countries safe from terrorists and drugs, so that we pet dogs can live in comfort and security.

We must also remember those dogs less fortunate than ourselves. We think of those who may not have had a Christmas table to scrounge at today and who may yet be unaware of the importance of Christmas. Many of you puppies will be new to your owners' homes this Christmas. My message to your owners is simple, a dog is for life but please remember to spoil him at Christmas.

For my own part I got the most fantastic Christmas present. It's a ball that talks when it senses motion. It's just so annoying. I guessed it was for me as we drove up the motorway yesterday and a bag in the boot kept talking whenever we went over a bump in the road. The Boss said it was very embarrassing when she bought it and then had to walk round with her shopping talking loudly enough for everyone to hear. I have my very own t-shirt as well. It's not as good as the one my cousin got that said 'I'm up and dressed. What more do you want?' Mine just says 'Security' which is of course a bit of a joke because I like nearly everyone.

Tuesday 26th December
We're off to stay with my Master's family. The Boss has already wound me up a bit by explaining that I can choose between whether I sleep in the car or the garage. So I said

I was happy with either, which did she prefer. It was only then I realised she wasn't planning to join me. It really is a dog's life. Still, to be honest, after all the turkey yesterday I may sleep most of the time.

Wednesday 27th December

Whose idea was it to build the M25? What a ridiculous road. Why build a road that goes round in circles? What is amazing is just how many people seem to want to drive round in circles. Maybe it would work better if instead of having 3 or 4 lanes that went each way, you had 6 or 8 that all went the same way. So you could only go in a clockwise direction. This may be inconvenient for those people who only wanted to go one junction the other way but they would do the whole clockwise journey so much quicker that it would probably work out better for them in the long term.

Friday 29th December

I was only naughty once while we were away and even then you couldn't really say it was very bad. I was left sitting outside in the garage so that I wouldn't chase the cats in the house. It was cold and I got peckish, as you do. For Christmas I was given a pack of 'begging strips' and I thought 'blow it, why should I beg for them, they're mine.' I knew what bag they were in and the bag was in the garage with me, so I got them out, opened the packet and ate them all. When I was found out I explained it was only like the children tucking in to the chocolate they'd been given. Fortunately, The Boss agreed and I wasn't in very much trouble. My dog biscuits were however wrapped up a little more tightly to ensure I was rationed.

Saturday 30th December

I have recently heard a new term and it sounds exciting. The term is 'moonlighting'. I'm thinking of putting my Christmas present to good use. You may remember it was a t-shirt that says 'security'. Now all I need to find is someone that wants to employ a completely docile puppy that is very well mannered and affectionate in the capacity of bouncer. I will still be a writer by day, but by night I'm going to 'moonlight' as a security guard. Of course there is absolutely no point in anyone asking me to do it that really wants anything valuable looked after, as I'm not at all fierce and make friends with almost everyone. In fact I only growl at my cousin and my great-aunt and I have even stopped growling at my cousin. He sort of scratched me under my chin a bit and I melted. So I will be most useful in the capacity of guard dog where you want something protecting from very elderly ladies. I am also experienced in keeping small boys amused and looking for lost rabbits. Unfortunately I do less well at controlling small boys and except on the occasions I pull the face that looks like the 'Taz' cartoon which is based on the Tasmanian Devil Dog, I don't actually scare anybody. Oh well, I've still got the Pet Dogs' Democratic Party, maybe my skills are better used there. Perhaps that is what I should do in the New Year, some serious campaigning on behalf of the PDDP. I'm still fed up that I couldn't go into service stations in England for lunch.

Sunday December 31st

Life is just not fair. If a dog made as much noise as a small boy they would be sent back to the Dogs' Home. If a dog was as disobedient he would have all privileges withdrawn. The worst of it is 'wind'. If the dog has wind he is confined to his room and only given boring things to eat. Small boys seem to think having wind is some sort of game and then worst of all, they blame the dog. I'm guessing the campaigning of the PDDP may have some difficulty stretching as far as this, but something ought to be done.

Well it is the last day of the year and what a year it's been. I started the year as just a tiny puppy and now it's almost wrong to call me a puppy at all. Although, The Boss says I'll always be her little puppy, which is rather nice. I have undergone a major operation and survived, although not with my male dignity quite intact. I have learnt to obey commands, on the odd occasions that it suits me. I have travelled to Switzerland and England as well as to lots of bits of Belgium. I guess as we go into next year I get to do a lot of those things all over again. I started to realise that was how life worked when the card came through the letterbox 'inviting' The Boss to go and have her car tested to make sure it's roadworthy. We had a good laugh remembering last year and the problems she had not knowing what to do and where to go. "It's ok" she said "at least we know where to go this time" then she turned the card over and it says she has to go to a different place. That about sums it up really. Each year we get to do much the same things, we just do them slightly differently.

Monday 1st January

I was thinking when we went to the vet's that one of the things that seems to be different between Belgium and England is that in Belgium lots of people work from home. It seems normal to run a small business from part of your house. There's the vet and some of the doctors and lots of other people too. It means they don't have to go far to get to work. In England there seems to be a lot of talk about the need to cut down on travelling, and there are lots of 'rush hour' traffic problems and yet everybody seems to work from bigger businesses that you have to travel to get to. Why don't they just encourage everyone to work from home? The other good thing then is they can have a dog to keep them company. Which gives more potential members of the PDDP.

Tuesday 2nd January
In the car when we're travelling, each person has half an hour of their choice of music and then it goes to the next person. I said I should have a turn, but no one took me seriously. I could have chosen something cultured by Bach for example or maybe I should get my own talking book. 'The Hound of the Baskervilles' must be available from somewhere. Time gets docked for bad behaviour, and as the judges of the bad behaviour are The Boss and Master it seems they always get their full half hour. In a full cycle of 5 half hours we get everything from a children's book (chosen by The Boss), to sports radio (my Master), to excessive pop music (chosen by the children). The four year old member of the team chooses whatever his brother or sister manipulate him into saying, for the most part. Although the other day he did have the good sense to ask for half an hour of quiet as he wanted to go to sleep, my thoughts precisely.

Wednesday 3rd January
So now with Christmas and New Year over we're back to work and normal life. The turkey is not quite finished, although for the sake of those of you that worry, it has

been in the freezer. The decorations are coming down and the bottles of Pimm's No 3 have been bought in bulk to take back for the cold winter's nights in Belgium. I caught a sneak look at The Boss's new year's resolutions and it seems she is committing herself to going to the dentist by the end of February. I will believe it when I see it. She has told me if I don't cut down in the marzipan I will need to go before long, but like any addict the risks are just something you have to take.

Thursday 4th January

Scrap the new year's resolutions, I've had a better idea. I'm going to devote this year to developing the cult of Alfie Dog. Snoopy and Garfield are famous, so why not me? I grant you 'Entlebucher Mountain Dog' is not quite so catchy as 'Beagle' but in years to come the name of Alfie Dog will be known around the world. There will be t-shirts with my picture on and people will come up to ask for my paw print. In my dreams I even appear on chat shows being interviewed, although I may need a little help from The Boss to cope with one or two of the details. Of course I'm not doing it for my own satisfaction, but for the good of the Pet Dogs' Democratic Party and all pet dogs everywhere.

Friday 5th January

I need your help. If I'm to become a worldwide cult figure the first step will need to be to get more people to have heard of me. I can do the whole writing to papers and maybe leave the odd business card lying around, but if it isn't any trouble could you send an email to some of your friends so they can read my diary too? If you just send a letter something along these lines...

'Dear xxxx (obviously you fill that bit in)

Immense good fortune will come to the pets of all those that read the diary of the great Alfie Dog (you can leave out the 'great' if you really have to). Please read his diary at www.alfiedog.me.uk If you like it, please send the link to five of your gullible friends, and their pets, so they can share in the good fortune too.'

That should just about cover it although you might want to add something along the lines of 'Alfie Dog' is the leader of the Pet Dogs' Democratic Party and spends every waking hour campaigning for more rights to be extended to pet dogs.' (I suppose it's just unfortunate that I don't have many waking hours.)

Do you think I should put something in about bad things happening to you if you don't pass the link on? I think that's how chain letters usually work. Alternatively, I could use the tactic of sending it out myself with a warning about some fake virus and see just how long it takes to go all the way round the world and come back to me. It's now your turn to do your bit and send it out. I shall know if you have by checking how many people are reading my diary. Thank you in anticipation and lots of frenetic tail wagging.

Saturday 6th January

How can the sixth day of the month be twelfth night? I suppose it's just another reason to mark humans down as being odd

I'm going to have t-shirts printed for my Master and The Boss saying something like "Owners of the amazing Alfie Dog. www.alfiedog.me.uk" Then all I will have to do is make them wear them. If they know it's with the objective of making me famous I'm sure they won't mind.

Perhaps I should have a whole load printed saying just "The amazing Alfie Dog" and the web address and give them away free to anyone who will take one. The only other option for becoming famous when you don't have any particularly notable skills seems to be to go on the 'Big Brother' television programme and quite honestly I think I might not fit in. For a start I don't' swear enough but in comparison to most of them, I am cute.

Sunday 7ᵗʰ January

It's funny here in Belgium they can only have sales on certain dates. It's to make sure they're genuine. This is as opposed to England where there are sales all the time and then at sale time there are still queues. I really don't understand humans at all.

When we were in England at a petrol station, I as usual was sitting in the car due to the severe prejudice in England against dogs. The Boss told me that when she went inside a lady had tried to carry her spaniel in with her. Now, disregarding the fact that spaniel's are largely irrelevant to the world of dogs and unless they are trained as gun dogs they are pitiable creatures that simply make everyone go 'aarrh'. Please don't mistake these feelings for jealousy, I have enough admirers of my own. Anyway back to the story of the spaniel being carried in. The assistant said "You can't bring dogs in here it isn't hygienic, there's food." At the time The Boss was coughing and sneezing over everything in sight and was allowed in, but the spaniel that was being carried and could touch nothing was told to leave. Something tells me there is something missing in the logic.

Monday 8th January

How should I know which particular item I found in the garden made me sick on the lounge rug? I'd read on my Master's 'Worst Case Scenario Calendar' that if I am stranded somewhere I should never eat white berries so it definitely wasn't any of those. It might have been the foul tasting stuff I found under the bush, but it might not have been. All I know is that I did not deserve to be shouted at by my Master. As always The Boss stuck up for me, even though she was left with the task of cleaning up. I was a bit subdued for a while and it was a few hours before I felt compelled to go back into the garden to see if I could find out what had caused it. I got to snuggle up on the bed with The Boss so it was definitely worth it.

Tuesday 9th January

I reasoned that if I was bad enough I wouldn't have to go with The Boss to get the cars road test completed. Think on. Despite my protestations that I would be in the way The Boss is working on the basis that I can be cute and if they are paying attention to the dog they might overlook the foibles of an eight year old car that has started to cough almost as much as she has. So now I have to 'act cute' on instruction. I suppose the fact that we had the whole security team at Eurotunnel round the car the other day may have something to do with it. On that occasion The Boss was mortified. She said it made it look like there was a problem and it needed the whole team to deal with it. In fact what happened was the first person thought I was cute and then called all her colleagues to meet me. So it made The Boss look like a criminal to an outside observer, but I just love the adulation.

20
A YEAR OF MY DIARY

Wednesday 10th January

Despite being apprehensive because the car's road test was at a different place, everything went really well. There were no signs telling you where to go, but The Boss wasn't going to be fooled and an arrow was all she needed to accidentally find herself at the front of the queue. I of course whistled and pretended she wasn't with me. She went prepared, we each had a book to read and a packet of sweets, but there wasn't time for any of that before we were whisked through. My little heart was pounding as they put the car through its paces. What if it failed? How would I persuade The Boss to get another impractical car that meant I could have the wind in my hair when we travel? When they put it on the machine that buffets it about I couldn't watch for fear some essential part would fall off. When it went up on the ramp I was whispering words of encouragement, as they shone lights in places no car should have to have prodded and poked. The Boss reassured me that it isn't the same as when I go to the vet, but she really mustn't talk about the car like that, it has feelings too. Then finally they said everything was ok and I hadn't even got past the chapter heading of my book. So that's that until next year. The people were even nice too and there was a lady mechanic. I got to nuzzle her a tiny bit, but the blokes weren't so easily swayed.

Thursday 11th January

Now we're for it. My Master has discovered bidding on Ebay. When I say discovered, that would be a bit of an exaggeration, he was more pointed in that direction. Personally I blame The Boss. If she hadn't bailed him out when he got stuck with the Belgian Flemish language Ebay site as his 'homepage' he would have given up and simply sworn at the computer. However, once she sorted him out there was no stopping him. Does it matter that we don't need the items he's bidding on, does it matter that we have almost run out of wall space to hang more pictures? Clearly not as far as he's concerned. Although The Boss did very gently tell him there really wasn't room for a signed guitar even if it was signed by his favourite musician. I offered to sign something for him and let him frame that, but it didn't seem to have the same appeal. He is going to regret that one day. When I'm famous, he's going to say I really wish I'd accepted Alfie's offer. Obviously with my desire for fame I do understand why people might want such memorabilia, but I struggle when it comes to a postage stamp that's over 100 years old. I could nip to the Post Office and get him one much cheaper. He tried explaining all about it's little perforations and wasn't impressed when I likened it to a teabag. Then he told me about the different coloured inks and about the stamps used to 'cancel' them. If I've got this straight he isn't even buying an unused stamp so it isn't even of any practical value. Once again I find humans completely beyond my comprehension. I might just scroll through and see if I can find any 'bones' for sale. I might be able to do it on my Master's account and charge it to his credit card.

Friday 12ᵗʰ January

I am distraught. It is with great sadness that I have to report the untimely and tragic death of 'pig'. Pig has been my constant companion for a number of months. Ok so I still take my Miffy comforter to bed, but pig has travelled all over Europe with me. There we were yesterday playing our usual game. I grab him in my mouth and present The Boss with a trotter to hold, while I tug. She has been so careful not to let me get a purchase on pig, so that nothing untoward happened to him, but yesterday I tugged before she was ready and that's when it happened. His whole little body ripped in two. Well as you can imagine, I just stood there. First I looked at pig, then I looked at The Boss. Then I stuck my nose inside him to see if there was anything there. Then I just sat down in disbelief. After a few minutes I picked him up as carefully as I could and took him to The Boss, tail wagging, saying "Of course you will be able to fix him won't you?" It was then that The Boss sat me down and explained that pig had gone to the resting place in the sky for plastic toys and he wouldn't be coming back. Pig was a present from Matilda the cat's family. The Boss says she'll try to get me another one if I can find out where it came from. Now I'm faced not only with my loss, but having to be nice to Matilda the cat so that I can find out where he came from. There are times as a dog that life just is not fair.

Saturday 13ᵗʰ January

Scarily I was watching some advice on television that was talking about the recent storms. Don't live close to big trees. What am I supposed to do now? Should I move house? Where I live is completely surrounded by big trees. Well if I remove the exaggeration there are big trees all round two complete sides of the house and yes they are big enough to fall on the house. I like trees. The Boss likes trees even more than I do, so she doesn't want to move. She reassured me that because my bed was on the ground floor it was less likely to be a problem, but what about when I sleep in her room? Of course I only get to do that when I'm ill or when my Master doesn't realise I'm there. I've done a full assessment and said I'm prepared to sacrifice my spot by the radiator for a cooler spot on the other side of the room – on the tree-free side. I've also devised a little plan. I've observed that when I pee on things regularly it seems to have a bit of a corrosive effect. The grass is absolutely dead in patches. So I was thinking if I started to pee on a regular basis on the side of the trees that are not near the house, then maybe if they weaken they will fall away from rather than towards the house and everything will be all right. Perhaps I should concentrate on a test area first to see if it makes any real difference. It might of course be easier to just move house.

Sunday 14th January

I tried an alternative tactic on the bed front last night. Well my Master is away so his side of the bed was empty and I do so hate seeing a comfortable bed going to waste. The Boss was a little surprised to wake and find a furry head on the pillow next to her, but I'd seen my Master sleeping like that so I thought I'd give it a try. I would normally go for the 'curled up in a ball' approach, but the pillow thing wasn't bad. Unfortunately, I got sent back to my own bed and have now been told it is my responsibility to change the duvet cover and pillow slip before my Master comes home and finds out.

Continuing along the theme of not understanding my

human companions, what is the point? Why go and buy new jeans 'because your old ones are a disgrace and have holes in them' and then continue to wear the old ones? It's the same with the slippers. Actually it isn't quite the same with the slippers to be fair, with them there's more hole than slipper, but the jeans are still holding together, except in one of two less noticeable places. I'm starting to think that The Boss actually likes to be scruffy. She calls it comfortable but I think she passed that stage a long time ago on the way to threadbare.

Monday 15th January

A trotter has been thrown in the bin. I wanted The Boss to repair pig not throw out his disembowelled pieces. That trotter still had good chewing potential. I suppose if she hadn't done it then my Master would have done when he came home. He seems unimpressed by all the bits of toys lying around. It seems that as a dog I'm not supposed to have feelings. Who is he kidding? Has he seen the wonderful cartoons by my favourite cartoonist Charles Barsotti that show amongst other things the problems dogs go to psychiatrists with, having been utterly destroyed by the whims of their owners. I can't bear to look at the ones that show the little dog with the tear in his eye, I just come over all emotional. How could any owner tell their dog that they regret getting them and they should have got a cat instead? It just breaks your heart. Anyway all that just goes to show I can have feelings too and the throwing out bits of my favourite toys is bound to leave me upset. Maybe I should have had a go at using the Superglue myself, but there seemed to be a few risks attached, not least of which was how to get the lid off the glue without sticking my mouth together.

Tuesday 16ᵗʰ January

I'm with the dog sitter for a couple of days. I was planning to be grumpy when I got here, but it turns out that Mackensey is pregnant and the shock really made me forget my mood. Having grown up a bit there are also certain things you know to do when in the company of a pregnant dog. First and foremost is of course to check you aren't the father. Fortunately the puppies are not due until the end of January and that rules me out because my operation was too long ago for me to have been responsible. It was a nice thought though, even if she is a different type to me. The second thing is to check whether they are still in a position to play with you or whether you need to back off, sadly there isn't going to be a lot of playing this week. Finally, you move into chivalrous mode and ask if there is anything you can do to help. Your main hope is that if there is anything it will be along the lines of fighting with the dog that did it, rather than running round completing domestic chores. As it turned out she just wants to be left alone and I can do that.

Wednesday 17ᵗʰ January

Do you think there is an organisation along the lines of 'Ebay Anonymous' to help wean addicts off their bidding tendencies? The Boss seems to bid for small value items and spends more on postage than on the item itself. She bought a mug the other day for $5. Then they wanted $26 to post it express mail. She's hoping they can find a slow boat to send it on that might be a little cheaper. This could of course be the time to buy shares in worldwide postal services.

Thursday 18th January

Just one small point of concern, what on earth do I do if Mackensey goes into labour? I'm not cut out to be a midwife. One look at the blood and I would be out of it completely. Imagine the trauma, it would be enough for me to need counselling. The good news is that the little ones aren't due until the 27th of January. The bad news is that I'm supposed to be staying here then too. I presume there will be someone else here and that I won't be expected to do anything. Surely if they need a dog then it should be the father rather than me. However, sadly as in so many cases there doesn't seem to be any sign of him. So much for pedigree, when the chips are down it really doesn't seem to make any difference in the dog world. It was the same for my mother. Was my father there to help? Did he even come to visit us when we were small? Did he take us for Saturday trips to McDonalds or even give any money to our mum to keep us? No. So what happens? She had to send us all to new homes. To be fair I like where I live and I'm still in touch with her, although I haven't seen her or my brother and sisters for a while, but I don't even hear from my dad. I suppose it's going to be much the same for Mackensey's puppies too. There really is so much work for the Pet Dogs' Democratic Party to do. The list of things we need to campaign for is getting so long it makes me tired just thinking about it. Perhaps Maintenance payments for puppies should be essential to allow puppies to be brought up at home with their mums. I suppose we would have to create a body like the Puppy Support Agency to track down absent fathers, or in some case mothers, and then try to get them to make payments. I think this one could be a tough job.

Friday 19ᵗʰ January

Well I'm home again and have discussed the whole absent father thing with The Boss. I'm shocked, it's worse than I supposed. Not only are there situations where dogs get bitches pregnant and walk away, there are even situations where money changes hands. Not between the dogs, that would of course amount to prostitution, no it's worse than that. The money changes hands between the owners. The owners of the dog actually receive money for him enjoying himself and walking away. It's outrageous. Perhaps this one is just too big an issue for the PDDP to deal with.

In my bid for fame and fortune, well fame anyway I have made some progress to setting up T shirt designs for you to choose from. I just need to think of some more designs and find if they do dog sizes as well as human. It would be an awful shame if I couldn't wear one of my own T shirts. So I have started my own shop at www.alfiedog.spreadshirt.net . Now all I need to do is include my paw print in some designs and think of some slogans.

Saturday 20ᵗʰ January

The things I do for you. There I was in the kitchen trying to come up with a decent paw print for a t shirt design. The Boss had the bright idea of using strong instant coffee as the ink. So there I was in the undignified position of sticking my paw in a saucer of decaf and then applying it to a piece of white paper. All I can say is that it was the wrong kind of paper as it didn't leave a nice neat paw print, more a splodge, which wouldn't work so well. I did leave some very fine coffee paw prints all over the kitchen floor as I ran off, but The Boss said the pattern of the floor made those impossible to use. I had another go with mud a little later but it seems I still have some work to do to perfect the design.

I'm wondering if I actually start to become famous and earn a bit of money whether I will need to become a tax exile somewhere. The point may be irrelevant if I can prove that as a dog I am not directly covered by the tax legislation in any particular country. It starts to open up a whole new possibility. If dogs are exempt from tax then any human who wanted to avoid paying tax could apply to become a dog. I don't know that we would accept all of them and in some case I guess it might take a bit of surgery but think of the upside for them. Of course the down sides do include the annual rabies jab and being micro-chipped and of course having to go outside to pee, but with some humans I can't see that being too much of an obstacle.

Monday 22nd January
I've asked The Boss if I can have one of Mackensey's puppies. I think I'm now old enough and responsible enough to care for a pet of my own. Unfortunately, The Boss has said no. Well more to the point my Master has said no to The Boss and she has simply had the pleasure of passing the message on to me. I don't think her heart was in it when she said it though. What she did say and she perhaps had a point was that she didn't know as much about Corgi's so didn't know how well one would fit into our lifestyle. My argument is if it's good enough for the queen of England it's good enough for me. Of course that didn't get me the Harrods collar for Christmas either.

I've been writing this diary for a year and despite not

being allowed a puppy of my own, I think I have grown up to be a mature and responsible dog. I do have my crazy moments, but then don't we all. If you don't, then you probably won't have understood most of the things that go on in our lives and if you've read this far will be wondering what it's all about. So let me tell you.

It's about living life as though you adore the people around you, no matter what they say and do. It's about enjoying every meal as though it's the first thing you've ever eaten, even if you have the same dog food every day of your life. It's about giving every new person you meet an enthusiastic welcome and not pre-judging them no matter what the colour of their skin or hair, the way they look or the way they talk. It's about chasing a leaf, just because the wind blows it and because you can. It's about chasing nothing at all because there's no leaf blowing at the moment you want to run.

Most of all, it's about being a faithful friend and companion to the person who lights up your world and never letting them down. For me that's The Boss and as long as I can be by her side, then no matter how crazy the things she does seem to everyone else, I will love her with complete and uncompromising devotion and would defend her to the last.

With much love to you all,

Alfie Dog

ABOUT THE AUTHORS

Alfie Dog

Alfie Dog is an Entlebucher Mountain Dog. He was born in Belgium in 2005 and his full name is Einstein van de Tiendenschuur. Although he lived in Belgium for the first two years of his life he moved to the United Kingdom in 2008 and has lived in North Yorkshire ever since. He started writing his diary at the age of 10 weeks and, with the exception of the odd day, when his human was in hospital and he couldn't find the password, he has written it every day since. You can find his diary at www.alfiedog.me.uk He is also the author of the novel 'Alfie's Woods', which he co-wrote with his human and the Pet Dogs Democratic Party manifesto

He lives with Shadow (Aisha Princess of Beauty) who, at the time of writing, is mother to 18 of the 50 Entlebuchers in the UK and due to have her final litter this year. His other companion is Aristotle, Shadow's wayward son, who terrorises Alfie whilst idolising him at the same time.

Rosemary J. Kind

Rosemary J. Kind is quite clearly mad. She has now co-authored three books with her dog and assists him with the technology for writing his diary. She is the only person we know who has called her business after her dog, and she is utterly devoted to developing the Entlebucher Mountain Dog breed in the UK, having first come across it in 1998 in the Encyclopaedia of Dogs.

She has published five books in her own right including one non-fiction book 'Negotiation Skills for Lawyers', one book of poetry 'Poems for Life', two novels 'The Appearance of Truth' and 'The Lifetracer' and a humorous look at travelling on the London Underground 'Lovers Take up Less Space'. She lives in North Yorkshire with her long-suffering husband and three dogs.

OTHER BOOKS BY THE AUTHORS

Alfie's Woods – Alfie Dog with a little help from Rosemary J. Kind

Alfie is fascinated when Hedgehog is recaptured following his escape from the Woodland Prison. Too young to understand money laundering, Alfie assumes that Hedgehog should be given sympathy for washing his money. Hedgehog, overwhelmed that any other creature should care about him, finds the strength to change his life. As an ex-convict Hedgehog meets with opposition at every step and it is only the faith of his friends and their unwavering support that enables him to turn his life round. Alfie's Woods is a story of the power of friendship and the difference it can make to all of us.

The Appearance of Truth – Rosemary J. Kind

Lisa Forster begins to trace her family tree. She very quickly discovers that the birth certificate she has had for thirty years is for a baby who died at the age of four months old and is not in fact her own. Her apparently happy middle class upbringing is a myth and her parents had a dark secret. With Pete Laundon's help Lisa sets about discovering the truth. Assuming she is adopted she follows up all possible routes, until with no options left she goes to the newspaper for help. After 30 years, who if anyone knows the truth?

The Lifetracer – Rosemary J. Kind

When Connor Bancroft is asked to investigate a death threat, sent on a countdown clock, he is unwittingly drawn into a complex story of revenge. He uncovers a series of murders, apparently linked only by the clock left with the victim.

Connor is more used to dealing with infidelity than murder and is nowhere close to solving the crimes. Now, his eight year old son, Mikey's life is in danger and Connor has little time left to find out – Who is The Lifetracer?

Lovers Take up Less Space – Rosemary J. Kind

Lovers Take up Less Space is a humorous review of the addictive misery of commuting on London Underground. A blow by blow account of everything from how to find breathing space on a packed Tube train, to the psychological torture of your fellow passengers eating a fresh hot bag of chips and not passing them round. It includes games to transform underground travel from a necessary evil to a spare time recreational activity, together with surprising facts and figures answering questions you had not yet thought to ask. Not for the faint hearted. This book will open your eyes to experiences your senses have long since ignored in the interest of sanity.

Pet Dogs Democratic Party Manifesto – Alfie Dog with a little help from Rosemary J. Kind

Man's best friend deserves to be heard. For too long pets have been seen as the underdogs, working tirelessly for little more than a pat on the head. It is time for the country to go to the dogs literally instead of metaphorically; for the prejudice we dogs face to be swept aside; time to vote for a more equal society, a more just society. It is time to vote for a society in which two-legs and four-legs stand together; a society in which man and dog work in partnership for a better future for us all. A vote for the Pet Dogs Democratic Party is a vote for your best friend, a vote for the most loyal companion you will ever have and one who wants what's best for dog and man together. Vote PDDP!

Alfie Dog Fiction

Taking your imagination for a walk

www.alfiedog.com

Join us on Facebook
http://www.facebook.com/AlfieDogLimited